INDIA
DARK

Praise for INDIA DARK:

"… an absorbing work of historical fiction based on a real Edwardian scandal… a sharp, accessible and atmospheric tale populated by memorable characters." **The Age, Pick of the Week**

"A powerful and convincing transformation of fact to fiction… a fascinating tale." **ABC Radio**

"Petty jealousies, ambition and unstable relationships are a heady concoction in a hot and foreign land. *India Dark*… is a dramatic, engaging and complex tale. Beautifully written and impeccably researched, it shows us that there is always more than one side to a story, particularly where emotions are involved. Murray has given us a real gem." **Good Reading**

"... will appeal to readers with a sense of history and adventure." **Magpies**

"This is a beautifully recreated, intriguing tale of trust, deceit, betrayal and love in an empire on the precipice of decline. Highly recommended." **Reading Time**

"Guaranteed to grab the attention of young readers... the novel chugs along like a powerful sub-continental steam train." **Viewpoint**

"Based on a true story, Kirsty Murray has opened up an amazing portion of history that will thrill readers who love historical fiction... left me thinking about the power of truth, lies, loyalty, friendship and gossip." **Pat Pledger, Read Plus**

KIRSTY MURRAY

templar

A TEMPLAR BOOK

First published in the UK in 2012 by Templar Publishing,
an imprint of The Templar Company Limited,
The Granary, North Street, Dorking, Surrey, RH4 1DN, UK
www.templarco.co.uk

First published in the English language by
Allen & Unwin Pty Ltd, Sydney, Australia

First UK edition

Mixed Sources
Product group from well-managed
forests and other controlled sources
www.fsc.org Cert no. SA-COC-1565
© 1996 Forest Stewardship Council

ISBN 978-1-84877-210-6

Printed and bound by CPI Group (UK) Ltd, Croydon, CR0 4YY

For Jocelyn Ainslie,
an angel at our table who always
holds the right thought

Contents

The Cast and Crew
of Percival's Lilliputian Opera Company

IN THE PERFORMANCE OF A LIFETIME:

INDIA DARK

OR

POESY'S ADVENTURES
AMONGST THE LILLIPUTIANS

CAST OF CHARACTERS

IN STARRING ROLES

Miss Poesy Swift......................... Aged 13 years
Miss Tilly Sweetrick.......................... 15 years

FEATURING

Master Charlie Byrne .... 13 years
Miss Eliza Finton .... 18 years
Master Lionel Byrne .... 14 years
Miss Tempe Melbourne......................... 17 years
Miss Ruby Kelly.................................... 17 years
Miss Clarissa Holden............................ 17 years
Master Freddie Kreutz .... 14 years
Master Max Kreutz................................ 14 years
Miss Valentine Percival (Usher)............... 14 years

WITH FULL CHORUS

Miss Eunice Finton .... 16 years
Miss Amy Piggot.................................. 15 years
Miss Lulu Baillieu................................ 16 years
Miss Beryl Kelly .... 15 years

Miss Pearl Kelly...12 years
Miss Rosie Taylor...16 years
Miss Myrtle Jones ....17 years
Miss Iris Percival (Usher) ....12 years
Miss Ivy White ....12 years
Miss May Molloy ....12 years
Miss Olive Blackwood ....13 years
Miss Ida Taylor..13 years
Master George Royce....................................11 years
Master Roy Blackwood ....12 years
Master Billy Waters......................................11 years
Master Henry Howard ....10 years

AND INTRODUCING

Baby Percival (Daisy Watts).........................7 years
Miss Flora Henley ....8 years

ADULTS TRAVELLING WITH THE TROUPE

Mr Edward Quedda
(Pianist, Stage Manager and ex-Lilliputian)

Mrs Eloise Quedda (nee Finton)
and two-month-old infant

Miss Enid Thrupp (matron)
and three-month-old infant

Mr Arthur Percival
(Manager and Musical Director)

Mr James McNulty (Carpenter
and Props Master)

Mr Michael Milligan (Electrician)

Percival's Lilliputian Opera Company
PROGRAMME

1

THE BETRAYAL
MADRAS HIGH COURT, APRIL 1910

Poesy Swift

Daisy opened her mouth and lies flew out. Her face so pink and white, her lips so plump and sweet, her lies so vile. I had to cover my ears. I shut my eyes too, wanting to block out the courtroom, to neither see nor hear the evil. The men in black gowns, the crowd of newspaper reporters, the swirling fans, Eliza weeping, Mr Arthur and his pale face, Daisy and her lies. Everything. But Tilly grabbed my arm and twisted my wrist in a Chinese burn.

"Poesy Swift," she whispered, her breath hot against my neck, "open your eyes, and take that look off your face. We will never get home if you ruin everything."

"You put her up to this, Tilly," I said. "You know she doesn't understand what she's doing."

Tilly twisted the skin on my wrist tighter and pulled my arm into her lap so no one could see her hurt me. Her blue eyes shrank to narrow slits.

"She speaks the truth, Poesy. You're the one that lied, not Daisy."

I tried to sit up straight but my eyes pricked with tears of pain. Then I did something I'd never done before. I pinched her. I pinched Tilly so hard that she squealed and let go of my arm. Mr Arthur's barrister, Mr Guruswami, turned to stare at us, his brown eyes full of judgement, and I knew he understood. Then I slipped off the bench and walked out of the crowded courtroom – past the Sikh guard and through the cool gloom of the High Court corridors, my boots tapping loudly on the black-and-white tiles.

The building was a maze of arches and stairwells, of echoing chambers and carved columns. I could hear someone following me as I turned a corner and ran down a long, gloomy hallway, past a line of turbaned Sikhs who stood outside another courtroom. All around me there were trials in session behind dark wooden doors, but I could think only of the one I had escaped, and of Daisy's lies and where they would lead us.

2

TRUST

Tilly Sweetrick

As I chased Poesy out of the courtroom, I remembered the first time she tricked me, that winter morning in a Richmond lane. I will never forget the way she looked, in her washed-out green pinafore and tatty brown boots. She had jumped down from a fence like a cat and stood right in front of me, batting her baby-blue eyes. Even though she was thirteen, she could have passed for ten with her china-doll whiteness, her pale buttery hair, those blonde lashes and brows – a pixie of a girl. It was only later I discovered she could be as tricksy as one too.

"Poesy Swift," I said. "You haven't changed at all."

She looked at me slyly and tipped her head to one side.

"I have grown a teensy bit, but I don't think Swifts get very big. I'll probably be this big forever."

I knew why she said that. Everyone had heard that the Percivals liked to hire petite girls. Everyone.

"Oh, Poesy," I answered, in all my innocence. "Some of the girls in the troupe grew inches and inches while we were in America and they look like great lumps now. Mrs Essie can't use them any more."

Then she said, "You've been in America?", as if she hadn't known.

"You are the pretty, prettier, prettiest I have ever seen you," she said to me and she leaned in close.

Then I made my mistake; I asked, "Do you still sing?"

"Some," she answered. That was Poesy. Always holding back, never saying yes or no – always might and maybe and some and s'pose.

So I told her to audition. I wish I'd kept my mouth shut. I wish so many things had happened differently. Poesy blushed and laughed in that way that made me remember her pretty singing voice. But later, after she became a Lilliputian, she was too quiet. You can't trust the quiet ones.

Now I was chasing her out of the High Court of Madras, hoping she would keep her big mouth shut. I could hear my heart pounding. At the top of the stairs, an angry barrister snapped at me, "Girl, how dare you run! This is His Majesty's court. Behave yourself."

I stopped. I couldn't help the tears. Suddenly, I was so tired of it all. I clung to the balustrade. The shadows from the fretwork made me giddy. Then Charlie was beside me. I should have known he wouldn't let her get away.

"What's wrong?" he asked.

"Help me, Charlie," I said, as the tears spilled down my cheeks. "She's being stupid. If she changes her story again, it will be terrible for all of us. Please, find her and fetch her back. Please."

Not that I needed to beg. It wasn't for my sake that Charlie had followed us. He nodded, a tiny tilt of his head in my direction. Then he was gone.

3

FALLEN FLOWER

Poesy Swift

I ran across the wide and dusty road, straight into Blacktown. I wanted to lose my way in its hot, narrow lanes.

Nothing had turned out as it should. I never meant for it to happen this way. Everyone had turned rotten and the stink was suffocating.

I ran, weaving my way between the rickshaws, the *tea-wallah*s and the crowd that flowed into the old town, into the narrow lanes of the flower bazaar. The sun flickered through the lattices above the stalls, and garlands hung like pythons from the cross-rails. The laneway was cluttered with buckets of flowers, petals lay strewn across the path, and the gutters spewed buds and stems.

I stumbled and fell at the feet of an old woman who was threading orange marigolds onto a string, and my stocking tore. The old woman spoke to me in that Hobson-Jobson language but I didn't stop. I was on my feet again in an instant, running blindly with no sense of direction.

I ran faster and faster, my feet slipping on piles of smooth leaves between the stalls. I thought of the first time I had seen Eliza, standing in the sunlight outside Balaclava Hall with Mr Arthur beside her. I thought of Charlie when we first met, pressed against me in the heart of an old gum tree and then later, lying beside me in the dark at Adyar. I thought of Mrs Besant, her arms open wide as she said, "Truth may lead you into the wilderness, yet you must follow her…" But I was lost, with no truth to follow.

4

THE PIVOTING MOMENT

Poesy Swift

I knew too much too soon. Once you know, you can't ever turn back to not knowing.

On Easter Sunday 1908, at 10.30 p.m., my father died at Sunshine railway station. Forty-six people were killed that night. In the dark, the express from Bendigo crashed into the back of a long train from Ballarat that had started to pull out of the station. The last four carriages, the extra carriages that had been added for the holidaymakers returning home, were crushed and twisted. I wasn't there but I can imagine the darkness and the noise and the screaming. A good imagination can be a curse.

The weekend Dad died, our house turned to glass. We had to be careful of each other after that. At night, when I lay in bed and listened to Yada and Mumma arguing, their voices spiralling up the stairs, I could imagine every pane in our terrace house shattering, breaking into tiny thin shards. And when my little brother Chooky wept and climbed into bed beside me, it was as if I could feel the fragments sticking out of our skins. We were like prickly animals – the hedgehog in Yada's picture book – but our quills were made of glass.

There are moments in your life when everything pivots. It should have happened when my father died. But nothing shifted in the long year after his death. Then I turned thirteen and everything changed.

Maybe everyone's life pivots when they're thirteen years old. In 1909, mine began to swing in a wide arc, away from the glass house, away from Chooky and Mumma and Yada.

It pivoted the moment Tilly Sweetrick came walking along our back lane. Her whistle, sweeter and higher than a boy's, carried through the wintery morning. When the lads catcalled and hooted at Tilly, she simply whistled louder until you had to cover your ears to stop the hurt of that piercing sound. She didn't care. She said whistling made her strong. Whistling was good for her voice, whistling would turn her into a famous singer like Nellie Melba, and she didn't care what anyone thought. I wanted to feel like that too. Not caring.

I hadn't seen her for two years but we had played together when we were little. In fifth grade, I stood behind her in the schoolyard while we said, "I love my country, I honour the King and the flag, I cheerfully obey my parents, teachers and the law."

Tilly didn't cheerfully obey anyone. She wasn't at school very often, but when she was she'd lead all the girls behind the peppercorn trees during playtime and make us watch her dance and sing. If you were lucky, she let you sing along. Then suddenly she disappeared. I waited for her under the peppercorn trees every lunchtime but she never came back to school and I didn't see her again until that wintery morning.

I caught the scent of Tilly long before she came into view. She didn't smell like Richmond. You could track your way around our lanes by the stink of things. You could tell that the mad old Misses Ryries kept goats and chickens out the back and that Mary Hall pissed in the street at the corner of Willow Lane. I knew I was nearly home when I smelled that sharp sourness. And the smell of the river ran through everything, dank and acrid, the background to our winter days. But Tilly brought the scent of sugar and lilies.

I jumped down from the back fence as she turned the corner.

"Poesy Swift," she said. "You look exactly the same."

I had lost my father since last I'd seen her and was hollow with misery. I couldn't think how I could look the same when I felt so small and broken.

"I don't think Swifts get very big," I said.

"Well, that's not such a bad thing. Some of the girls in our troupe grew inches and inches while we were in America and they look like great lumps now."

"You've been in America?"

"How could you not know?"

When I looked at her, the years we'd been apart compressed into a tiny moment, as if I had seen her only yesterday. Yet somehow, as if by magic, Matilda Sweeney had become Tilly Sweetrick while my life grew bleaker by the day. Her bottom lip looked red and ripe, like a cherry. She wore her dark hair loose, and it was longer and thicker than I'd remembered. Everything about her was fuller and richer – as if she had ripened in the seasons away from Richmond.

"You've changed. You've got pretty, prettier, the prettiest," I said, stumbling over my own tongue.

She reached out and teased a lock of my hair away from my face, wrapping it around her finger. She stood so close to me that her sweetness made me dizzy.

"You've grown pretty too. Do you still sing? The way we

used to on Sundays at my house?"

"Some," I said.

"You should come and try out for the Lilliputians."

"You mean the music-hall people?"

"Of course! Did you think I meant midgets? That's who I've been touring with – Percival's Lilliputian Opera Company – singing and dancing our way across America. They're putting together a new troupe now we're home. Some girls are leaving and some have got too old. But you're still a little darling. Mrs Essie will think you're delicious. You could stay a Lilliputian for years. You must audition."

"I couldn't!"

She wrapped her arms around my waist and kissed me on the forehead.

"You don't want to go to that dull old Continuation School," she said. "You'll have to be a fusty, dusty teacher then, and never get married. Men don't make passes at girls who wear glasses. Come away with me and all the boys will make eyes at us and think we're darling sweethearts."

"I don't care what boys think," I said.

I could feel the hot flush of blood rising up from my chest and burning my cheeks.

Tilly tapped my chin with one finger and laughed. "Or you could go to Bryant & May and burn your fingers off like Elsie Taylor did. Imagine. Who'd want a wife with a finger missing!"

"I don't care if no one wants me," I said, pushing myself away from her. But I looked at my hands and thought about Elsie Taylor's missing fingers, about the stink of sulphur and the high red-brick walls of the match factory. I saw the fire and the darkness that lay ahead.

5

THE LILLIPUTIANS

Poesy Swift

The morning of the auditions, I went to Tilly's house early but she had already left. Her ma explained that she had caught the tram with the Kelly sisters in Collingwood. Maybe she felt bad that Tilly hadn't waited for me. I climbed on the tram at Smith Street, but I didn't sit with Tilly and her friends. After a while she walked to the back of the tram and took my hand.

"Why are you hiding up here all by yourself?"

"You're with your friends," I whispered, looking down into my lap.

"Well, if you're going to audition, you should meet the Kellys. C'mon."

She led me to where the others were sitting, their skirts spread across the green leather seats.

"Ruby, Beryl, Pearl, this is Poesy. She's auditioning."

I could see Tilly wasn't sure of me. Not like when we were in the laneway. She wasn't sure that she wanted to own me.

Beryl and Pearl barely nodded in my direction, but Ruby looked me up and down and then clapped her hands.

"What a darling little creature," she said, "You are clever, Tilly. If she can sing, Mrs Essie will be rather pleased, even if the child is raggedy."

I glanced at Tilly and saw her purse her lips, as if she'd sucked a lemon. I smiled uncertainly and tried not to mind when Tilly sat down and pulled me roughly onto her lap, as if I were her new doll.

Ruby was the eldest Kelly sister but she still wore her honey-blonde hair long and loose. It curled around her shoulders and her heart-shaped face. She was so pink and white and dimpled that she reminded me of the girl in the posters for Kodak. But then all the Kelly girls were picture-book pretty in their crisp white clothes, new black stockings and shiny, black-buttoned boots. I smoothed the fabric of my brown dress and wished I was invisible. Ruby leaned forward and her breath was sweet and minty but her words were meant only for Tilly.

"You remember that gentleman who followed us from city to city to see all our performances?" she asked. "Well, he's been writing to Tempe and he wants her to go back to America and marry him."

"But he was peculiar," said Tilly.

"Of course he was awfully odd. She won't go. But it's rather nice he asked. Do you remember he kept sending chocolates backstage and Tempe wouldn't touch them?"

"Oh, yes, and the boys stuck their fingers in all the soft-centred ones." Tilly laughed.

Chocolates and flowers and gentlemen admirers. America – it made me shiver to think of it. I'd been to Ballarat once, before Dad died. Only once. Yada and Mumma seemed to think Richmond was the whole world.

The tram rattled through Northcote and stopped at a flat, dusty intersection in Thornbury. I followed Tilly and the

Kelly girls along Darebin Road. My stomach began to ache.

Balaclava Hall was a white weatherboard building with long windows and a small porch at the front that was crowded with children and their parents.

"Tilly?" I whispered, in awe of everyone's stiff curls and layers of lace.

"Don't worry," she said breezily. "You'll be better than the lot of them." She grabbed my hand and dragged me up the front steps of the hall.

"This is Poesy Swift, Mrs Essie. The girl I told you about."

I tried to keep my gaze steady and look Mrs Essie squarely in the face. She had grey hair pulled back in a tight bun and she studied me in a way that made me burn, as if she saw straight through me, as if she saw straight into my heart, and knew I was hopeless. Beside her stood her brother, Mr Percival. Mr Arthur Percival.

He looked kind, that first day, and so smoothly handsome with his sparkly blue eyes that I felt too shy to meet his gaze. He wore a silvery-grey jacket, lovely slim-legged trousers and a dove-grey tie. You'd never have thought he and Mrs Essie were brother and sister. To look at, Mr Arthur could have been her son, even though he was thirty-five years old, old enough to be my father. He tipped his soft derby hat onto the back of his head and smiled at me, and his eyes grew crinkly with cheerfulness. He took off his grey reindeer gloves and he spoke my name, as if we were old friends.

"Poesy, you mustn't be shy with us," he said, touching my chin lightly. "The children in our company have a marvellous time with singing, dancing, costumes, everything a girl enjoys. And if you pass muster when you audition, we'll train you to be a proper little actress. Is your mother here?"

"My mother had to work today and my grandmother is taking care of my little brother. But they're very happy for me to be here," I lied.

"And have you prepared a song for us?" he asked.

I felt the blood drain right down to my boots. I hadn't thought about a song. What *had* I been thinking? I'd been thinking about being given boxes of chocolates and America and sailing away from Melbourne and never having to change Chooky's wet sheets ever again.

"Oh, Poesy knows thousands of songs," interrupted Tilly. "At our musical Sundays, at my place, she was always larking about and showing off and singing louder than everyone else, weren't you, Poesy?"

I grinned and nodded like an imbecile. Had I been a show-off? I always thought it was Tilly who stole the limelight. In school they had called her 'Little Miss Noticebox'. I never felt anyone took notice of me.

On Mr Percival's instruction, I stepped up onto the low stage at the far end of the hall. My head exploded with songs but they were all hymns from Sunday School. 'Onward Christian Soldiers' didn't seem the sort of song the Lilliputians would sing. I looked at Tilly and made my eyes wide. She was mouthing something at me and miming the gestures of a song behind Mrs Essie's back but I couldn't think what it was. What on earth had made me imagine I could be like Tilly, with her dark, glossy curls and her wide, laughing mouth? All of a sudden, I wanted to go home.

So I sang the only song I could think of: 'Home, Sweet Home'. I knew that Tilly always acted out her songs so I put my hands together as if I was begging to be taken to my home, sweet home, and disdaining the pleasures of palaces for my humble home. No place like home. And that was true, there was nowhere like my cottage. Nowhere as empty and as full of misery.

I let the song fill me up, the notes swelling in my chest. I loved the way singing made your head feel lighter, as if the breath and the sound were one and the same. As if you became the sounds and the song. I knew I didn't look so mousy when I sang, I knew my cheeks turned pink and my eyes shone, and I hoped, I prayed, that maybe I looked a little more like Tilly. Mr Arthur watched me closely, noting every gesture I made, taking in every aspect of my figure, but Mrs Essie tipped her head to one side and listened with her eyes shut as if all she wanted to gauge was the sweetness of my voice.

Afterwards, I played chasey around the back of the hall with two of the littler girls who were waiting outside. When we were tired, we sat underneath an old ghost gum.

"Have you had your audition already?" I asked.

"Thilly!" said the smallest one, her lisp so thick I wasn't sure if she was exclaiming Tilly or silly. "We're already with the Lilliputhianth. We don't have to audition."

"What's it like travelling with the troupe?" I asked.

"It's jolly hard work," said both the girls at once.

"Oh poo," said Tilly, sitting down beside me. "Don't listen to Daisy and Flora. It's much harder having to sit in a stinky old classroom. What would you know, either of you? You've never done anything else."

Tilly turned to me and held my face in her hands.

She studied me closely, as if there was something about me that she needed to discover, something that puzzled her.

"This is your chance, Poesy. I heard Mrs Essie and Mr Arthur talking about you. They like you." I could hear a faint note of incredulity in her voice, as if, despite her promptings, she'd thought I would fail. "Now all you have to do is make sure your mother agrees. They won't take you if your mother doesn't sign the papers. If she does, we'll be able to sing and dance our way across America."

I hoped she couldn't feel me trembling. Trembling with longing.

"It could be the making of you, Poesy," she announced. "If you join up, we could be friends again."

"Aren't we friends anyway, even if I can't come?"

"Don't turn my words around. Of course we are, but if you can make your mother sign the papers, we'll travel the world together. All you have to do is tell her. Tell her tonight."

A DREAM UNSPOKEN

Poesy Swift

I didn't tell Mumma. I didn't breathe a word. That night I sat quietly at teatime and squashed my egg into little pieces while Yada and Mumma argued back and forth across the table. Fat tears rolled down Chooky's face and plopped onto his plate but I couldn't feel anything. It was the same argument they had been having since the start of the year.

"Poesy doesn't need to finish the term," said Mumma. "It won't make any difference to whether she finds a job. Dimmeys are hiring. This is her chance."

"Dimmeys are looking for girls of fourteen!" Yada slapped the table with her skinny hand. "Why, she looks no more than ten!"

"But she's not ten. She's thirteen and old enough to earn her keep. Dimmeys put the smaller girls in the back of the shop. If she starts now, she could work her way up."

"She's still a child, Adeline!"

"Ma, you make it sound as if I'm forcing her into slavery," said Mumma with the bitterness that always tinged her voice when they fought over me. "I'm not suggesting Bryant & May."

I thought of Elsie and the other girls who lied about their age and found work dipping matches or stirring jam at the factory across the bridge. But no one would want me. No one except the Lilliputians. Yada was right. I did look like a ten-year-old, even though it was three months since I'd turned thirteen.

"I want her to get an education," said Yada. "Poesy is more than clever enough for the Continuation School."

I should have said something then. I no more wanted to go to the Continuation School than I did the match factory. I wanted to sing. I wanted to be with Tilly. I wanted her world. But Yada would have been horrified to have a granddaughter on the stage. And Mumma would have misgivings. She'd never liked Tilly. I cleared my plate and left the kitchen.

While they argued, I stood in front of the mirror in Yada's bedroom and bunched up the back of my nightgown so the front stretched smooth and flat against my chest. My narrow shoulders looked like the spiky nubs of wings and my face was as pale as a new moon. How could I ever be a star of the stage?

Chooky came into the room and stared at me, his face sticky with dirt and tears.

"Do you think I'm pretty enough?" I asked him. He put his thumb in his mouth and nodded. I turned back to the mirror but there was nothing pretty in the face of the girl who stared back at me. Her face was heavy with sadness.

Downstairs, the fight grew louder, the angry voices sharper, aiming to wound. A door slammed, and another, and then Mumma screamed. It set Chooky sobbing again and sent me running to the top of the stairs. Mumma was kneeling at the bottom, holding her wrist with the other hand. She looked up at Chooky and me. "She didn't mean it.

It was my fault. I put my hand in the door. She didn't mean to slam it so hard." But Chooky and I knew. It wasn't the first time Yada had hurt Mumma.

Yada opened the kitchen door and stared.

"Darling," was all she said, before she fell to the floor. Then the seizure came over her, as it always did when she was afraid. As it had that night the policeman came to tell us Dad wasn't coming home. Mumma gave a little shout of alarm and crawled towards Yada, trying to shield her head from hitting the skirting boards. All the while Yada's body writhed and shuddered. Her skinny, black-stockinged legs kicked against the wall. My skin prickled and I wanted to turn away, to pretend I hadn't seen her at all, to go back to the mirror and stare at my reflection, but my feet kept moving, taking me down the stairs until I was kneeling on the floor beside Mumma, waiting for Yada's fit to end. While Mumma nursed her and Chooky wept, I waited.

Finally, Yada lay still. A trail of saliva shone silver on her cheek. She looked up at us with glazed eyes. She had stopped shaking but she was still somewhere else. I put my arm underneath her and tried to make her sit up but she pushed me away. It was too soon.

It took ten minutes before Mumma and I could help Yada to her feet and steer her back into the kitchen. I made a pot of tea and doused a cloth in cool water to wrap around Mumma's bruised hand. Chooky came and sat under the table and rocked his body in a soothing rhythm, his thumb in his mouth.

I loved them all but it hurt too much. I loved them but I knew I would leave them.

HOLD THE RIGHT THOUGHT

Poesy Swift

Next morning, I woke to the sound of Yada calling, "Chook, chook, chook," and scattering scraps in the backyard beneath the plum tree. Chooky was out there too, shooing the hens towards the food, as if they couldn't find anything without his help.

The kitchen was quiet. Mumma was still in bed, nursing her bruised hand. There was no butter but I scraped a thick lump of dripping from the tin by the stove and spread it on yesterday's bread, set the kettle on the hob and measured tea-leaves into the old brown teapot.

Yada and Chooky sat either side of me and no one spoke. We were all listening to the house. It was as if last night's argument was still echoing around the kitchen. Finally, Yada said, "I hope you held your mother in your thoughts."

Chooky nodded but I stirred my tea and listened to the chink of the spoon against the china. I'd been holding my family in my thoughts all my life but it hadn't saved my dad or healed Mumma's broken heart or stopped Yada's seizures.

Yada knew me too well. She knew the closed expression on my face. She took my hand and folded her fingers over mine.

"Poesy," she said, "remember when I took you on the tram into the city to hear Mrs Besant?"

I nodded, ashamed that I remembered the excitement of walking past all the theatres more than anything that was said in Mrs Besant's lecture.

"There is no religion higher than truth," said Yada. "That's what she told us. Your mother and I, we argue because we seek the truth. It is a fact that we would have more pennies if you sacrificed yourself to the dreadful match factory. But in truth it would not lead us closer to happiness."

I took a sip of tea and tried to avoid meeting Yada's gaze.

"But if there was some other way I could bring us pennies, everyone would be happier then, wouldn't they?"

"Pennies can't make our happiness, child. Mrs Besant said the whole world, the whole universe, is only a Thought of God. Sometimes my thoughts overwhelm me but I am trying to treasure the strength of God to help me hold the right thought and discover the truth. If Adeline and all of us would simply hold the right thought, then we would defeat the forces that trouble us. Pennies won't solve our problems. Each of us makes our world through our thoughts."

Yada spoke softly, as if afraid that Mumma would hear. Since Yada had converted to Theosophy there had been battles for my faith as well as my future.

It made my head hurt to think anyone could change the world through their thoughts. But I held the thought of the Lilliputians in my mind. I held the moment where I had stood singing in Balaclava Hall and tried to imagine it happening again. Perhaps it worked. Later that morning, Mrs Essie came to the door.

Mumma and Yada shook their heads in disbelief when Mrs Essie explained why she had come. I stood very still, like a deaf–mute, waiting for Yada to start an argument, but she was too shy of Mrs Essie. She listened with her head to one side, her expression horrified. After Mrs Essie had left them with some papers to sign, the fight began in earnest.

Yada took the papers by one corner and dropped them in the basket for fire waste, as if they were filthy rags fit only for burning.

"Oh Mother, it's the stage or the match factory for her," said Mumma. "Why can't you see that? The woman said thirty shillings a month. Thirty shillings! What would you have Poesy do here in Melbourne that would earn a fraction of that? And we'll be spared her board and lodging if she's away."

"Board and lodging! You talk as if she were a stranger, Adeline, not your own sweet child!"

Mother slumped in a chair and put her head in her hands.

"More schooling for Poesy won't put bread on the table," she said, "but if she takes to the stage she could save Chooky. Look at the boy. Look at him. What's his future? You worry about the girl, but Chooky will be a man and have no way of supporting himself. You talk as if Poesy will be able to provide for this family on a teacher's wage. What happens when she marries? But she can help us now. Thirty shillings a month for two years would mean Chooky could stay at school for as long as needs be."

"You'd sell your daughter for thirty pieces of silver!"

Mumma turned to me.

"Poesy," she said. "What do you want to do?"

I couldn't look at Yada. "I want to join the Lilliputians. I want to go to America."

America, America, America: the words ran around the

inside of my head like music. Whenever I could cadge a penny I'd go down to Mr West's cinema and watch the American movies, and it seemed as if everything alive and exciting and worth living for was in that country. It's all I wanted, to feel more alive. I didn't understand what it meant to be 'careful what you pray for'.

Early next morning, I took the billycan down to the fence and hung it from a nail by the front gate. The milkman would fill it in the dark early hours and lower it to the ground by its string. The street was quiet. I could smell the damp from the river and the fog rising. I tried to think about the power of thought, about making my future with my thoughts, but my mind felt blank. There wasn't a single thought I could hold that made me feel I had made the right choice.

I walked slowly up the path, tapping out a rhythm with my feet. In the still dawn, my voice sounded clean and sweet as I sang a little skipping rhyme I'd made for myself about the Lilliputians: *"Tilly, Flora, Daisy. Ruby, Beryl, Pearl. Lulu, Iris, Valentine, soon these girls will all be mine. Soon they'll be my friends."*

On Monday, Mr Smith the milkman called with his account. He usually kept sugared almonds in his pocket, but that last Monday he had run out.

"Next time, Poesy," he said.

"There might not be a next time," I said, almost not believing my own words. "I'm leaving, Mr Smith. Going away with the Lilliputians. Right around the world!"

It wasn't until I said it out loud that I felt I understood what it might mean. But in truth, I understood even less than I imagined.

8

Rehearsing the Future

Poesy Swift

Tilly was always at Balaclava Hall ahead of me but I liked to take my time. I liked to stand at the top of the road and stare at the hazy blue Dandenong Ranges, dreaming about the future. And the other good thing, if I waited, was that I could walk with Charlie Byrne.

Every morning, Lionel and Charlie would step down from the tram at Darebin Road. Lionel was fourteen and one of the eldest Lilliputian boys, though he could pass for much younger, and showed no sign of whiskers or muscles or anything manly. He always pushed past me, he never wanted to talk to any of the new girls. Charlie was a year younger but he was happy to chat with me. In the beginning, I imagined that if he had been a girl he could have been my sister. I don't think I understood what it meant to have a sister.

We both knew that when we arrived at the hall, we wouldn't speak to each other again. As soon as the others came in sight, Charlie flapped his arms and ran at the boys. Then Lionel would go to hit him and they would tussle like two puppies. I suppose it kept them warm. It was icy in Thornbury on those winter mornings. I tucked my hands beneath my arms to stop them turning blue and watched the boys wrestle.

Mr Arthur hated it when the boys fought. It was the only time I saw him cross during those Melbourne days. Sometimes he'd send the stage manager, Mr Eddie, or the props master, Mr Jim, into the yard to sort them out. But no one took Mr Jim or Mr Eddie seriously because they looked so young. Mr Jim was only nineteen and Mr Eddie had been a Lilliputian only a few years ago, though now he was twenty-one and married with a baby. When they stepped between the boys, it looked as though they were simply playing along with them.

Mr Arthur hardly ever shouted at us girls. The only time you could tell he was angry was if he dropped his gaze and the cleft in his chin grew deeper as he gritted his teeth. It almost made him look even handsomer. The line of his jaw was so strong and sharp, it was as if a sculptor had carved it and chiselled his high cheekbones and smooth brow. But mostly he was jolly because we all wanted to please him. When he was directing the chorus line every girl sang as sweetly as she could, and when we danced for him it was as if we were floating on air.

In those winter months at Balaclava Hall, I remember Mr Arthur smiling all the time. Even his eyes grew smiley when he was pleased with our singing. When Mrs Essie called him 'Baby', as she often did because once he'd been the youngest in the troupe, you could see the boy in him, even though now he was a proper grown-up man.

Perhaps that's why I found it easy to talk to him. I'd always been shy of talking to men and boys but Mr Arthur was different. So was Charlie Byrne.

The first time Charlie and I spoke, it was an accident.

I was sitting in the big gum tree that grew beside the hall. Charlie came pelting outside as if his tail was on fire. He scrambled into the lower branches and was up next to the roofline before the other boys had even made it out of the doorway. At first he didn't notice me sitting with my back against the trunk and my stockinged legs stretched along a branch. I gave a little cough so as not to startle him, but he nearly lost his balance when he saw me.

"Sorry," I said.

"It's not the place you expect to find a girl," he said.

"Who are you hiding from?" I asked.

"I'm not hiding. Not yet. Anyone can see us from the ground."

I glanced down through the leaves. "What will they do if they spot us?"

"They won't. Least they won't find me." Then he stepped into a deep fork in the heart of the old tree. I hadn't noticed it before. He had to wriggle down to get inside the hollow.

I climbed across from my branch and peered into his hidey-hole. "I never thought of that. No one would know you're there."

He turned his face upwards. His eyes were like green jewels, the way the sun lit them. He had a tiny pale scar above one eyebrow and a wide, soft mouth. It was like looking down into the face of an elf.

"Is there room in there for me too?" I asked.

Even though there wasn't really any space left he said, "Yes. It fits two." And then I slid down beside him, trying to hold my skirt in place as my body scraped against his. His face was only inches away. I kept my arms very still, pressed against my side, and we both held our breath and listened. We could hear the sound of footsteps, of the other boys pelting past the gum tree. I heard Freddie and Max Kreutz shouting and I shuddered a little. They were the biggest boys – a pair of tawny-haired twins with big fists like hams and long, meaty cheeks – and Tilly had warned me about them.

"Why are they chasing you?" I whispered.

"I foxed them with a bit of magic, and Kreutzes don't like being foxed. Freddie Kreutz, he's the boss of the boys."

"Why is he the boss? I thought your brother Lionel was the boss."

"Lionel?" I could feel his breath warm against my cheek as he sighed. "Never. The Kreutz twins have been on the stage since they were six. They've got two big brothers who were in the Lilliputians and now they're actors in London and San Francisco. Kreutzes reckon anything they don't know about theatre isn't worth tuppence."

"Tilly told me those Kreutzes won't be allowed to go on tour soon," I confided, "because they're too interested in the girls. When Freddie caught Tilly all alone behind the hall, he tried to kiss her. And when Max watches you, it makes you want to pull your skirt down to your toes and fold your arms across your chest."

Suddenly, I realised I was pressed up close to Charlie without a whisker of space between us. I sucked my tummy in and tried to make a little gap between him and me but it didn't work. I could feel his chest moving in and out as his breath quickened and our silence seemed to make the hollow even more snug.

"You're not like the other boys," I said. "They smell funny, like chalk and boy-sweat – sort of dusty and gritty and a little bit sour."

"You reckon I smell sour too?"

"No," I said softly. I rested my chin on Charlie's shoulder so my nose was almost touching his ear. I could feel the heat of him against my face. "You smell like matches and liquorice."

He put his hands on my shoulders and pushed me away, so at last there was a little sliver of space between us. "Maybe we should climb out now."

From outside, we could hear the babble of girls talking as they left the hall and drifted into Darebin Road. "Not yet," I said. "I want to wait a little longer. Just until Tilly has gone home."

"You don't like Tilly? I thought she was your friend."

"I do like Tilly. It's just that sometimes it's hard being a Lilliputian."

"You mean the routines? I can help you with those, if you like."

"No, it's not the dances or the songs that are hard. They're fun. The hard bit is trying to understand who you're meant to be friends with."

Charlie furrowed his brow, as if he wasn't quite sure of what I meant.

"You see, everyone likes Tilly," I explained. "But she doesn't like everyone so I don't know who is safe to talk to. I thought I'd be friends with Valentine, but Tilly told me Valentine was *her* best friend and it wouldn't do for one of her second-best friends to try and steal her very best one away. Who *should* I like?"

Charlie didn't answer. He was listening to the voices

outside, as if part of him was somewhere else, thinking about some other problem.

"They're gone. Tilly and that lot," he said.

"Help me out then," I said. "You'll have to give me a boost."

He made a stirrup with his hands and when I put my foot in it, he laughed.

"What?"

"Your feet. They're so small. They're like tiny pinecones."

I could feel the blush rising up right from the heel of my foot as he boosted me out of the hollow. We sat in the open branches and looked down into the yard. Most of the children had disappeared and only the grown-ups and a few older girls stood on the steps of Balaclava Hall.

"Who is that one? The beautiful lady?" I asked, pointing at a girl with long, soft brown hair and skin like white satin touched with the softest pink. She stood beside Mr Arthur and when she laughed at something he'd said, her voice was like a lovely bird song.

Charlie shrugged and his mouth turned down, as if he were disappointed. "She's not a real lady. That's only Eliza."

"She's very pretty. You have to admit she's pretty."

He shrugged again. Perhaps it wasn't right to ask a boy about other girls. "Maybe she's pretty," he said. "Maybe she's dangerous."

"Dangerous?" It was such a peculiar thing to say. I looked down at Eliza again, at the neat turn of her tiny waist, at the way she tipped her head back when she laughed, her long white neck and her sweet, round face.

"I hope I'm dangerous when I grow up," I said.

9

SETTING SAIL FOR LILLIPUT

Tilly Sweetrick

I simply adored that moment when the ship's steward called, "All visitors ashore!"

I'd already said goodbye to Ma long before the call. I think she was glad to see the back of me, but not as glad as I was to be going away from Melbourne. Away from listening to her moan about my father, away from her drunken shouting at the empty seat in the kitchen where he used to sit, away from her weepy apologies the morning after as I made peace with the neighbours and tidied up the horrid mess she had made of our lives. At the beginning of every Lilliputian voyage, I felt as though all the strings were being cut, a kind of giddy weightlessness that meant I was free again.

Poesy was still holding on tight to her family. She clung to her granny, while her little brother kept butting her hip, trying to make a space for himself between them. Her mother had the good sense not to come to see her off. It was dismal having to watch all the mothers weeping on the dock. I slipped an arm through Poesy's and drew her towards me. She definitely looked like someone who needed rescuing.

"You write to me. From everywhere," whispered the brother, in his strange baby voice. "Promise. Postcards, especially."

"Yes, darling," said her granny, "write to us from every port and hold us in your thoughts."

Poesy nodded, as if it were too hard to speak. I wished they would leave. I knew she'd start to blub if they stayed any longer. Two years might have seemed a long time to them. To me, it was nothing. Only two more years – it made my heart sing. By the time we came home, I would be seventeen and everything would be different. I'd be old enough to put my hair up, old enough to audition for the variety shows, choose my own clothes and find myself a real beau.

I took Poesy below deck to the cabin she was to share with me, Valentine and Eliza. The beds had shiny brass railings with the Currie line emblem on them and the flowery curtains could be drawn right around the mattress. I could see her eyes grow big with the sweetness of it – our girls' cabin. It was rather nice to be the one to introduce her to her new life. We stood side by side and stared at our reflections in the mirror above the washstand. She was so happy. Whatever she said later, at that moment I knew Poesy was happy. The strings were loosening.

"My dad sailed the world," she said. "He brought me back dolls from some places. I have them with me for good luck."

She took a green-and-silver cloth-covered storybook and two funny, ugly little figurines out of her old tapestry bag. She tucked the book under her pillow and sat the dolls on the edge of the washbasin. They were no longer than my finger and had grubby little clay faces and worn sackcloth dresses. I could see she thought they were lovely, so I had to pretend.

"They're darling," I said, picking one up between two

fingers and trying to look interested. "But you don't still play with dollies, do you?"

Poesy blushed, a slow creeping pink that started at her throat and then turned her face bright red. She snatched the dolly from me and held it as if it were the most precious thing in the world. I didn't mean to upset her, but she had to realise that we were all getting too old for dolls and toys and storybooks. I hugged her close and stroked her flushed cheeks.

"This is a whole new life, Poesy. You're about to sail around the world, like your dad. You're almost a grown-up, seeing ports and the seven seas and the wide, wide world. You can be free now."

Poesy rested her head on my shoulder and sighed. For the loveliest moment, we understood each other.

Then Eliza walked in and Poesy changed. Even then, there was something between them, though Poesy swore there wasn't. It was as if she thought Miss Eliza Finton was someone special.

Eliza lay down on one of the lower bunks, her face to the wall, hardly noticing us.

"Are you all right?" asked Poesy.

Eliza lay there rubbing the edge of her shawl against her cheek, like a baby comforting herself. It was a pathetic little show. She couldn't possibly be sad at leaving Melbourne. She didn't even have any family there. Maybe she was having a sulk so that Mr Arthur would change the cabin arrangements. She couldn't have been happy about sharing a room with three younger girls. But it was her own fault. She'd said she didn't want to share with Ruby and Tempe and Clarissa, and now she was stuck with us.

"Go and play," she said, her voice flat and uninterested.

Poesy stepped closer, as if she wanted to comfort her.

"Yes, c'mon," I said, grabbing Poesy's hand and pulling her into the corridor. We ran up on deck and stood watching Melbourne disappear from view as the *Ceylon* steamed across the flat waters of the bay. Suddenly, Poesy let out a little sob.

"You should be happy. I thought you wanted to come away," I said.

"I did. I do, I still do. But can't you feel both things? Happy-sad and sad-happy at the same time?"

That was the problem with Poesy. Nothing was simple. She saw the good and the bad in everything.

Suddenly, out of nowhere, Flora Henley and Daisy Watts careered into us, squealing with excitement. I was annoyed but Poesy apologised to them. Apologised – to seven-year-olds! She couldn't see past their top-of-the-chocolate-box sweetness to put them in their place. I suppose they were pretty enough, Flora with her chocolate curls and bright green eyes and Daisy with her pudding face and plump lips that she liked to nibble when she was thinking. Not that either of those two did much thinking. They spent more time giggling than letting any ideas slip through their airy heads.

"Haven't you two got somewhere that you have to be? Someone else that you have to annoy?" I said.

"We're exploring," said Daisy. "Do you want to play, Poesy?"

"No, Poesy doesn't want to play baby games. Off you go, shoo!"

As the two flighty imps cantered down the deck, I made

Poesy turn to look me in the face.

"We are going to have a great adventure, Poesy Swift. Now we're away from our mothers and Mrs Essie and all the nay-sayers, we can do what we want."

"But we have to work too, don't we? Mr Arthur said we have to rehearse in the dining hall every day, and that matron, Miss Thrupp, she seems very strict."

"Pish-posh! Mr Arthur is easy to please and Miss Thrupp is a little mouse. A bit of singing and dancing in the morning and then the rest of the day we can do as we please."

"Aren't we meant to have lessons in the afternoon? Mrs Essie told my grandmother there was a teacher."

I put my arm around her shoulder. "That's the beauty of being away. They've said Myrtle Jones is our teacher but Myrtle is really a Lilliputian. It's all a blind. Myrtle is only seventeen and she never even finished school."

"No lessons?" said Poesy, her little mouth falling open in surprise.

"Don't worry. We've got better things to do. C'mon, the ship is ours!"

I hooked her arm through mine and we strolled along the deck. All the adults had gone below, but the Lilliputians were out in force. The boys kept to the forecastle and hung over the side, barking at the waves like a pack of silly dogs, but Charlie and Lionel Byrne stood a little apart from the other boys. I saw Charlie glance towards us and I grabbed Poesy's arm and turned her away. I wasn't fast enough.

"Oh, there's Charlie," she said, swivelling to wave in his direction.

"Don't make such a fuss!" I said. "He'll want to come and

talk to us."

"What's wrong with that? I like Charlie."

"Charlie is all right but Lionel is beastly, with his creepy puppet and his bossy manners. And you don't get one Byrne without the other. Besides, you can't count Charlie as a friend. He's a boy and he's younger than you."

Poesy sighed, as if I was explaining something terribly complicated.

Valentine stood at the rails with a gaggle of the middling girls, tittering like sillies as they watched Melbourne grow smaller and smaller. I adored Valentine but sometimes she could be simply too giggly.

The older girls sat in deckchairs, arranged in a closed circle. They wrapped their coats tight and folded their arms across their chests as they leaned their heads together. The wind carried their gossip away. I dragged Poesy towards them and we perched on the end of Tempe Melbourne's deckchair. There was nothing that Tempe was afraid to talk about. A girl could learn a lot from someone like Tempe.

That first night at sea, the ship's doctor insisted that a whole party of girls sit at his table. I knew exactly what that slimy old quack was thinking. I'd been 'examined' by his type before. I asked Poesy to swap seats with me. It wouldn't hurt her to learn a thing or two about dealing with men like that.

I saw it – the moment she discovered what sort of medicine the doctor dished up. She had a forkful of food halfway to her mouth when she suddenly froze. It must have been the instant when she felt his hand settling on her knee. Then her face flickered with confusion. Perhaps she imagined he was only pinching to see if she was healthy. You could tell by the burning blush that spread across her face that his horrid, bony fingers were kneading her leg, working their way up her thigh. She let her hair fall forward to cover her scarlet cheeks and wriggled away from him. I giggled and Poesy knew I understood. She stared at me, her baby-blue eyes as big as saucers. She really was too betwixt and between. It was about time she grew up.

I laughed again and made a little stabbing gesture with my fork at a slice of meat on my plate. Poesy curled her fingers around her knife and her knuckles grew white. For a moment, I thought she might plunge it straight into Dr Whitehead's hand but she simply laid it across her plate. Then she turned to the doctor, smiled that slow, cat-like smile of hers and excused herself from the table. I was glad. Glad that she had found out. She was becoming a real Lilliputian.

10

Locked Doors

Poesy Swift

The door to our cabin was locked when I came below deck. I knocked lightly and pressed my ear against the metal. Tilly and Valentine were still in the dining hall so it had to be Eliza in there. At first, I thought she must have been asleep. But I could hear someone making a low humming noise. Or was it the echo of the ship's engine? After five minutes of tapping and calling her name, I wandered aimlessly up onto the moonlit deck. I simply couldn't go back to the dining table and that doctor person. It was too horrible. I clung to the rails as a biting wind swept off Bass Strait.

"Is that you, Poesy?" said Eloise. She jiggled her baby, Bertie, to stop him mewling. "What are you doing up on deck?"

Eloise was Eliza and Eunice's sister. She'd been a Lilliputian once, but now she was nineteen, married to Eddie Quedda and had Bertie to look after.

"I felt sick." I couldn't tell her about the doctor. "So I went to my cabin. But Eliza won't open the door. At least, the door won't open. Maybe she's not there."

Eloise took me by the wrist and pulled me towards the stairs. "What can she be thinking?" she muttered.

While I held baby Bertie, Eloise rapped loudly on the

door of the cabin.

"Lizzie, open this door at once."

There was a murmur of voices from the other side. "Lizzie," said Eloise again, her tone more threatening.

The door opened a crack and Eliza's pale face appeared in the gap.

"Poesy was up on deck, freezing, because you wouldn't let her in."

"I was sleeping," Eliza said, rubbing her eyes. "I didn't hear her knock."

Eloise tried to push against the door but Eliza held it firmly. "I'm not dressed, don't push."

"Is there someone in there with you?" asked Eloise.

Eliza glanced at me as I held baby Bertie awkwardly in my arms. "Why aren't you both in the dining hall? What are you doing wandering about the ship?"

Eloise took the baby from me. "I was trying to settle Bertie and Poesy is unwell, but that's not the point, Lizzie. We've talked about this before."

Talked about what? I thought.

"Go away, Lo. Just leave me alone. Don't worry about me. Worry about that baby of yours." Then she turned to me. "Poesy, darling, be a chum and go and ask the steward for a jug of water, please. I've used up what was here. I'll have everything straightened up by the time you come back." She pushed the door shut.

I looked at Eloise questioningly, but her lips were drawn thin as she jigged her baby in her arms, trying to still his sobs.

"Go along then," she said, waving me away.

"But can't we ring for the steward?"

"Maybe the bell isn't working," said Eloise. "Go."

I was halfway along the hall when I heard Eloise knock again and the argument with Eliza begin afresh. I could hear the rise of their voices and then the sharp retort of flesh against flesh. I felt my own cheek sting at the thought of Eliza being slapped.

By the time I got back to my cabin, Eloise was gone. I rapped softly and Eliza opened the door immediately. Everything in the cabin was as I'd left it before tea, but there was a funny odour in the air, warm and salty with a musky undertone. I crinkled up my nose. "What's that smell?" I asked.

"Ships have lots of funny smells," said Eliza. She wore a long ivory nightgown with white sateen trim. She slipped into her bed again. "I'm sorry, Poesy. I was asleep when you knocked the first time. You'll have to take the water from the steward when he comes. I don't want him to see me in my nightie."

"But why are you in bed again already? It's not very late."

"I always feel a little woozy on the first night at sea," said Eliza. "I'll have my sea legs soon."

She did look odd, but not unwell. Her eyes were bright, like two dark blue marbles with silvery flecks, and her cheeks were shiny pink.

After the steward brought the water, I climbed up into my bunk above Eliza.

"You're a quiet little stick, Poesy. I think we're going to like each other."

I hung over the edge of my bunk and looked down at her. Her face was so lovely, so luminous in the moonlight.

"Are you all right, Poesy?" she asked, as if she could read everything that had happened to me, as if it were written on my face. "Come down here, climb into my bunk and tell me what's the matter."

And so I did. She lifted the blanket and I slid in beside her, as if we were the oldest friends in the world. I told her about wanting to leave Melbourne and how guilty I felt, about Mumma and Yada and Chooky and them needing the thirty shillings, about all my fears about not being good enough for the Lilliputians, and even about the creepy doctor and not knowing how to stop him. After I'd finished, she stroked my hair and whispered to me softly.

"You'll be right, little Poesy. You're a peach of a girl and the audiences will love you. And I'll watch out for you too. I think you and I will be great friends, and if you've any little troubles, you can tell me. Telling your troubles always makes them lighter.

"But I think maybe we should be even better friends if we didn't have to share with Valentine and Tilly. Perhaps we could ask to have a little cabin for two. Just you and me. Would you like that?"

I didn't know how to answer her. I liked the idea so much, it felt wicked to want it.

"Would they let us?"

"If you asked Miss Thrupp, she could arrange it for us. Because it's your first trip."

"Can't you ask?"

"My sister might intervene. She has opinions about everything, but she's not the one in charge. It's up to Miss Thrupp and Mr Arthur. Will you ask, Poesy dear?"

In that moment, I felt I would do anything for her.

"Even if Eloise thinks she knows best, it must be nice to have a sister," I said, wishing that Eliza was mine.

"There are nice bits and not so nice bits," replied Eliza.

"How do you mean?"

"Oh, I'm too tired. You get up in your little bunk now. I'll tell you about it another time. When we have our own cabin."

Snuggled down in my bed, I listened to Eliza's breathing change as she fell asleep, but for a long time I lay awake, feeling the rhythm of the ship as it sailed up the dark coast; feeling the rhythm of my new life.

11

Runaway Girls

Tilly Sweetrick

We docked in Sydney but no one was allowed to go ashore, not even Eloise, Eliza and Eunice, whose parents lived in Paddington. Only Miss Thrupp, that odd little matron who was meant to be in charge of us children, she took her baby nephew with her and disappeared. I watched her figure merge into the crowd on the docks and rather hoped she wouldn't come back.

I really couldn't take to that woman. Nor could I understand why she'd signed on to travel with the Lilliputians. She was such an unlikely matron. Everything about her was so tiny and birdlike – her hands, her wispy light-brown hair, her bright dark eyes that darted this way and that when anyone misbehaved. She was nothing like Mrs Essie. As soon as Mrs Essie walked into a room, every one of the children fell quiet. You knew you had to obey Mrs Essie. She never needed to raise her voice or even speak crossly to us. It wasn't that we were afraid of her – it was more that she commanded our attention. But Miss Thrupp was like a sparrow, hopping about the edge of the troupe and twittering in a tiny voice. When we were all together rehearsing in the dining hall, it was as if she became invisible, fading into the wallpaper. Perhaps it was because of her baby. She said Timmy was her dear dead sister's orphaned boy and she had promised to care for him. Maybe that was why he was a fractious little thing that hadn't taken well to the sea voyage. Or maybe it was simply Miss Thrupp. She handled him as if he would explode at any moment, as if she were frightened of him. I think she was frightened of us too. I was almost surprised to see her struggling up the gangplank again later that evening. If she'd known what lay ahead, she would never have returned.

As we steamed out of Sydney Harbour and through the Heads, Poesy and I stood at the rails. I slipped my arm around her shoulder and she rested her head against me, nuzzling in closer, almost as if she were my little sister. I rather liked that about Poesy in the beginning. There was a sweetness to her that made you want to take her under your wing.

"First, we'll probably stop in Brisbane," I said. "And then from Brisbane, we'll sail in one great big smooth line all the way to Honolulu in Hawaii. Then we'll go to Vancouver and start a tour of Canada. They love us there. We'll play St John and Winnipeg and then Montreal and Quebec City – oh, you'll simply adore those French-Canadian cities. They're so sweet. And then there's Ottawa and Toronto and then we'll do America properly." I counted the cities on my fingers, as if I was tapping out the beats of a lovely song. "New York, Boston, Chicago, Portland, Seattle, San Francisco. Mr Arthur has a house there, you know. We might stay in San Francisco for quite a while."

Poesy looked up at me, almost breathless with wonder. I felt it too – that it was utterly wonderful to be going back to America. I'd been such a baby when Mrs Essie had taken me on my first world tour. This time I was an old hand; this time I was a thoroughly modern girl.

"Aren't you glad I told you to audition?" I asked Poesy, expecting her to thank me. But instead she turned everything upside down.

"So you are pleased Mr Arthur picked me, aren't you? You don't mind that he likes me so much?"

She said it in such a way that I felt quite uncomfortable. I let go of her shoulder and leaned over the railing to let the wind catch my hair and whip it out behind me.

"You ask the silliest questions, Poesy."

Next morning, Mr Arthur told everyone to be in the dining hall at ten o'clock sharp, as if it were an ordinary day, but he should have known better. Leaving Sydney had made everyone skittish. Perhaps it was because now the voyage was to begin in earnest and we knew we wouldn't set foot in Australia again for two years. Whatever the reason, no one wanted to rehearse.

Mr Arthur came below deck to ferret out every single Lilliputian, though it should have been Miss Thrupp's job to fetch us. He banged on cabin doors and was rather sharp with Freddie Kreutz and told him he was an insolent cur when really Freddie was only grumbling about having to put his boots back on.

Once rehearsal began, Mr Arthur seemed less grumpy. He worked each of us through our songs carefully. I'm ashamed to admit that I rather liked the way he tipped his head so his face was level with mine as I sang. It's hard to believe, but in the beginning I liked the way he made you feel you were the only girl in the room.

We worked our way through 'A Runaway Girl'. I was

growing tired of all the other old musicals but this one was still my favourite. Even though I was only in the chorus, I was sure that at some stage I would play Winifred Grey, the beautiful Englishwoman who runs away to sing with bandits. It was exactly the sort of part that suited my voice.

Poesy stood behind Mr Arthur's chair as we both watched Eliza sing her solo. When she'd finished, Poesy leaned over and whispered close to his ear, "Do you think, Mr Percival, sir, that one day I might sing a lead role? One day, like Eliza, I might play Winifred?"

I wanted to pinch the sly minx. Her whisper might as well have been a shout. I heard every syllable. It simply wasn't done, to wheedle your way into a part like that. I expected Mr Arthur to rebuke her, but instead he turned around and took one of her hands and gave it a little squeeze.

"Poesy, you mustn't keep calling me Mr Percival or 'Sir'. 'Mr Arthur' is much friendlier, don't you think?"

Poesy blushed, her usual, endearing ploy – and then muttered in a babyish voice, "Yes, Mr Arthur."

When we stepped up to sing the next number with the rest of the girls, I tried not to think about Poesy. The lyrics swelled inside me and burst out so I could hear my voice above all the rest of the chorus and it felt as though it were my song, mine alone. "I'm only a poor little singing girl…"

ABRACADABRA

Poesy Swift

On the third day out from Sydney, Charlie came and leaned against the rail beside me. We hung over the side, staring into the churning seawater. Tilly was in one of her moods again and Eliza was having afternoon tea with Lo, so I was glad of his company. Sometimes, when he was sitting, watching the other boys, he reminded me of Chooky, or the sort of boy I hoped Chooky might become.

"Queensland is out there," he said in that soft voice of his. "You can almost smell it. Once we get past the last of the coast, everything will feel different. No more Australia. We're nearly through the Coral Sea and at the Torres Strait but we won't stop again now until we get to Surabaya."

"Sura-what?" I asked.

"Surabaya, on the island of Java. We cross the Arafura Sea to get there."

"But I thought we were going across the Pacific to America."

"Eventually, we'll get to America," said Charlie, not looking at me.

"What do you mean 'eventually'?"

"Lionel reckons we can't afford to go to America yet. Old Man Percy told him we have to make some money first. This troupe isn't as good as the last. Too many of the worst from the old lot and too many green ones that don't know what they're doing."

"Do you mean me?"

Charlie shrugged. "You're all right," he mumbled.

"I'll be better by the time we get to America."

"I expect so. That won't be for a year or more. We'll be going to India first."

I caught my breath. Tilly had told me so much about America that I could see it, taste it, long for it – but India? I'd read Mr Kipling's books. India was wild and strange, full of boys and men, wolves and tigers. Yada had told me it was a country of great souls, and her hero Mrs Besant had said that India was the mother of all religions, but in my mind it was a dark place full of monkeys and snakes, holy men and soldiers.

"Don't you think they're like magic words?" asked Charlie. "Arafura, Surabaya," he chanted. "It's almost as good as abracadabra."

"What are you talking about?"

"That's some of the route we're taking. When we get through the Malacca Straits we cross the Bay of Bengal to reach India."

He smiled and looked at me as if I felt as he did. "Say it," said Charlie, his green eyes shining. "Say it, Poesy. It's only ten words. Say it like a magic spell. *Arafura-Surabaya-Java-Sea-Malacca-Straits-Bay-of-Bengal-INDIA!*"

"Arafura-Surabaya-Java-Sea-Malacca-Straits-Bay-of-Bengal-India," I repeated, trying to make the words sink in, willing myself to feel the magic that Charlie heard in those names. But inside, I trembled. The future had grown dark and unknowable.

13

SISTERS

Poesy Swift

That night, Tempe Melbourne came storming into the new cabin that Eliza and I had to ourselves. I was a little intimidated by Tempe. She was so tall and aloof. I knew she had been friends with Eliza once but her expression was anything but friendly now.

"Have you heard?" she said, almost shouting as she stood in front of my bunk. "He's messed it up already and we haven't even left Australian waters."

"You mean about having to go to Java?" Eliza said, and I was relieved she seemed so calm.

"Not only Java. We'll have to do Singapore and Georgetown and then India. India! You know one of the Lilliputians died in India when they toured there in '97. My mother never agreed to me going to India! Your mother will be angry too, Poesy," she added, almost as an aside.

"Stop it, Tempe," said Eliza. "You are not to spread lies. It's not true."

"What's not true?" said Tempe.

"That one of the troupe died."

"How would you know? You weren't on that trip. Everyone knows he caught leprosy and they left him in India to rot."

"You're being ridiculous. And melodramatic. Nobody

died, I tell you. Not a child. It's a lie. And it's a lie that your mother didn't agree. Every mother gave the Percivals permission to make decisions on our behalf. All our parents trust him."

Tempe went red in the face. "You think your parents would trust him if they knew about you?"

Eliza stepped forward and slapped Tempe. Hard. "Get out!" she said, pushing Tempe out of our cabin, slamming the door behind her.

We looked at each other for a long, terrible moment and then Eliza burst into tears. She sat beside me on my bunk and put one arm around me as she sobbed. "It's not true. Nothing she says is true. It wasn't a child that died. It wasn't. It was poor Mr Arthur's brother. Why does everyone have to twist things and make lies?"

But it wasn't the dead boy that I was thinking about.

"What did Tempe mean about not trusting Mr Arthur?" I asked.

"Nothing. She's a stupid, spiteful girl. I can't believe I used to trust her."

"But wasn't she your friend, Eliza?"

"Don't call me Eliza, darling Poesy. Call me Lizzie. Call me Lizzie and let's always be true friends. Friends that believe in each other and trust each other."

My head exploded with questions but Eliza was trembling so much I was afraid to ask any of them.

"Please don't turn against me, Poesy."

I squeezed her hand. "Don't worry. I would never turn against you, Lizzie." And I meant it.

That night, when Lizzie and I climbed into our bunks, she

told me stories about growing up with the Lilliputians. She told me of all the places she'd visited and the best shows and the most beautiful gowns. And then, when we turned the lights down, she sang to me. Even though she was almost too old to be a Lilliputian, they kept her in the troupe because of her beautiful voice. With just the two of us in our little cabin and the sea washing against the steamer, it felt as if Lizzie's voice spun a silky cocoon of songs that would bind us together forever. When she wrapped her arms around me, I felt I would love her with all my heart until my dying day. She was the big sister I never had, the friend I'd always longed for. There was nothing I wouldn't do for her. She was everything to me, everything I wanted to become. I would trust her with my life.

I fell asleep and dreamed we were together on stage, holding hands as applause rained down around us.

14

SPINNING ACROSS
THE ARAFURA SEA

Tilly Sweetrick

We didn't do it out of spite. It was sheer boredom that started
me off. There was nothing more to it. I came up on deck to
find my poor little Valentine hanging over the rail, staring
down at the sea as if she'd been hypnotised. That's how dull
we both felt. So dull that a wave could capture our attention.

All Valentine's brown curls had grown frizzy and her face
was sticky with sweat. I pulled her away and made her spread
her arms wide. "Turn your face up to the sky and copy me,"
I said as I began to spin.

Our skirts swirled as we spun around and around. A
line of deckhands stopped work and turned to watch. They
folded their arms across their chests and their faces had tight,
hungry smiles. It made me feel even giddier, to know that
spinning could change the way they saw us. I loved it that we
could act like little girls and yet be something more.

Poesy stood with the boys and gawped at us. Ever since
she'd changed cabins, she'd drifted away whenever I tried to
talk to her. She was always on the edge of things now, always
with Eliza or Charlie, never with me any more. I grabbed her
arm. "Come and spin with us, Poesy, we're getting giddy,"
I said. "It's like floating!"

"Giddy, giddy, giddy!" said Valentine, laughing as she spun towards us and fell dizzily into my arms. I stroked her hair away from her face and set her on her feet again. One sailor, a young one with dark eyes, was watching us, his mouth slightly open, as if at any moment he might have to step forward and take a bite of one of us. It made me giggle.

"See, Poesy, it's fun." I twirled on my tiptoes so my skirt filled with air and floated above my knees.

"Mr Arthur will be cross," was all she said.

"Oh pish-posh. No one's going to dob us in. Come on."

But she looked to Charlie and then he looked to Lionel and I knew she wouldn't play. She shook her head and stepped away from me. And so Valentine and I stuck out our tongues and then threw ourselves into a spin again, spinning and spinning until it felt as if the ship was spinning too and we fell down on the deck, clutching our stomachs as we gasped and laughed and kicked our legs in the air.

"Get up, Tilly, quickly."

It was Poesy, suddenly beside us as if she knew Mr Arthur was coming. A second later he was towering over me. I didn't care. I clutched Valentine's arm so that she would stay down.

Mr Arthur dragged us to our feet. His fingers felt hot and sweaty as they encircled my wrist. His mouth was set in a tight grimace and he pulled us towards him.

"What do you think you're *doing*?" he said, his eyes swivelling from the row of hungry sailors and back to me.

"Playing. We were only playing."

"You will act like young ladies," he hissed. "Not little tramps."

He held me too tightly. My wrist ached. "Get your hands

off me," I said, trying to shake myself free.

"Don't take that tone with me, young woman," he snapped. Then he spoke softly, his voice full of menace. "Don't think you're too big for a spanking."

I wanted to slap him, but I was glad he was angry. I wanted him to be furious. As furious as I was at being cheated, at being taken to the East instead of going to America. I hung my head, as if I felt contrite, though inside I was bubbling with rage.

He turned away and gestured for Lionel to come to him. As if nothing had happened between us, he started talking to Lionel, instructing him to tell everyone to go below deck for rehearsals.

In the dining hall, Eddie banged away on the piano and Mr Arthur talked at the boys, working them through one of their scenes from *Florodora*. Miss Thrupp twittered away at us girls and finally managed to get the little ones to pay attention, but Valentine and I sat on a bench and fanned ourselves with our hands. Although it wasn't ten in the morning, the air was stifling in the dining hall. Eloise turned on the fans but that only made the two babies squall and Mr Arthur shouted at her to make them cease their infernal racket.

An hour into the rehearsal we were all pulling at our collars and slippery with sweat. Mr Arthur threw his hands up in despair and shooed us out of the dining hall. By eleven we were on deck again, most of us hanging over the rails to gaze at the blue sea and feel the breeze against our damp clothes.

Ruby, Tempe and Clarissa stood with their arms locked

and leaned against a wall while a crescent of sailors gathered around them. They didn't have to spin for anyone to notice them.

"Those girls," said Poesy, shaking her head. "They know they shouldn't fraternise with the sailors."

I laughed. "Fraternise? They're flirting. Miss Thrupp will have puppies if she sees them."

Just at that moment, Miss Thrupp stepped out on deck looking pale green and walked straight to the railing beside us. She handed her baby to Poesy to nurse and then vomited over the ship's side. I suppose I should have felt sorry for her, but when the breeze blew back in our direction it was hard to muster a whit of sympathy.

Ruby, Clarissa and Tempe all laughed at something the steward said and Miss Thrupp didn't even raise her head.

Finally, Mr Arthur came on deck. He looked straight at the big girls and their sailor-boy admirers and his face took on that bloated, red look that he'd turned on me when I was spinning. He strode past the boys playing quoits – didn't even glance at me – and spoke so sharply to Miss Thrupp that she jumped. The greenish hue in her cheeks gave way to pink as she followed Mr Arthur's gaze to where the wicked three were standing.

"Ooooh, they are going to get such a serve," I whispered to Poesy. But she didn't seem to hear me. Her little face grew pinched with worry.

We watched Miss Thrupp wipe her mouth and nod at Mr Arthur, as if to reassure him, as if it were her decision to step in and not his instruction. While he stood watching, she crossed the deck to the girls and the sailors. "Girls!"

The sailors flinched, suddenly embarrassed, and Tempe and Clarissa glanced at her nervously but Ruby laughed and rested one hand on the steward's forearm.

Miss Thrupp stepped closer, her face red with irritation. "Ruby!"

This time her voice was so loud that everyone on the top deck heard her. The boys stopped flinging quoits and the passengers dozing in their deckchairs woke suddenly, craning their necks to see what the fuss was about.

"Ruby," said Miss Thrupp. "I'd like a word with you. In private, please."

Ruby smiled insolently.

"Not now, Miss," she said.

"Yes, Ruby, now," said Miss Thrupp. She stepped into the circle of sailors and took hold of one of Ruby's hands. Ruby tried to shake free but Miss Thrupp held fast and began dragging her away.

Tempe and Clarissa stood back, as if trying to put some distance between themselves and Ruby. Everyone on the deck watched, waiting for the fireworks, but Ruby allowed herself to be pulled towards the stairwell. Tempe and Clarissa followed meekly behind.

"C'mon," I said, "let's follow."

We tried not to let our feet clatter on the metal stairs as we scurried after Miss Thrupp and her charge. Later, Poesy would say she didn't like to take sides and that she'd only been there because she was carrying Timmy for Miss Thrupp. But she wanted to see what happened as much as me.

We were about to turn the corner into the long corridor when we heard their raised voices.

"You will listen to me, Ruby Kelly. You will listen and you will obey."

Ruby laughed, her best catty laugh. Even though I didn't really like Miss Thrupp much, there was something in Ruby's laughter that made my stomach turn in a tight, anxious knot. It was a troublesome laugh, like a warning that you simply had to heed, a sound you hear before disaster strikes.

"You're a charlatan. You can't try and tell me how to behave! Why everyone knows that baby is your son, not your nephew. How dare you preach to me! I'm not the one with a brat and no husband. I'll talk to the stewards whenever I feel like it and I won't make the same mistakes as you."

Tempe and Clarissa had crept up behind us and they gasped, "She's really done for now."

We all jumped off the last steps and stood in the narrow corridor watching as Miss Thrupp chased Ruby down the passageway.

"Ruby, Ruby, you will go to your cabin. You will not go on deck again this afternoon. Ruby!"

But Ruby paid her no attention, marching down the passage until Miss Thrupp grabbed a handful of hair and yanked it hard. Ruby's shriek caused cabin doors to fly open. Next thing we knew, Miss Thrupp and Ruby were slapping each other furiously. Miss Thrupp looked desperate. She tried to wrap her arms around Ruby but was pushed to the ground as Ruby stood over her and shrieked, "You can't stop me!"

Miss Thrupp grabbed Ruby's ankle. In a fury of unbalanced rage, Ruby tried to wrench her ankle free and kicked Miss Thrupp in the stomach, hard. That's the truth. As I remember it, the plain truth. Ruby kicked Miss Thrupp but only while trying to escape.

At exactly that moment, Mr Arthur came clattering down the stairwell and pushed past us. He grabbed Ruby by the wrist, spun her around and boxed her ears so soundly that Ruby howled and clutched her head on either side. She stumbled against the wall but Mr Arthur caught her. Keeping one hand on Ruby, he reached down with the other and helped Miss Thrupp to her feet. Then he piloted them both down the passage.

"Tempe, Clarissa, take Ruby to your cabin and stay there until you are sent for. Poesy, as you've got Timmy you can help Miss Thrupp back to her cabin. Tilly, go and fetch Dr Whitehead and tell him Miss Thrupp needs his ministrations."

I was annoyed that I was given the least preferable task. "But what about Ruby? The doctor should see her too."

Mr Arthur looked at me, his eyes narrow. "The girl was hysterical but she's unharmed. Remember, she attacked Miss Thrupp. She got what she deserved."

I stared at him as if he were a stranger. I was starting to see Mr Arthur Percival in quite a different light. As he ran his hand through his hair and smoothed it back into place, I saw a glimpse of something dark and cruel in the set of his mouth.

"What are you waiting for, child? Do as you're told, or there will be consequences."

But there are always consequences for every little thing we do. One day Mr Arthur would suffer some serious consequences himself. One day, Mr Arthur would find out all about consequences.

15

THE PUPPET SPIRIT

Poesy Swift

It was late in the day when we sailed into Surabaya. There was no breeze and the air felt sticky, as if I could hold it in my hands and wring the water from it.

Tilly, Valentine and I watched as the gangplank was set in place. The port was tiny compared to the docks of Melbourne and there was noise and dust and people of all different colours bustling about everywhere we looked. Underneath the smell of coal and oil was the odour of fish. Down on the dock, a dark-skinned man stood beside a cart laden with golden mangoes. Further away, a group of small boys played in the shade of a coconut palm. There were men in strange costumes with little hats and odd skirts tied about their waists. Voices crying out in strange languages wafted up to us.

"I don't want to get off," said Tilly. "I don't think I'm going to like this place."

"It's all right," said Valentine. "It can't be so different to Manila. Americans are lovely wherever they are."

"But there aren't any Americans in Java," said Tilly. "Really, Valentine, sometimes I think your head is full of fluff! The Dutch are in charge and they hardly speak English, at least that's what Freddie told me. It's going to be awful."

I stuck my fingers in my ears to block out Tilly's voice and tried to think of something cheering that I'd read about the Dutch, but all I could think of was clogs and windmills.

The hotel smelled of dust, boiled ham and something sharp and spicy that made my nose itch. There weren't enough beds for all of us and Eloise said we would have to sleep two to a bed. Lizzie asked for me, because, she said, it was only fair to pair the big girls with smaller ones. But I knew it was more than that. It was so easy between us now. We slept together like a pair of spoons in a drawer, side by side. Though perhaps I was the little teaspoon and she the dessertspoon.

That evening, the advance booking agent, Mr Shrouts, met us outside the hotel. He led the way as Mr Arthur, Jim and Eddie herded us down the main road. In the dusky twilight, natives stopped what they were doing, fell silent and stared at us. Others came out onto their verandahs and watched our procession as if the circus had come to town, not a proper theatre company.

When we came to a wide, open field, I felt my heart sink. I hadn't thought about having to perform in tents. All of a sudden, I had a picture in my head of the freaks' pavilion at the Royal Melbourne Showgrounds. I looked down at my dress and smoothed my hand across my tummy to stop it flip-flopping about.

Maybe my body knew what my mind couldn't. Maybe my insides understood that the evening would bring disaster. Lizzie said that Mr Arthur wasn't to know, that he'd acted in good faith.

We stood in our costumes at the rear entrance to the tent

and slapped away at the mosquitoes. From out in the dark fields, we could hear the bark of geckoes. Little Flora began to cry and pull at her costume.

"I don't want to be in a tent. I don't like tents."

"You have to think of it as a rehearsal," said Freddie Kreutz. "We're only doing a revue, after all. We can't do a proper show until all the props and costumes are unloaded. Besides, it's not as if there's anyone important in the audience."

"That's not very professional," said Lizzie. "Every audience is important."

"Oh, what a trooper you are," said Freddie in a fake-jolly tone that made me squirm. "You know Lionel is opening the show tonight? Mr Arthur said he could do his ventriloquist act, for fun. What a toady, eh?"

Lizzie pulled out a handkerchief and wiped Flora's tears away. "You don't have to be snide about everything, Freddie. Just because you don't have anything special to do doesn't mean other people should hide their light under a bushel."

"Ooooh, so are you going to give us a nice little flash of what's under your bushel, then?"

Lizzie spun about and slapped his face. Freddie's hand flew to his cheek, to cover the pink mark on his flesh, though I'm sure she hadn't hit him very hard.

"What was that for?"

"For being a nasty, rude little brat," she said.

I hated Freddie for provoking Lizzie, for making her act that way. It wasn't really what she was like. She was the gentlest soul in the world and it was awful to see her so angry.

I took Flora by the hand and led her away behind the tent to sit with Charlie. I wished Miss Thrupp would come and help us with our costumes but no one had seen her since her fight with Ruby. She and baby Timmy had stayed locked in their cabin. They hadn't even come ashore with us.

While we sat in the makeshift backstage area, Lionel carefully unpacked Danny McGee. I know it was babyish to be frightened of a doll. That's all Danny was – a ventriloquist's dummy – but when I saw him perched on Lionel's knee I shuddered. In the dim glow of the gaslight, he looked like a shrunken corpse.

"You wait," said Lionel, grinning. "Everyone's going to be astonished by my Danny."

Mr Arthur frowned. We knew he thought it was bad luck to boast before you went on stage. Better to be nervous. Maybe he was right. He lifted the tent flap and gestured for Lionel to follow him.

"C'mon," said Charlie. "Let's watch."

Even though it wasn't allowed, Charlie and I carefully folded back a piece of canvas and peeked. Lionel sauntered onto centre stage carrying Danny McGee and made himself comfortable on a stool before introducing himself. Then he turned to Danny and told him to say hello to the audience.

Danny's eyes swivelled about in his ugly little head and his jaw dropped open. Lionel wasn't very good at throwing his voice. It sounded as if someone was strangling him, his words growing even squeakier and higher as he tried to force the sounds out from between tightly stretched lips. There was a murmur of unease from the crowd.

Except for the front row of Dutchmen sweating in their over-tight suits, the tent was full of dark-skinned men. There were a few women sitting with their children at the very back. They were wrapped in strange pieces of coloured cloth instead of ordinary clothes. I had never seen anyone like them. Their skin was coppery brown and every single one of them had dark eyes. It was hard not to stare.

"How do you think he's doing?" asked Charlie anxiously, leaning so close to me that I could feel the heat coming from his body. "Do you think they like him?"

"Nobody is laughing."

"They probably don't understand the jokes. I told him he'd have to be careful with the jokes."

"No, it's not that," I said. "Something's wrong."

The murmur of the audience grew louder and a small boy began to wail. When Lionel made Danny McGee jump up and do a little song-and-dance routine, the whole of the native audience leaped to their feet and fled, pushing the benches over in their hurry to leave the tent. Mr Arthur shouted at Mr Shrouts and Mr Shrouts started yelling in Dutch at the man who'd been selling the tickets, who ran out after the retreating crowd of Javanese people as they disappeared into the night.

Lionel sat frozen on stage, his mouth trembling. Backstage, we all stared at each other. No one knew what to do. Mr Arthur lifted the back flap of the tent and crossed the stage.

"What did you do, boy?"

"Nothing. Only what I always do."

A short, round Dutchman got up from his seat at the foot of the stage and approached them.

"It's not the boy's fault. You know, here in Java they believe in magic. They think the boy has bewitched the doll. Black magic. An evil spirit is inside the mannequin and the spirit is speaking, not the boy."

Lionel's face crumpled and Arthur slapped his forehead and exclaimed, "That's scuppered it, hasn't it? We won't be doing a second show, not now they're all terrified."

But as he spoke, a small group of Javanese returned to the tent, shepherded by Mr Shrouts and the ticket-seller.

"You must show them it is only a toy," Mr Shrouts said, breathless from his pursuit. "Show them it's mechanical, show them how you do it. Then they'll be all right and we can get on with the show."

Lionel slipped off his stool and held Danny McGee up, showing how his hand fitted neatly under the dummy's coat. He took off Danny's clothes and laid them on the stool; the red-and-black checked jacket, the green bow tie and the dusty grey pants. All the time he spoke to the audience about how the dummy was made. Then he took Danny's head apart and showed them the workings and how he made the dummy's eyes roll and mouth open.

Charlie and I watched the audience anxiously. They still looked apprehensive but it seemed that they were starting to trust Lionel. It was only when the head rolled off the stool and hit the floor with a crash that a few people jumped to their feet again. But Lionel simply leaned over and picked up the head, holding it out to the audience to show them it was an empty object, not the vessel of an evil spirit.

When Lionel came off stage, his shirt was soaked in sweat. His eyes were bloodshot and his mouth was set in a grim line.

"Are you all right, Leo?" asked Charlie, putting his hand on his brother's shoulder.

"It killed him. It killed Danny."

"What do you mean? You're being silly," said Ruby. "He wasn't ever alive."

"He was for me. And now he's finished." He shoved the head of the dummy at Charlie and ran out into the night.

Charlie turned Danny McGee's head over in his hands and we all saw the ugly black crack in his forehead from where he'd hit the stage. One of his eyes sat at a skewed angle while the other stayed shut.

"Perhaps he can fix it," I said dubiously.

"I don't think so. The fall has damaged its mechanisms," said Charlie.

"Poor old Danny McGee," I said.

"It's not the dummy I'm worried about," said Charlie, looking to where Lionel had departed through the open tent flap.

After the show, we walked silently back through the streets of Surabaya. Mr Arthur carried Daisy asleep in his arms. The dim gaslight outside the hotel sizzled as bugs flew into its glow. Nightjars swooped through the eaves of the verandahs. Then, from between two buildings, we saw a flickering movement, a flaring light and a collage of shifting shapes. Beyond the laneway stood an odd little temple of some sort. Seated on the ground, a crowd of Javanese watched shadow figures move across a screen. We heard a babble of foreign words while the shadowy forms on the screen fought and danced, their shadows lengthening and then shrinking as if by magic.

Standing at the edge of the laneway, silhouetted against the soft light, was Lionel. Charlie called to him but Lionel ignored him, transfixed by the play of shadows. Mr Arthur handed the sleeping Daisy to Eddie Quedda. Then he walked over to Lionel and put an arm around his shoulder to draw him away. For a brief moment Lionel resisted, but then suddenly he slumped against Mr Arthur and allowed himself to be led over to where Charlie and I waited. Behind them, the shadow figures writhed and twisted in an intricate play of movement.

At the steps of the hotel, Lionel stumbled and Mr Arthur caught him gently and guided him towards the entrance.

"It's all right, young Lionel," said Mr Arthur. "You did your best."

Lionel turned his stricken face upward to gaze at Mr Arthur and his expression grew soft with gratitude.

"Thanks, sir," he said. "I won't never let you down again."

It was such a tender moment. I wanted to cry out, "I won't let you down either, Mr Arthur." But it would have been a promise I couldn't keep.

16

LOVING LIZZIE

Poesy Swift

The next morning we were back on board the steamer. Mr Arthur had said he couldn't afford to pay for another night's lodging in Surabaya if we weren't doing a show, and that meant we'd have to sleep on the ship. Some of the girls wanted to wander about the town, but Mr Arthur said it was improper, so they sat restlessly fidgeting on the deck.

I went to my cabin and lay on the bed. I tried to write a postcard home:

Dearest Chooky and Yada and Mumma,

This morning as we walked back to our ship, Mr Arthur insisted Eliza and I stop at a roadside stall and try a piece of an awfully peculiar fruit called durian. It smelled so unpleasant I had to peg my nose but when I popped a piece in my mouth it was sweet and juicy and oddly delicious. You can always trust Mr Arthur's advice.

Then my pencil hovered above the card. I didn't really want my family to know I was in Surabaya. Could you buy durian fruit in America? Would Yada realise that I hadn't gone where Mr Arthur had promised to take me? How could I explain it? I sighed and pushed the unfinished postcard under my pillow.

"What's the matter, darling Poesy?" asked Lizzie.

"Do you think Mr Arthur was right to bring us here?"

"You mustn't be disheartened, Poesy," said Lizzie. "We only stopped at Surabaya because the *Ceylon* had to deliver cargo. This isn't what things will be like everywhere we go. Batavia will be much better. It's bigger and prettier."

"Have you been there before?"

"No, but Mr Arthur has and he said it's very civilised. And after that there'll be Singapore, which I have visited and it's lovely. There's a big theatre and plenty of white people to come and see us so we won't have to worry about the audiences."

"Don't they let the coloured people come?"

"Oh, I can't remember. Perhaps there are Chinamen up in the gallery, but the stalls and balconies are full of the nicest people and they give you presents and ask you for afternoon tea."

"Tilly says they only ask the prettiest girls. She said I shouldn't expect too much. She said she might let me come along with her because she usually gets a lot of invitations, doesn't she?"

Lizzie laughed. "Tilly? Do you really think Tilly is one of the prettiest? Prettier than you?"

She stood up and leaned in close to my pillow. She put one finger on the tip of my nose and put her face next to mine, so close that I could smell the minty sweetness of her breath. "You are far prettier than Matilda Sweeney or Sweetrick or whatever she may call herself now. That girl can't hold a candle to you, dear one." She kissed me on the cheek. "Don't let Tilly or anyone else make you doubt yourself, Poesy Swift. You're pretty and clever and a wonderful little actress."

I wanted to fling my arms around her and hug her. I wanted to bury myself in her lovely soft embrace but she had thrown herself down on her bed again and was flicking through the pages of a magazine. I hung over the side of my bunk and my hair fell like a pale waterfall about my face.

"Can we be friends forever, Lizzie?"

She raised one hand and gently touched my cascading hair.

"Yes, my little pixie. We shall be friends forever and we shall both live happily ever after."

And I believed her.

17

HEADS AND TAILS

Poesy Swift

The next day, I sat alone in the forecastle, watching the coast as the steamer churned its way north. Tilly and Valentine found me there.

"This air, it's so sticky, don't you think?" said Tilly. She lifted her petticoats and flapped them into the wind.

"Tilly!" I cried. "You've got no knickers on!"

"It's delicious," she said. But Valentine shook her head. "You won't like it when we're ashore. Your thighs will stick together when you walk."

I covered my ears. Those two could talk about the rudest things.

As we steamed towards the town of Batavia we passed hundreds of small islands. Some were no more than a single palm tree standing up out of the sea quite by itself. When we passed through the entrance to the harbour, Batavia came into view. Dark green hills dotted with elegant mansions rose on either side of the town. A rickety boat pulled alongside the steamer and we all squealed when we discovered we were going to take the journey ashore in a *sampan*.

Batavia was nicer than Surabaya had been but people still stared at us as we travelled through the town in open carriages. As we rode into the central square, Freddie Kreutz pointed at an odd tower set into a well in the ground.

"That's where the Dutch execute prisoners," he said with spiteful glee. "They take them underground from the court house and then…" He made a slitting motion with his fingers across his throat and a horrible gargling noise.

Max laughed and put his hands around Freddie's neck. "Now, you are my prisoner…" Then the two of them were wrestling with each other on the floor of the carriage and all the girls had to raise their feet up onto the seat. I pulled my skirts over my knees and shivered at the thought of men having their heads chopped off under the ground while above them people were promenading with their parasols in the tropical heat.

Outside our hotel, we clustered in the shade of the verandah. For some reason, we weren't allowed inside. Mr Arthur stood at the counter, arguing with the manager, while we waited. Daisy and Flora kept tiptoeing over to the door, peering into the cool darkness of the foyer and giggling. The boys sat on the edge of the steps scuffing their feet in the dust and we girls flopped on benches, fanning ourselves with our hands.

It was almost too hot to talk. I wandered across the verandah and stood behind Charlie and Lionel, watching over their shoulders. They were doing a trick with a shiny silver coin. Charlie had it in one hand and then, as if by magic, it passed through the skin of that hand and into the other.

"See, it's easy," said Charlie, handing the coin to Lionel. "You have a go."

"I still can't see how you do it. You're not showing me properly," said Lionel, wiping the sweat from his forehead. He glanced up at me. "You should go away, Poesy. Magicians can't let other people see their magic."

"But Charlie's letting you watch. He's teaching you and you're not a magician."

"That's different. He's my brother."

"Please, Charlie," I said, jumping down from the verandah to stand in front of the boys. "Show me too."

"Lionel can show you. Go on, Leo – give it a go."

Lionel scowled as he fiddled with the coin, passing it clumsily from one hand to the other until finally he lost control altogether and it slipped out of his hand and landed in the dirt with a plop. The sun bounced off the image of the King's head and I picked it up.

"Can I try?" I asked.

"No," said Lionel. "Girls don't do magic."

"It's all right," said Charlie. "She probably won't be able to work it out."

The coin was slippery with boy-sweat, and warm from Lionel's hand. I shut my eyes, picturing the movements that Charlie had made. In my mind's eye I could see exactly what he had done.

I took a deep breath and laid the coin on the palm of my left hand and then ran my right palm over it. The first time, the coin stayed there, but on the second try I managed to 'palm' the coin away so my left hand was empty. This time, I moved my hands so swiftly that no one but a magician would have known the coin had moved from my left hand to my right palm. I quickly placed my left hand on the back of my right and pressed hard, as if pushing the coin through flesh and bone. With a flourish, I turned my right hand over to reveal the shining shilling. I looked up at the boys for approval. Charlie smiled, but Lionel's face grew dark. He scowled at Charlie.

"You've showed her that before, haven't you? You two are trying to make me feel stupid. I don't have to stand for that." He turned away from us both and stomped into the darkness of the hotel foyer.

"Now look what you've done," said Charlie.

"You can hardly say that's my fault!" I said, handing back the coin.

"Don't be cross, Poesy. Lionel was right. Girls aren't supposed to learn magic. It's against the magicians' code."

He looked both serious and stupid in equal measure. I couldn't help but laugh. Suddenly, he laughed too. "That's the last time I let you close to me when I'm doing a trick." Then he reached up behind my ear, and when he drew his hand away he was holding a coin.

"That was clever," I said.

"I've been practising. Mr Arthur said that if I get really good, maybe I can do a magic act next time we stage a revue."

"Tilly says we'll never do a revue again. Not after what happened in Surabaya."

Charlie shrugged. He was funny like that. He never liked to talk about anything that he thought was gossip or start an argument, not even with Lionel. Not like the Kreutz brothers. Mr Arthur was always having to pull Freddie off Max or Max off Freddie. They were like two bears that set upon each other without the least provocation.

As we waited outside the hotel, Max and Freddie began to shove each other restlessly. The little girls began to whine. Why weren't we allowed inside?

Mr Arthur strode out onto the verandah looking haggard and called all the grown-ups into the hotel foyer. A few minutes later, Miss Thrupp scurried out and began flapping her arms, shrilly rounding up children and making us march into the street. Everybody grumbled but Miss Thrupp wouldn't say why we had to leave in such a hurry. She wouldn't even let us wait for the carriages to return.

The few bags we'd brought with us from the steamer were loaded onto another cart and we were all forced to walk back along the dusty roadways to the waterside again. As we tramped past the fish markets towards the dock, Tilly sidled up to me and grabbed my arm.

"Did you hear?" she asked. "Cholera – it's been through the hotel and they're not letting anyone stay ashore."

The stink of the fish market suddenly seemed horribly rank. "Cholera?" My stomach lurched and my limbs felt weak. "Why didn't Mr Shrouts warn us?"

"He sailed straight to Singapore – that's what advance agents do. They travel ahead of us for most of the tour."

She spoke in such a snappy tone that I lowered my head and decided to keep my thoughts to myself.

"I don't want to go ashore in Batavia ever, ever again," she said. "I can't wait until Singapore. At least it's a British colony. Really, the Dutch aren't like us. They simply aren't like us at all."

I couldn't see that the Dutch were very different or what that had to do with cholera, but it wasn't worth saying that out loud with Tilly in such a huffy-puffy mood.

We scurried towards the *sampan* as quickly as we could, jostling to be first. Mr Arthur stood by the ramp and handed the girls onto the old boat one by one. When Ruby Kelly nearly lost her balance, he caught her in his arms and lifted her gently on board. She blushed a little but she didn't thank him.

"Did you see that?" whispered Tilly, more to Valentine than to me. "Did you see how Mr Arthur was with Ruby? Perhaps Ruby's given him ideas."

"Tilly!" I said. "How dare you talk like that about Mr Arthur!"

Then she laughed, long and loud. She took my hand and kissed the back of it, as if to placate me. "Mercy, Poesy Swift. That wasn't meant for you. You have such jug-ears! But why shouldn't he like Ruby? He was jealous when she was flirting with those sailors. That's why he boxed her ears."

"No, that's not right. It was because she hurt Miss Thrupp."

"Mr Arthur isn't what he seems, Poesy. He's a married man. They say he has two children. Somewhere. But he gives all the girls ideas. Even I used to fancy him once, when I first joined up."

"He doesn't give me any ideas," I said hotly. "Besides, he's a grown-up and we're children. He's old! How can anyone fancy him?"

"That doesn't mean a thing," piped up Valentine. "Lots of girls have older men fall in love with them. Men can't help themselves."

She put her face close to mine, talking in a hurried, breathless way. "When we danced for Mr Carnegie in New York City, I think he fancied me. Mr Carnegie, that is, not Mr Arthur. But with Mr Carnegie, it was more fatherly. Perhaps he would have liked to adopt me. You know, that's probably why he sent money for the Northcote Library. He sent flowers backstage too. They were addressed to all of us but I was the lead that night in *The Girl from Paris*. Of course, Mrs Essie wouldn't let me meet him. There's always a sign on the stage door when we're touring saying that no one's to meet the children, in case they're not proper, but sometimes when you look down into the audience, you know the gentlemen fancy you. It happens all the time."

"But Mr Arthur isn't in the audience. Mr Arthur – he's like an uncle to us, isn't he?"

Tilly narrowed her eyes and shook her head at both of us.

"You are adorable, Valentine, but sometimes you say the most fanciful things. While you, Poesy, you are simply a baby."

I looked out at the smooth blue Java Sea and hoped I would never grow up.

18

THE INQUISITION

Poesy Swift

We were only eight hours out of Batavia on our way to Singapore when one of the crew collapsed. I was playing chasey with the little girls and we all saw him fall. He was one of the coal-shovelling men who stoked the engines. He came staggering onto the deck and collapsed right in front of us so that Daisy nearly tripped over his body. She let out a squeal. The man was black and sooty with coal dust, sweat was running in rivulets across his face and he was twitching, almost like Yada when she fitted. Dr Whitehead came running and Miss Thrupp hurried us away from the man.

Half an hour later, there was a meeting of all the passengers in the dining hall. Dr Whitehead announced that the stoker who had collapsed had died of cholera. Miss Thrupp and Eloise both gasped and clutched their babies, and all the girls began to talk at once. Mr Arthur had to stand on a chair and shout at the top of his voice to make us quiet down.

"There is no need to panic, ladies. I presume none of you have been mingling with the crew. This man would have caught the disease because he stayed ashore in Batavia while we returned safely to the ship. But I want everyone to stay in their cabins until Dr Whitehead gives the all-clear. We will suspend rehearsals until such time as the good doctor deems it appropriate for us to mingle again."

As soon as the announcements were made, Miss Thrupp burst into tears and ran from the dining hall. Mr Arthur turned his face up to the ceiling and sighed.

"Eloise," he called. "Please go and assist Miss Thrupp. She hasn't had much sleep, it seems."

"And who, may I ask, has?" said Eloise. Her baby was only a month older than Timmy Thrupp. She handed Bertie to Eliza and stood with her hands on her hips, facing Mr Arthur. "Can't you see, Arthur? She's frightened. But she's not the only one with a baby, or a cross to bear. You can't keep all these kiddies locked up all the way to Singapore."

"I don't *want* to lock them up," he said, exasperated. "But they can't mingle with the crew or any other passengers. God knows what will happen if one of them comes down with cholera."

We were given a list of instructions. We must keep ourselves clean, wash our hands, drink only tea, avoid the passengers who weren't in the troupe and keep to our cabins until we were notified by Eloise or Miss Thrupp that we could go to the dining hall.

Tilly and Valentine hooked arms and went off to their cabin in a hurry. I looked across at Lizzie and felt my heart sink. I knew she hated being shut up in the cabin. She was always going up on deck in the evening to watch the sea, or sending me out so that she could have time to herself.

In our cabin, the air was like warm soup. I pushed at the porthole, but even with the window open I felt as though I could hardly breathe. Eliza lay on her bunk with a wet flannel over her eyes.

"Has this ever happened before, when you were touring?" I asked.

"People have got sick before. In Manila, Tempe got some tropical sort of fever and I had to take her part. But we were never quarantined. I'm glad I'm with you, Poesy. Imagine if we were stuck in a four-berth cabin with Ruby and that lot."

"Don't you like Ruby?"

"Do you?"

I didn't answer because I wasn't sure how I felt about Ruby. She was one of the prettiest girls in the troupe – no one could compete with her honey curls and dimples – and she had been kind to me. Once, during a rehearsal, she offered to help me with some dance steps. Mr Arthur had been rather wry about it, saying it would have been nice if she could show the same courtesy to her little sisters, but I'm sure she helped them too occasionally.

It wasn't Ruby that worried me but her two best friends, Tempe and Clarissa. All three girls were seventeen but Tempe was their leader. When she looked down her nose at me I felt uncomfortable inside my own skin, and even if she smiled at me, my teeth were set on edge as if I'd eaten something too sugary.

As for Clarissa, there was nothing sweet in her – she was like something sharp and pickled that left a dry, startled taste in your mouth.

It was odd that I should have been thinking about them at that moment. I was thinking about Clarissa in particular when there was a knock on the door and there she was, as if I'd conjured her.

"Come and visit us, Poesy," she said, taking my hand and

drawing me out into the hall. "You must be lonely all by yourself."

"I'm not by myself," I said. "Lizzie's here."

Clarissa didn't say anything but she raised one eyebrow and pulled the cabin door shut, leaving Lizzie to her rest.

She kept a firm grasp of my wrist as she led me down the hall to the big cabin that the older girls shared. I tried to twist my arm free but she kept a resolute grip.

"I'm rescuing you, you stupid creature," she said, shoving me through the door of her cabin.

Tempe and Ruby were sitting on a bunk, looking flushed and frowsy in the equatorial air, their bare feet making a row of twenty neat pink toes. They'd stripped down to their petticoats and were taking turns fanning each other with little Chinese paper fans. Clarissa made me sit on a chair opposite them, as if I was on trial. Then she peeled off her outer clothes as well and lay down on the empty bunk above them.

"We need two things from you, Poesy," said Tempe. "We need you to tell us what Eliza and Mr P. were doing on deck together late last night. And we need you to be our agent and do a little bit of snooping for us."

"What do you mean?" I asked warily.

"First question, please," said Tempe. She pulled her petticoat up higher and then leaned forward, putting her pretty face close to mine. "What happened last night?"

"I don't know what you're talking about. Lizzie always goes for a walk on deck in the evenings."

"Surely you're not such a dunderhead that you didn't notice Eliza was missing for *hours*," said Clarissa.

"She wasn't missing. She was with Lionel. He saw her back to our cabin."

"Not Mr Arthur?"

"If she was with Mr Arthur, she was with Lionel as well."

The jury looked at each other knowingly, as hideous as three witches.

"Do you think she's in love with him?" asked Tempe.

"With Lionel?" I asked, incredulous. "She pities him, that's all."

There was something lumpy about poor Lionel. Lumpy and clumpy and a little bit sad. It didn't seem possible that anyone should fall in love with him, least of all Lizzie.

"No, silly. Mr Arthur, of course!" said Clarissa.

"No!" I shouted. "How can you be so beastly, Clarissa! Lizzie's not like you. She's good and kind and pure of heart."

"Hush, hush," said Tempe. "We didn't know you and Eliza had become quite so thick. We thought you were Tilly's little friend."

"I'm Tilly's friend too. But I'm not a sneaking hound," I shouted.

Fighting back tears, I dashed out into the corridor, away from their awful insinuations, away from the horrible inquisition, away from their nasty secrets and dirty lies.

19

CABIN FEVER

Poesy Swift

I went back to our cabin but Lizzie wasn't there and I was glad. I couldn't bear to face her. What if she asked me why Ruby and Clarissa and Tempe had wanted to see me? She would be appalled.

I picked up my two dollies, Topsy and Turvy, and pressed their little bodies against my cheeks. Yada had tried to clean them once with eucalyptus oil, and ever since they had smelled of gum trees. It didn't make me long for home. It made me think of Charlie and us being wedged side by side in our tree outside Balaclava Hall. I tucked them into my apron pocket and stepped out into the passageway.

I knew I'd be in terrible trouble if I was caught but I simply couldn't sit on my bunk waiting for Lizzie. I tiptoed down the corridor with my heart in my mouth and knocked on Charlie's door. I hoped he'd be alone because Lionel was nearly always shadowing Mr Arthur. When no one answered, I opened the door myself.

"Poesy!" exclaimed Charlie. He was sitting on his bed in his undershorts. He jumped up quickly and turned his back on me while he pulled on his trousers.

"I knocked," I said, stepping into the room and shutting

the door behind me. I suppose I should have been embarrassed to catch him half-undressed but I felt oddly pleased. It made me feel we were like brother and sister.

Charlie and Lionel's cabin was tiny, no bigger than a cupboard with two little bunks set into the wall. I looked around with curiosity, trying not to stare at Charlie's naked chest, while he pulled on his singlet.

"I was sewing up my trousers so the pockets make a cone shape, rather than squares," he said. "It makes it easier to find things when you're doing a trick. Would you like to see?"

"I thought you said girls shouldn't know about magic."

"You're not like the other girls," he said. He snatched an old Gladstone bag from beneath his bunk.

"I want to show you everything. You see this, this is my *servante*, my magic bag of tricks."

He patted the bunk and we sat down opposite each other with the *servante* between us. One by one, he showed me his props: hats, balls, dice, cards, eggs, wands, coins, handkerchiefs and two tiny jars of white powder. Then he took out a shiny red book with a wizard dressed in a long shroud on the cover and rubbed his hands over it. The title, *The Magician Annual 1909*, was embossed in silver letters.

"It's science, really," said Charlie. "Not mumbo-jumbo."

I leaned closer to him as he flicked through the pages, pointing out news of the world of magic and explaining the tricks. Suddenly, he looked up.

"Why are you here, Poesy?"

"If I have to be locked in a cabin, I'd rather be locked in with you than anyone."

He smiled but he wouldn't look at me. The silence between

us grew until I couldn't bear the weight of it. My eyes began to sting with tears.

"It's just I hate the way all the girls do nothing but talk about men and boys in a really horrid way."

Charlie pulled a face. "That's what they do, that lot. They flirt and tell stories. If you don't like 'em, don't listen. Then it won't matter what they say."

"But they tell lies! They pretend that men like them and they think every girl wants nothing but to be kissed and it's all they want to talk about."

Charlie shrugged. "I don't pay those girls no mind. All a storm in a teacup, if you ask me."

"Do none of the boys listen to them?"

"I should think not," he replied. He reached into his *servante* and pulled out a red velvet bag.

"Let's not talk about all that rubbish any more. I'll show you a trick. Have you got something I could do a vanishing act with?"

"I wish you could put all those girls' terrible lies in that bag and make them vanish."

Charlie rolled his eyes.

"I've got Topsy and Turvy," I said, pulling my dolls out of my apron pocket. "But you won't really make them disappear for good, will you?"

"No," he said, scrunching up his nose. "I'm going to make them come to life and actually be like Houdini. You watch. There's more to these dolls than meets the eye."

Charlie took Topsy and Turvy from me and turned them this way and that, studying them closely. He smoothed their wiry black hair down and adjusted the fall of their dresses.

When he finished examining them, he winked at me and then he made Topsy and Turvy dance about on the top of his *servante* while he whistled a little tune. Next he made them peek over the edge of the case to look at what was hiding inside. He animated them so well, it was almost as if they were really alive. When they'd finished studying all his things, he sat them both in the crook of his arm while he shook out the soft red velvet bag and showed Topsy and Turvy how it was lined with black silk.

Before I could stop him, he'd tumbled them both into the bag.

"Now look into my *servante* and fish out that long green ribbon," he said as he held the bag firmly shut with both hands. "We don't want them to escape. We want them to prove that the magic has taken hold of their souls."

My heart fluttered in my chest but I did as I was told and tied the ribbon in a tight knot around the top of the bag. "Now you keep hold of both ends of the ribbon, Poesy, so you can be sure that Topsy and Turvy are safe inside."

While I held the long ribbon stretched in either direction, Charlie pulled out a silk scarf and covered the bag. I could feel my heart beating faster. The air in the cabin suddenly seemed very close. I pulled the ribbons tighter and tighter, almost afraid that Topsy and Turvy really were going to come to life and wrestle their way out of the bag. And then, that's exactly what they did.

Charlie put one hand under the scarf and up jumped Topsy and Turvy. I let out a shout of surprise and at the same moment he threw away the silk scarf and I was left holding the two ends of the ribbon with the bag still firmly hanging in the middle. It was extraordinary. I grabbed the bag and untied the ribbon. Of course it was empty, for Topsy and Turvy were sitting on Charlie's knee. I studied the bag to see if there was some secret hole that he had slipped them through, but it was neatly sewn on all sides.

"How did you do that?" I asked.

"If I told you, it wouldn't be magic."

"Please, Charlie. I can't bear not knowing. You mustn't lie to me."

"I'd never lie to you, Poesy," he said, suddenly hurt and shy in the same instant. He hung his head and picked at Topsy and Turvy's clothes. "I just can't tell you all my secrets."

Even though I longed to know how he'd done it, I nodded. Gently, I prised the dolls from his fingers. I kissed each of them tenderly and then tucked them back in my pocket. All the while, Charlie sat watching me.

"One day, perhaps I might tell you," he said.

We stared at each other for a long moment.

"One day," I said, "we might tell each other everything."

20

LITTLE PIGGIES

Tilly Sweetrick

It was dreadful being cooped up. I felt like a wild bird trapped in captivity. Every time I tried to creep out of my cabin, Mr Arthur or that awful sneak Lionel would be patrolling the ship and would shoo me back into my cage.

We steamed across the Java Sea and crossed the Equator during the night. When we reached Singapore, a health inspector came on board, took away the body of the dead stoker, and declared the *Ceylon* was to be quarantined for two weeks.

"Two weeks!" The pronouncement shot through the troupe like a whipping, a prison sentence.

That same afternoon, Mr Arthur called a meeting in the dining hall. The air was steamy and everyone was thirsty, but the doctor said we had to keep drinking nothing but tea until the all-clear was given. Everyone sat slumped in their seats, utterly miserable.

"Rehearsals will continue so you won't be confined all day. I want you in the dining hall every morning by ten o'clock sharp but at other times you'll keep to your cabins. We've booked the Victoria Theatre here in Singapore and we must be ready to open our season as soon as we're off the ship."

"We can't spend another two weeks in our cabins," I said.

"You simply can't treat us like cattle, only allowed out for milking." I looked at Mr Arthur pleadingly but he ignored my warning. His face was drawn and his mouth set in a grim line. If only he'd listened to me.

At the end of our first week in quarantine, I was quietly making my way to the dining hall for rehearsals when it happened. As I turned onto the main deck, a dozen girls came pelting towards me. Ruby was in the lead, her tawny hair loose. She threw her arms up in the air to slow her pace and nearly collided with me. While the others streamed past, she put her arms on my shoulders, breathless with laughter.

"C'mon," she said. "We're playing Stampede." She grabbed my hand and broke into a run again, dragging me through the crowd of girls. "Charge!" she yelled and the whole retinue of big ones, middlings and even little Flora and Daisy went racing to the stern, their shoes slapping loudly on the wooden deck. The steamer seemed to rock under the force of us and I found a bubble of laughter moving up through my chest. It was the silliest race in the world, twenty girls running on the deck of a steamship.

Out of the corner of my eye I saw a crowd of sailors standing above us – even the black-faced stokers had come up from the furnace to watch the horde of girls and their flying skirts. And I saw Miss Thrupp and Eloise standing by an open door, shouting and waving for us to stop. But no one listened. The only voice that rang clear over the sound of the sea and the steamer was Ruby's. "Stampede, stampede!" she cried, and the girls squealed and shrieked and slid recklessly towards the other end of the ship.

We had turned for the next race when Mr Arthur came

striding down the deck towards us. Ruby held my hand tighter. "Let's charge him," she said, her eyes bright and fierce. That's when I tried to twist free.

Some of the middling girls stopped running and began to murmur, disappearing around the stern of the steamer. Suddenly there were only a handful of us. Ruby hesitated. Mr Arthur grabbed her by both arms.

"Stop that. You're hurting me," she cried out.

"You stupid girl! What do you think you're up to? You're leading a riot."

"We were only having fun. Playing," she said. "You said, 'Go and amuse yourself, Ruby.'"

"You know perfectly well what I meant. Stop being childish."

"If you treat me like a child, why shouldn't I act like one?"

"You will go to your cabin and stay there for the rest of the day."

"You can't keep us cooped up in those poky cabins any longer. What do you think we are? Pigs? You think you can keep us in our little piggy pens and then trot us out when you fancy?" Then she started to oink, snort and squeal as if she really was a pig.

Mr Arthur grew bright red in the face. Then he did it. He slapped her face sharply with his open hand. I was standing so close to them both that I could feel the swish of his hand moving through the air. Instinctively, I raised an arm to protect myself. Ruby ducked, too late, covering her cheeks with both hands. That didn't stop him, though. He boxed her ears twice until she was bent over with the shock of the blows. Then his hands flew like great ugly wings, slapping

Ruby as she crouched down on the deck, trying to fold in upon herself. She fell to her side, panting and crying out like a wounded animal. I couldn't bear it. I jumped at Mr Arthur and grabbed him by the arm.

"Please, sir, please." I hung on his forearm with all my weight but he was much too strong for me. Ruby tried to crawl away while I shrieked for him to stop. Suddenly, we were surrounded by people. A group of sailors restrained Mr Arthur while Miss Thrupp leaned over Ruby and tried to raise her to her feet. Ruby was howling now, with her mouth open and a stream of saliva running down her chin. She tried to push Miss Thrupp away too. Her hair fell wild and tangled across her face.

"Tilly," cried Miss Thrupp. "Fetch Tempe and Clarissa, quickly."

And I ran. Down below the decks, along the corridors I ran, calling out, shouting for the other girls. But only Poesy came. I fell into her arms and sobbed.

21

Dancing on a Watery Grave

Poesy Swift

I know what we did was wrong. I know Yada would have disapproved because we didn't tell the truth. But if we'd been forced to stay on the boat any longer, something even more dreadful might have happened.

Since the stampede, nothing seemed right with the troupe. We sat in our cabins and picked at our clothes and skin and at each other. Tilly filed her nails into tiny sharp points that made me want to cover my eyes. The boys acted as if they were at war, raiding each other's cabins at night, setting trip-wires across the corridors and launching into skirmishes for the least little offence. Charlie said the Kreutz twins were set to murder each other if they were cooped up in their cabin any longer. As it was, we witnessed another sort of crime and I saw my first dead body.

The last night before the quarantine was lifted, we went on deck to look at the lights of Singapore, imagining that soon we'd be ashore. Everyone was longing to see the yellow cholera flag taken down from the mast. Then we heard the terrible news. Another crew member had fallen ill. Not simply ill. He'd up and died in the heat of the afternoon. If the authorities found out, it meant *another* two weeks in quarantine. The adult passengers, the captain and Dr

Whitehead had a meeting and made a plan.

Next day, we were all on deck to greet the inspectors' party, as instructed. We were meant to make the ship look busy and happy, so we played quoits on the upper deck when the quarantine officer, the harbourmaster and his men came aboard for the inspection. The dead sailor was dressed in fresh clothes and sat in a deckchair with Eddie Quedda, Mr Arthur and our electrician, Mr Milligan, sitting on either side and in front of him. They pretended to be playing cards together and they angled the dead man's hat as if his hand had been played out and he was having a nice little catnap.

I squeezed my eyes shut tight whenever I had to walk past the corpse. It was too dreadful to see his white, waxy hands folded casually across his belly.

The men nodded at the health inspector and his assistants as they passed into the crew's quarters. Before they could return, the dead man was lifted out of his seat and put inside a cupboard on deck while Charlie and Lionel were sent to the top of the stairs to keep guard. Then Tempe and Clarissa were stationed in front of the cupboard door. Tempe leaned against it in a way that looked so natural you'd never believe there was a dead body on the other side. She and Clarissa smiled and nodded at the quarantine officers as they passed by and I realised that those girls really were very good actresses. I don't think I would have looked so easy with a corpse weighing heavy against the thin metal door behind me.

In the dining hall, we lined up for inspection. Daisy batted her lashes, trying to look sweet, but the health inspector suggested she needed glasses. Ruby looked hollow. Lionel's hands trembled. The dining hall wasn't big enough to contain all the unease in the passengers and crew. You could smell our desperation. But the doctor declared everyone fit and the captain invited the quarantine officers to stay on board for a celebratory dinner and performance. We'd promised the rest of the passengers a show ever since we left Melbourne. Before the sailor died, I'd been looking forward to it, but knowing there was a corpse in a cupboard on the upper deck made the ship feel like a morgue.

Yada's voice kept echoing in my mind: "Acting and theatre are cheap folly; only ritual is important." I didn't want her to be right but it didn't feel seemly to sing 'Hurrah! The Master Comes!' when someone was passing over into the other world. It made me shudder to think of the poor dead sailor's ghost wandering the ship as we sang and danced so gaily.

If we had to do a show, I was glad Mr Arthur had picked *Florodora*. It was set in the Philippines and there were lovely songs for the chorus of Florodora girls and even some good parts for the boys. Max was the detective, Tweedlepunch, and Freddie played the villain, Gilfain. Charlie played the romantic lead, Frank, to Ruby Kelly's Dolores. I'm sure he hated having to pretend to be sweet on Ruby. She was too big to be playing opposite him but Mr Arthur was trying to make up to her for losing his temper by giving her a lead role.

Charlie looked so dashing, dressed as a captain in a lovely uniform with gold braid and a blue-and-gold captain's cap set jauntily on his dark hair. Halfway through the first act he sang a duet with Ruby. It gave me the strangest feeling when he swept off his hat and knelt before her. I had to shut my eyes. I couldn't bear to see him holding her hand and staring into her face with a sloppy expression. I tried to imagine that it was someone else, not Charlie, making love to Ruby. My stomach began to churn. My chest grew tight, as if I might suffocate. When we reached the finale of Act One, I slipped out of the dining hall.

I was standing on the rear deck when I saw two sailors taking the dead man out of the cupboard. The steward put his finger to his lips. "We have to dispose of the body before the ship gets any closer to shore, miss, otherwise they'll know it's from the *Ceylon*."

"What are you going to do with him?" I whispered.

"Slip him over the side."

The sailors carried the body aft. If you didn't know, you would have thought they were throwing a bag of rubbish overboard. I heard a 'plop' as the body hit the sea and was swallowed into the watery darkness. I couldn't help myself. I ran to the side and stared at the place where the corpse had disappeared beneath the waves, but it was as if the man had never lived.

Back in the dining hall, I was in time to put my costume on for the closing scenes. When we started singing 'The Island of Love', part of my mind was out on deck, at the stern of the steamer, gazing into the black waters of Singapore harbour, thinking of the sailor's corpse and his bitter, lonely end.

I wanted to say a prayer for the sailor's soul. Even if no one else heard it, I wanted to help his ghost find peace. I looked into the laughing, happy faces of the passengers and my mind was so jumbled with song lyrics that I couldn't find the right words. As I curtseyed to the audience, a scrap of a poem that Yada used to read to me filled my head. Even though it wasn't a prayer, I hoped it held the right thought:

> *No more the wild confused main,*
> *Is tossed about with storms of fear.*
> *The sea is singing; and the rain,*
> *Is music to the ears that hear.*

22

Playing Favourites

Tilly Sweetrick

Feeling earth beneath my feet was heavenly.

I hooked my arm through Poesy's as we waited for Mr Arthur to organise a dozen rickshaws to take us to our hotel.

"This is more like it," I told her. "I feel so much safer now we're in the British Empire again."

"But they have cholera here in Singapore too," said Poesy.

I gave her arm a little pinch. "Don't be like that, Poesy. Don't spoil things."

"How can you not think about that poor dead sailor?" she whispered.

I glanced around the docks, at the crowds of Chinamen, Malays, Europeans and sailors of all nations. There were so many cheerful people in the world, it was awful the way Poesy wanted to spoil my chink of happiness. I was sorry that other people died but it was lovely to be alive. Thinking of dead people made me queasy. I shook off the feeling and climbed into the rickshaw, squashed between Poesy and Valentine.

As the rickshaw trundled through the streets, I leaned out and savoured every bit of the town. Hawkers shouted at passers-by and the air was filled with strange smells, spicy oils and sweet-smelling smoke. I wanted to shout, "Singapore, I love you!"

Our rickshaw had huge penny-farthing wheels, a black leather shade pushed back and long poles that the driver clasped in his sinewy hands. He was skinny and bare-chested with a lank scarf around his neck, ragged trousers and bare feet. I couldn't see his face beneath his straw coolie hat but I'm sure he was a Chinaman.

"I hope we don't have too many natives or Chinamen come and watch us," I said. "My mother would faint if she knew that I was being watched by Orientals."

Poesy gave me a snitty little look and said, "I can't imagine that Mrs Sweeney has ever fainted in her life."

"No one likes a snide miss, Poesy Swift," I said.

Poesy sucked in her lower lip and frowned. "I'm sorry. I didn't mean it to come out like that."

"She's been spending too much time with Clarissa, Tempe and Ruby," said Valentine.

Poesy hung her head and fidgeted with her hands.

"What did Tempe and that lot want with you anyway? You never did tell us why they invited you into their cabin. And what's been going on between you and Eliza? You've turned into quite the little pet of the big girls, haven't you?"

"I don't know," she said. But of course she was lying.

"Well, now that we're in Singapore, things will be different. You can share with me and Valentine again. You don't have to put up with those older girls bossing you around."

"Lizzie never bosses me."

"But she took you away from me. If it hadn't been for me, you wouldn't even be a Lilliputian, Poesy."

She looked at me with those big blue eyes as if I had said something outrageous. Why couldn't she admit that but for me she never would have joined up?

"Can't you see? Eliza doesn't really like you," I said. "She's only using you. She used to be best friends with Tempe and Ruby, but since they squabbled Lizzie refuses to share a cabin with them, so she's made you her little puppet. It's not fair. You're my friend."

Poesy frowned again and took a long time to reply. Sometimes I had to wonder if she was a bit of a duffer. "Why can't I be everyone's friend?"

I nearly snorted in irritation. Then Poesy slipped her damp little hand over mine.

"You have to understand, Tilly. Lizzie is like a big sister to me. She's almost a grown-up."

"No she's not," I said. "She simply thinks she is."

"Let's not argue," said Poesy, doing her trick of turning things away from what was important. She leaned forward to look out at the street. Valentine began prattling about Ruby, Tempe and Clarissa again, worrying at all the details of whether Mr Arthur would go on giving Ruby the best roles simply out of guilt. Poesy didn't say anything; even though she must have seen and heard things that we hadn't, she kept her little mouth shut tight.

I could have wept with relief when we reached our hotel, to have a proper roof over our heads. At last! A room where the floor didn't creak and move beneath my feet! The whole building was white, with deliciously deep-set verandahs, and it overlooked the water. Palm trees grew in the small garden out the front and vermilion flowers tumbled down a trellis. We piled into the hotel, all the girls talking at once and the noisy boys shouting as they raced each other up and down the marble staircase. Twenty-one girls with stage voices and dancing feet. Eight boys with too much energy and not enough sense. Miss Thrupp covered her ears in despair as our voices ricocheted across the foyer. Her Timmy began to howl, as usual, and she disappeared, leaving Mr Arthur to organise everything.

Our trunks were unloaded and porters carried them upstairs to the rooms while Lo sorted us into our new groups. I wasn't sure I even cared whether Poesy was put with us again, I was still feeling so cross with her. But Lo obviously had ideas of her own about Poesy and Eliza sharing a room. She placed me, Valentine and Poesy with three younger girls. Our room was on the second floor, above the tradesmen's entrance. When I saw that the French windows opened out onto a balcony, I let out a shriek of pleasure. Valentine and I dragged two rattan chairs onto the balcony and sat with our arms resting on the railing, watching hawkers in the bustling street below. Poesy and the other girls took off their boots and flopped onto the white beds, pulling mosquito nets around themselves.

"This weather is beastly," said Valentine, patting her brow with her hankie. "I hope it's not like this everywhere we go."

"It will be hot in Manila too," I said. "But I still think it's my favourite place in the East. Those American soldiers simply love giving chocolates and flowers."

Suddenly Poesy piped up, contradicting me. "We're not going to Manila at all."

"Oh, how would you know, Poesy?"

"While everyone was shouting down in the lobby, I heard Mr Arthur talking with Mr Shrouts. Mr Shrouts had just come from having tea with someone from Liddiard's Lilliputians. And Mr Shrouts told Mr Arthur that the Ramos brothers had all of Manila sewn up and no one wanted to see another child troupe so soon after Liddiard's."

"Yes, but we will get there eventually," I said.

"That's not what I heard," she said.

Valentine and I looked at each other and then at Poesy, still lying beneath the mosquito netting, so wise, so smug. "What else do you know, Poesy?"

"Lizzie says we'll be in India for a very long time and then go to China. We probably won't get to America until 1911."

"1911! That's years away. I thought we were only going to visit Calcutta, not tour the whole ruddy sub-continent. I can't wait until 1911 to reach America."

"You might have to," said Poesy. "We all have to do as we're told."

Then she turned on her side and put her pillow over her head, as if she couldn't bear to hear what I would say next.

I stormed across the room and snatched the pillow away from her. "Listen here, Miss Poesy. I've had quite enough of your airs and graces. How dare you tell me that I have to do as I'm told, as if you're the one who knows all about being a Lilliputian. And why didn't you tell me the minute you heard we were going to be stuck in the East for years?"

"I did tell you," whined Poesy.

"Don't contradict me," I said. "I don't know what's happened to you, Poesy. You're not the girl I knew in Richmond."

Poesy climbed off the bed, pushing her way past me as she walked to the door of our room. "Perhaps I'm not that girl any more. Maybe I'm not who you think I am. I might have my own ideas about things."

"Perhaps, might, maybe and s'pose," I called after her. "Make up your mind, Poesy Swift! Whose friend are you?"

23

STAGEDOOR JOHNNIES

Poesy Swift

We played the Victoria Theatre that night. Carriages picked us up from outside our hotel and drove us through the wide, open street along the foreshore. The Victoria was a beautiful wedding cake of a building with long white columns like a Grecian temple and a grand entrance – a real theatre. Backstage, in the dressing rooms, there were proper mirrors to use when we put on our make-up and racks for hanging our costumes. Miss Thrupp helped Daisy and Flora into their dresses while the rest of us helped each other. May Molloy started to cry but Ruby said she was much too big a girl to make a fuss and she should be able to fix her costume in place herself.

As soon as Ruby left the dressing room, I went over to help May. Her outfit was the fiddliest arrangement of frills and bows and I couldn't see why anyone would expect her to be able to fix it at the back.

"It's all right, May," I whispered. "You look lovely."

"I miss my mum," she said, sniffing and wrinkling her nose. "I wish we was home."

"Me too," I said. But as I said it, I knew it wasn't true. Not a single part of me wanted to be back in Richmond. I would have liked to see Mumma and Yada and Chooky here in Singapore, sitting outside in the theatre waiting for the moment when I came on stage. It would be grand to see their upturned faces admiring me. But I shuddered at the thought of having to go home with them, back to the dank streets of Richmond, back into my mouse-brown dress and our drab grey life.

"Ruby's mean to me and it's not fair," said May sulkily. "She's got her sisters with her. Not like you and me. We've got no one."

"That's not true. We all have each other. Friends can be like sisters," I said, pulling the big blue sash around her waist tight and patting it into place. "Now you stop sooking, May Molloy. We've got a show to do."

It was funny I was so confident on the outside, because inside I felt like blancmange. When the red velvet curtain parted and I saw a sea of faces in the theatre, I wanted to freeze. This wasn't a rehearsal. This was a real audience in a beautiful, grand building and the expectation in their faces sent a tingle through every nerve in my body.

The moment I found myself was when we sang 'Tell Me Pretty Maiden'. I was one of six Florodora girls in white lace with ostrich feathers on their hats who danced out onto the stage to meet their six beaus. When Charlie went down on bended knee to me, I felt lighter than air. I sat on his knee, my arms around his neck, and I sang 'If I loved you, would you tell me what to do to keep you true to me?', and bubbles of happiness fizzed through me from the soles of my little white dancing shoes to the feathery tip of my bonnet.

After the performance, as we stepped out through the stage door, a crowd of admirers stood waiting for us, exactly as Tilly had said they would: little children with their mothers clutching autograph books, young men with bouquets, old people with boxes of chocolates. Flora was given a huge bouquet, a five-pound box of candy and a doll almost as large as herself that opened and shut its eyes. I'd never felt such a wave of longing. I couldn't take my eyes off that doll. It made Topsy and Turvy seem raggedy and ugly.

Tempe Melbourne had her eyes on other things. One young man stood a little away from the crowd, his dark hair glossy in the half-light. Afterwards, I came to think of all those backstage boys as oily, but perhaps that was only because of what happened later.

The young man was carrying a simply enormous bouquet of flowers. He made his way over to Tempe.

"Excuse me, Miss," he said, offering her the bouquet, "I can't tell you how wonderful you were tonight."

Tempe looked over her shoulder, her eyes narrowing as she checked to see if Mr Arthur was about.

Lionel was behind me. He leaned in close and whispered in my ear. "You watch out for those stagedoor Johnnies – they're a bad lot for the most part. The ones that go for the big girls make big trouble."

"I'm not big," I said.

"Not yet. But look – look at Tempe. That's trouble, if I don't mistake it."

Tempe stood to one side and chatted sweetly with the dark-haired young man. She didn't see Mr Arthur stepping out of the stage door carrying sleepy Daisy, nor Lionel hurrying over to speak to him.

Mr Arthur set Daisy on her feet where she swayed, only

half awake. "Hold her," he said to Lionel as he marched up to Tempe and the young man, grabbed hold of the flowers that Tempe was cradling in her arms and thrust them back at the stagedoor Johnny. "Flowers may be sent to the hotel."

He dragged Tempe to one of the waiting carriages. The young man looked flustered but Tempe's eyes glittered with rage. When I climbed into the carriage beside her, Clarissa, Ruby and Tempe had their heads together, their voices full of jagged barbs.

"I'm sick and tired of him," said Tempe. "I'll be eighteen before the year is out and still he treats me like a child. That young man was lovely. And probably rich. Mr Arthur's own sisters married men they met in the East. Even Mrs Essie!"

"I could put up with him playing chaperone," said Clarissa, "if he'd let us sing what we want to sing. He's never going to let us do anything. We're stuck with these fusty old musicals while everyone else is singing vaudeville. He doesn't give a fig for our futures."

Ruby stamped her feet and the carriage rattled. "Oh how I hate him! If I were a man, I'd horsewhip him for how he beat me. He's simply vile."

I wished I had climbed into another carriage. I wished I was with Tilly, even if she was cross with me, or with Charlie or Lizzie. The air between the three girls sparked with rage.

When I looked out into the night, I saw the oily-haired young man standing in the light outside the theatre, watching our carriage drive away. He had thrown his bouquet into the gutter and was smoking a cigarette, as if he had already forgotten about Tempe. I wanted to make the others look back, to see he didn't care, to show them that Mr Arthur had been right, but I was afraid to speak.

"He's just like a butcher," said Ruby. "He wants to squash us and mince us up so we're all the same, to turn us into sausages. A butcher."

Tempe and Clarissa nodded and the word seemed to echo around the inside of the carriage. *Butcher, butcher, butcher.*

24

BOY MAGIC

Poesy Swift

The train from Singapore to Kuala Lumpur snaked through long stretches of green jungle and then wet open fields edged with palm trees. I pressed my face against the glass and watched the tropical green flash past. I was glad to be leaving Singapore. Every time we'd gone to the Victoria Theatre, I'd been afraid of seeing the stagedoor Johnnies. They made me feel strange and not myself. The way they looked at me made me wish I was too little to draw their eye, and yet, to my shame, I wanted them to see me too. I wanted chocolates and flowers from them. But then I thought of what Mr Arthur would think of me and I burned with embarrassment. When we left the theatre at night I kept my head down and tried not to meet anyone's gaze.

On our first morning in Kuala Lumpur, Miss Thrupp and Lo harried everyone into a crocodile and we walked in pairs to the theatre next to the Town Hall for the morning rehearsal. Even though it was only a short distance, we were all bathed in sweat by the time we reached the theatre. Ruby grumbled all the way there. "We should be going by carriage. Why is he making us walk? Mrs Essie never made us walk."

It was cool and dark inside the theatre. I threw off my hat and shook my hair free. Daisy looked especially flushed and she whined in a baby voice when Flora tried to make her play chasey.

Eddie Quedda sat at the piano and ran through the overture for *Florodora*. We all massed on stage to sing the opening chorus, and then the boys stepped forward to perform the clerks' song.

"Cripes, it's so old-hat, this rubbish," grumbled Clarissa. But it was easy to ignore her. Everyone else liked *Florodora*, especially me. I sang in the chorus as Miss Lucy Ling, but I longed to be cast as Dolores or Angela, the two principal girls. Ruby had been moved into the chorus again and Valentine's younger sister, Iris, sang Dolores while baby Daisy lisped her way through the role of Angela. It seemed sad that some of the bigger girls, who had such beautifully strong voices, were now in the chorus. It put you off wanting to grow up, as if the big girls were being punished for becoming women because the audience wanted little girls.

Tilly was the only bigger girl who looked cheerful, though she was still acting cool with me. Since the trouble with the stagedoor Johnny, she'd been given Tempe's role as Lady Holyrood. The only bad thing about this was she had to pretend to fancy Max, whom she couldn't stand. It was hard to like the Kreutz twins. They were so rough and prickly and they kept their blonde hair cropped so close you could see their pink scalps.

When Max puffed out his cheeks and played his role for all the laughs he could get instead of being romantic, Tilly slapped him on the neck. Max let out a howl and then grinned sheepishly at Tilly.

"Go on, Tills," he said. "You don't want me to be all soppy

on you, do you? Or do you?" And then he winked at her!

If it had been me, I would have died of embarrassment. But Tilly laughed. It was almost as if she were flirting with him.

As the morning wore on, Daisy became more and more peculiar. She kept stuttering her lines, and shiny sweat beaded on her forehead. Miss Thrupp wiped Daisy's brow and then crossed the stage to talk to Mr Arthur. A moment later, Daisy's role was given to Flora, and Daisy was bundled into a gharry with Miss Thrupp and taken back to the hotel.

It was after midday by the time Mr Arthur let us stop rehearsing. This time there were carriages waiting for us because the heat was so intense. Lunch was ready in the dining room of the hotel but no one apart from the Kreutz twins had much appetite. Across the table from me, Flora pecked at her rice like a little bird and then laid her head on the white tablecloth and drifted off to sleep.

Up in our rooms, we peeled off our layers of clothes and lay on our beds in our vests and knickers. The fans whirled overhead and made the white mosquito netting billow like clouds. I tried to write a letter to Mumma and Yada but the sweat from my hands smeared the ink and then made a stain on my white knickers.

I looked up to see Lionel standing in the doorway, grinning. I felt my tummy do a little flip-flop of alarm.

"Go away, Lionel," I shouted, pulling the bedsheet up to my chin.

"I'm looking for Lizzie," he said.

"I don't know where she is! Go away!"

He stood staring at me. The grin fell away and there was

something peculiar in his expression. Then he pulled the door shut. I leaped up and dressed myself and slipped out into the corridor. I felt all jumpy inside my skin.

As I walked past the other rooms, I saw Miss Thrupp and Lo arguing beside Daisy's bed while Daisy lay sprawled across the sheets, breathing shallowly. I saw Max and Freddie wrestling on the floor of their room in a mock punch-up. I saw Lionel, his head bowed, listening to Lizzie as they stood outside Mr Arthur's room talking in low voices. And I saw Tempe, standing alone on the balcony of her room, dressed in nothing but her underwear. She was leaning on the rail and calling out to someone passing in the street. It seemed both shocking and yet ordinary. It was as if everyone was caught in a different play but I couldn't understand the stories or guess how the dramas would unfold.

It had started to rain. Not like Melbourne rain, which you could walk through as if it were fairy drops, but great sheets of thick water that tumbled earthwards from the flat grey clouds as if Heaven were in flood.

I stood on the front verandah of the hotel and stared out at the deluge. When Charlie came and stood beside me, I realised I had been looking for him all along.

He held a book with one finger wedged between the pages to mark his place.

"I've a new trick," he said. "Would you like to see?"

We sat together on a rattan seat as the Kuala Lumpur rain flooded the streets and he opened his book and smoothed the crinkled pages.

"My uncle gave me this before we left Melbourne." He showed me the cover: two hands holding a deck of cards and *The Boys' Book of Conjuring* embossed on the brown cloth. Then he laid the book in my lap with the page open and drew out a deck of cards from his pocket. They were battered and dog-eared and I don't know how he managed to make them flow like a waterfall from one hand to the other. Then he held them up in a fan with the deck facing me and asked me to pick a card – any card. I pulled out the Knave of Hearts and pressed it against my chest so he couldn't see which one I had chosen. He shuffled the cards one more time and then held the deck shut while he closed his eyes, concentrating hard.

When he opened them and looked into mine, I felt my heart flutter like a trapped butterfly. His eyes were the loveliest shade of green, with little hazel flecks set deep in his irises. He held my gaze for a second or two as if it were the first time we had seen each other.

"Knave of Hearts," he said.

25

TYGER, TYGER

Poesy Swift

Yada always said, 'Discretion is the better part of valour', but there was no point trying to explain to Tilly about discretion. She seemed to think I should run and tell her every tiny detail of what happened to me, every ripple of gossip that fluttered through the troupe. She was livid when Valentine told her that Lionel had been to our room while she was asleep and stared at me in my underwear.

"Why didn't *you* tell me, Poesy?" she said. "Why do you have to be so prim and proper?"

I said I didn't want to talk about it and then I went and asked Lo to shift me to another room. I was hoping she'd let me share with Lizzie again but Lo said Pearl Kelly was happy to swap places with me. Pearl didn't want to share the same room as her older sister, Ruby. Unwittingly, I jumped out of the frying pan and into the fire. There were six of us in my new room. The big girls, Tempe, Clarissa and Ruby, had their beds on one side while I pushed mine onto the other side close to May and Iris.

Every day after lunch we were sent to bed to sleep for two hours before the show. Miss Thrupp would come to each room and admonish anyone who wasn't lying down. "Even if you can't sleep, you must lie still and rest your body."

We opened the windows and turned the fans up so they spun as fast as they could, but our bodies still felt sticky against the bedding.

Ruby always fell asleep within minutes of lying down, her petticoat hitched up and her long legs creamy against the white sheets. Everyone was drowsy that afternoon, except Tempe. She stood at the window, watching the laneway that ran behind the hotel.

"He's here," she hissed, her face flushed.

"Should I wake Ruby?" asked Clarissa, dressing quickly.

"No, better with just us two," said Tempe.

I sat up in my bed and pushed the mosquito netting aside. "Where are you going?" I asked. That was my mistake. I should never have asked.

Clarissa and Tempe looked at each other and then back at me.

"It's too hot to sleep. We're going downstairs," said Clarissa.

"But we have to stay in bed," I said.

"We're not babies," sighed Tempe. "We're going motoring. We're going into the jungle and it will be cool and lovely. Mr Tolego, that nice man who gave me flowers the other night, is taking us for a ride in his car."

"Not another stagedoor Johnny."

"He's not a stagedoor Johnny. He's a gentleman."

"But you'll get into trouble. Mr Arthur says talking to gentlemen is 'improper' if you don't have a chaperone."

"Shut up, Poesy. We'll only get into trouble if you tattle." She paused for a moment and put one finger to her chin, as if considering me more closely. "You can come along, if you like. Then it won't be 'improper' at all, because you'll be our chaperone."

I didn't really want to go with them but I couldn't think what else to do. If Miss Thrupp asked me where they were, I'd have to tell the truth. As I pulled on my dress and pinafore and laced up my boots, I told myself I was saving them from disgrace. I hated lies. But sometimes I told lies to myself.

As we tiptoed along the hall, Valentine poked her head around the door of her room. "Where are you lot off to?"

"None of your beeswax," said Clarissa.

"Can I come? I don't mind where you're going. Everyone's asleep in here and I'm bored."

Tempe rolled her eyes. "In for a penny, in for a pound. Come along, then, you can keep Poesy company."

We were almost at the top of the stairs when little Flora called out. "Where are you *going*?" No one answered. "Take me with you. There's nothing to do when Daisy is sick."

"Oh for heaven's sake," said Tempe. "Just what we need. We'd better take her along too. At least, if we get caught, we can say we're giving all the littlies a treat."

She ran to the end of the hall and grabbed Flora by the arm.

"Oh good," said Flora. "Are we going on an outing?"

Valentine and I held Flora's hands. She skipped along merrily between us as we followed the big girls through the foyer. Mr Tolego's car was parked out the front, long and sleek and black as a panther. We climbed into the back, four girls squashed in a row and Flora sitting on my lap, with Mr Tolego in the front seat all by himself. He turned around and smiled at us and his teeth were very white and ferocious-looking in his swarthy face. He had a strange accent and I felt too shy to listen closely to him when he spoke to us. Tempe leaned forward to hear his conversation as the car made its way slowly through the crowded Kuala Lumpur streets. We drove past strange buildings with little golden hats and spires, down sleepy streets with tumbledown shops. Finally, when we were out of town and on a long stretch of road lined with palm trees, Tempe giggled and climbed over the seat to sit beside Mr Tolego.

If I'd been a proper chaperone I would have put my arms around her waist and hauled her back from the precipice, but I was afraid she'd jeer at me for being prudish. I'd never been motoring before and the thrill of it all must have muddled my thinking.

The car had dark burgundy leather seats with little button-holes and Flora put her fingers in the dimples and laughed. I laughed too but it sounded as though it were the laughter of a different girl, not me. The town gave way to rubber plantations and rice paddies and then jungle, until there was absolutely no one in sight. Parrots called out from the dark, leafy greenness. Monkeys shrilled in the jungle canopy above us. The air was cool and moist, and smelled of earth and growth and things rotting. It made my nose tingle and my skin felt swollen with the sound and the moisture.

"Where are we going?" I asked, feeling anxious. I remembered Yada's warnings to be careful of strangers, and Lizzie talking about the white slave trade, saying that white girls were captured and sold by traders to be slaves to wicked men. Suddenly, I was afraid.

Mr Tolego turned around in his seat. "It's cooler in the jungle. Once upon a time there were too many tigers for anyone to be safe here, but don't worry, you will be safe with me." He grinned at us.

"Tigers! Oh no!" Flora squealed. She squeezed my arm. "Tell him to turn back. I don't want to see a tiger."

"Charlie told me the last tiger in Singapore was shot at the Raffles Hotel," I reassured her. "He said it was hiding under the billiard table and they killed it, so there are no more tigers."

"That was Singapore, Poesy-poo," said Clarissa. "I'm sure there are tigers in Kuala Lumpur. Look at all that jungle – can't you imagine their stripes hidden in all the stripy light through the ferns?"

Flora began to make low, whiny sounds.

"Don't listen to her," I whispered into Flora's ear. "There are no tigers, only monkeys. You like monkeys."

"I don't like monkeys," said Valentine, being particularly unhelpful. "The hawker outside the hotel has one on a leash and it bared its teeth at me. I wouldn't want to see a monkey that wasn't on a chain."

Flora nuzzled her head against me and sobbed softly. We drove on in silence through the darkening jungle. The light was soft and dappled, as if it were already late afternoon.

Mr Tolego steered the car onto a tiny cart road and parked in a glade.

"Isn't it getting on? Shouldn't we be turning back?" I asked. But neither Tempe nor Mr Tolego seemed to hear me. "Tempe?"

"We're going to go for a stroll. Teddy says there's a lovely walk up here, a little stroll to a grove or something."

I felt a leaden weight in my stomach. Mr Tolego opened

the door on the passenger's side and held out his hand to Tempe, holding hers a moment too long. She laughed lightly and stepped away from him towards the jungle path.

Flora started to cry again. "I don't want to go for a walk," she said, burying her head in my lap. I knew she simply needed to sleep. Why had we brought her with us? Why had I come along? My own choices were a mystery to me.

"I'll stay here with Flora," I said, hoping they wouldn't be too long.

Valentine shrank back in her seat and scanned the jungle nervously. "I'll stay behind too. I don't feel like walking."

Clarissa climbed down from the car but Mr Tolego didn't offer his hand to help her. Her face was tight and closed and she fiddled fretfully with the bow of her hat.

Tempe turned and said, "Clarissa, perhaps it's best you stay too, so the little ones don't feel frightened."

"I won't be frightened," I called out. But Tempe only laughed. "She's such a funny little creature, that Poesy. Valentine's afraid, so you had better stay with her." Clarissa stomped back to the car, her face like thunder.

She didn't speak to us the whole time Tempe and Mr Tolego were in the jungle, but she picked away at the ribbon of her hat until the satin edge was shredded.

When Tempe and Mr Tolego came back along the path, Tempe's eyes were bright and feverish and she carried her hat crushed against her front with clenched hands. Her fawn dress was crumpled and her hair was frizzy from the damp heat.

"Why were you so long?" demanded Clarissa.

"Oh do shut up, Lissa," said Tempe. She slumped in

the front seat and watched Mr Tolego with a slightly wary, calculating look as he climbed in beside her and started the motor.

Mr Tolego said nothing on the drive back to town but his face seemed swarthier than ever. No one spoke. Only Flora was cheerful. She had slept in my lap while Tempe and Mr Tolego were in the jungle and she was happy to be heading back to the hotel.

"We might be late for the evening show," I said, worrying out loud.

Tempe was silent and Mr Tolego didn't once turn to speak to us. When I repeated my concern, Clarissa set upon me.

"Stop it, Poesy," she said. "You are such a worry-wart. If you lot keep your mouths shut, no one will even know we were gone."

The afternoon light had turned to gold by the time we arrived at the hotel. At the entrance, Mr Tolego finally decided to pretend to be a gentleman and he handed each one of us down from the back of the motor car, lifting Flora all the way to the ground. Valentine giggled and Flora did a little curtsey, as if he were someone special, someone to bother with rather than simply another stagedoor Johnny. But I kept my eyes downturned and followed the other girls around to the back entrance of the hotel. I couldn't bear to look at him. I hoped I'd never see his pirate's face again.

26

WHIPPING GIRL

Tilly Sweetrick

Was it Poesy's fault? Sometimes I wonder. She always seemed to be there when things went wrong, to be caught up in the worst of everything. I was sitting on the terrace finishing off a slice of cake when I heard the fight begin. Every girl looked up, like frightened deer. Miss Thrupp was on her feet in an instant, ushering everyone from the terrace, shooing us up the stairs and back to our rooms. Which was probably rather lucky, because from our balcony I saw everything unfold.

"Temperance Jones," roared Mr Arthur. His voice rang out along the dusty roadway. Tempe and Clarissa stood in a frightened huddle at the tradesmen's entrance to the hotel. They must have been creeping in from some naughty adventure. But Flora and Poesy and Valentine were there too, standing next to Mr Arthur. Poor little Flora burst into tears of confusion and dear Valentine was white with distress, while Poesy's face was contorted with horror, as if she had opened Pandora's Box. Clarissa and Tempe looked as guilty as sin.

Tempe flushed deep red and shut her eyes. Very slowly she spat her words out at Mr Arthur, like sharp little darts.

"Don't call me that. Don't call me Temperance. My name is Tempe. Tempe Melbourne."

She turned her back on him and started down the path that led to the street. Mr Arthur leaped off the verandah and pursued her. He grabbed her by the arm and spun her around to face him.

"Temperance, of which you have none. Do you have no sense of what men like that want from you?"

"He doesn't want anything from me that I'm not glad to give. I'm no different to Eliza. Or perhaps she doesn't give as gladly as I do."

That did it. Mr Arthur raised his cane and brought it down hard across her face. A gash opened above her eyebrow where the cane had slashed but Mr Arthur didn't stop. As Tempe cried out and cupped her hands around the bleeding wound, Mr Arthur started to drag her back to the hotel. Despite her injury, Tempe fought him every inch of the way until he turned on her again and brought the cane down across her legs and back, again and again, blow after blow. Natives and Chinamen gathered at the back gate and stared at him. A crowd from the hotel spilled out from the side verandah to watch, but no one intervened. Mr Arthur kept beating Tempe until suddenly the cane snapped and the end piece went flying into the undergrowth.

Clarissa, stupid girl, stood wringing her hands. She didn't have an ounce of sense inside her feathery head. But I should have thought Poesy would have done something. Instead, she stood slack-jawed, clinging to Flora's hand. At least Valentine had the wit to scream.

It was Ruby who came to Tempe's rescue. She went pelting down the stairs and flew off the verandah. She grabbed Mr Arthur's arm and suddenly the two girls and the man became lost in a tussle of torn clothes and shouted abuse.

Finally, Mr Arthur dragged both girls up to their room and slammed the door on them. Clarissa, who had been loitering on the stairs, was forced inside too, to complete the wicked trinity. Then he took out his set of keys and locked them in. His shirt was drenched with sweat and he was breathing hard. Miss Thrupp and Eloise stood in the hall, staring at the closed door. From behind it we could all hear Ruby shouting swear words at the door, at Mr Arthur, at the whole troupe. We couldn't hear Tempe at all.

All the adults assembled in the corridor outside the girls' room: Miss Thrupp, Eloise and Eddie Quedda, even Jim McNulty, the carpenter, and Mr Milligan, the electrician, whom we hardly ever saw except at the theatre. Mostly they looked numb with shock. Only Mr Arthur had anything to say.

"This is your doing, Miss Thrupp," he said, his breath coming in short gasps. "Your disgrace. How did they leave the hotel without your knowing? You are employed to control these girls. And by God, if you can't, then you force me to measures most unpopular. Someone has to save them from ruin."

Lo's face twisted in a snort of outrage. "As if you care when a girl is ruined," she said, but then she looked stricken, as if she wished she'd never spoken.

Miss Thrupp hitched her baby higher on her hip. Little Timmy's face was a funny shade of yellow and his head lolled around on her shoulder in a peculiar way.

"I cannot be involved in these histrionics. I have a sick child to care for. You employed me as matron, not as a prison guard."

She turned and walked stiffly back to her room.

Tempe couldn't perform with us for the closing show in Kuala Lumpur. On the platform at the station the day we left for Ipoh, she sat on top of a trunk with a scarf wrapped around her head to hide her bruises. Ruby and Clarissa stood either side of her as if they were her bodyguards, but they needn't have worried. No one wanted to talk to them.

I was glad to be on the train again. If you shut your eyes to the jungle you could imagine you were anywhere in the world. The rhythm of the wheels, the smell of coal and the feel of the leather seat beneath us were comfortingly familiar, like any other tour. Valentine and I held hands and pretended we were somewhere else other than on a steam train riding through the dark jungles of the Malay Peninsula. My poor little Valentine. She was quite shaken by her terrible adventure. I told her she should never, ever go anywhere without me, ever again and she swore she never would and sobbed on my shoulder.

After Ipoh and Butterworth, we took the ferry across to Georgetown on the island of Penang. It was a pretty little town and the audiences were kind to us, even if there weren't many of them in the theatre.

Next morning, when we came down for breakfast in our hotel, Tempe and Clarissa were sitting in the foyer, their arms folded across their chests, their faces like thunder. Outside the hotel, Mr Arthur organised for their suitcases to be loaded onto the back of a bullock cart. I knew instantly that he was sending them home. He was talking with an older, matronly-looking woman. She didn't seem very excited at having been appointed as chaperone to the two vixens, but

Mr Arthur slipped a small wad of money into her hand and she smiled, a horrible glossy smirk.

We'd just sat down for breakfast in the dining room when Mr Arthur walked straight to our table.

"Are you ready, Valentine?"

Valentine couldn't look at me. She hung her head and a big tear rolled down her cheek and plopped onto her skirt. "I'm sorry, Tills. I didn't know how to tell you. I'm being sent home too."

"But you didn't *do* anything," I cried. I put my arms around her neck and clung to her. I didn't care about the others leaving but I couldn't bear the thought of losing Valentine.

"Enough nonsense," said Mr Arthur. "Come along, Valentine."

"I'll only be a minute," she said to him, and she hugged me tightly. "It's all right, Tilly dear," she said, kissing me on the cheek. "I don't want to go to India. I want to go home."

"But why must he choose you? Why not Poesy? She was in the car too."

"Poesy told him we'd been with Mr Tolego instead of saying we'd been out for a stroll, silly girl. Clarissa wants to scratch her eyes out. Besides, Poesy doesn't want to go home."

"But why do you want to?" I cried.

"I'm going to stay with Mrs Essie and if Tempe and Clarissa try to say bad things about Mr Arthur being too rough, I will say otherwise."

"You'd lie for Mr Arthur?" We both looked into the foyer where Mr Arthur was tapping his foot, waiting for Valentine to finish her goodbyes. He pointed to his watch impatiently and Valentine nodded.

"It wouldn't exactly be lying to say Tempe and Clarissa exaggerate everything. I've been with the Percivals since I was five years old, Tilly. They're like family to me. You have to stick up for your family."

I gripped her arm as she tried to leave me. "You can't go. You can't leave your sister behind. Iris is your real family." I wanted to say she couldn't leave me but everything was turned upside down. For the first time in our lives, I wasn't sure of her.

"Iris can take care of herself. She is twelve years old, for goodness sake. Besides, Mr Arthur can't spare her. She's the best in the troupe."

I flinched and dropped her arm. She might as well have slapped me. She'd always said I was the best actress in the world. I watched her walk out of the dining room.

Out in the street, I stood to one side as Tempe and Clarissa said their farewells. Valentine didn't look back at me as she climbed onto the wagon.

"He can't be doing this," said Ruby, wrapping one arm around Clarissa's neck and the other around Tempe's and drawing them close to her. "You can't go. I won't let you."

Tempe turned her ruined face away. "I'm glad. Williamson's will have me, and I won't try out for the juvenile company either. I'll be a real showgirl. I'm sorry you're not coming with us, Ruby. When you come home, you can audition for Williamson's too and we'll all be together again. Then we'll be real actresses, singing songs worth singing."

"I want to come now, but he won't let me," said Ruby bitterly. "He doesn't want my parents to find out that he's a brute, in case they come after Beryl and Pearl."

The three girls huddled together for a moment, nestling into each other's bodies like a kindle of kittens. Clarissa looked up at Poesy and scowled.

"What are you staring at, poo-faced Poesy," she said. "Go away."

Poesy stood a little apart from the rest of us. Her yellow hair fell limply around her shoulders and there were purple shadows under her eyes. "I only wanted to say goodbye," she said.

"If you'd kept your big mouth shut," said Clarissa, "we wouldn't be leaving. You're a tattler, a tell-tale-tit, and I hope all the nasty monkeys come to take a bit."

Even Tempe thought that was too harsh. She put her hand out and stilled Clarissa's sharpness.

"You sound like a five-year-old, Lissa. It's all right, Poesy. This is not your fault. But be careful, all of you. No one can trust the Butcher."

That was the first time I heard anyone call Mr Arthur 'the Butcher'.

As Valentine, Clarissa and Tempe climbed onto the wagon, they turned to wave goodbye and Tempe's scarf slipped to one side. The sight of the long gash down her face seared the word 'butcher' into my brain. *Butcher, butcher, butcher.* He'd taken my Valentine from me and cut me to my heart.

27

THE SHOW MUST GO ON

Poesy Swift

Nightmares plagued me. Sometimes Mr Arthur came storming through the jungle, sometimes I could feel Mr Tolego's hands sliding up my body, and all the while I could hear Clarissa's voice shrieking, "Tattler!" Then everything would turn red and I would wake trembling.

After Kuala Lumpur, some of the girls refused to sleep in the same room as me. I was moved in with Lizzie again. It was such sweet relief to be with her. Once, I woke from my nightmare confused and sobbing. It felt like the middle of the night but it must have been early because Lizzie was coming in through the door and the light spilled across my bed. She lifted the mosquito netting and climbed in beside me. Even though it was hot to have two bodies so close, I fell into a deep and dreamless sleep once she held me. Sometimes I felt Lizzie was the only one who believed I hadn't tattled. All I'd said to Mr Arthur about the trip with Mr Tolego was that we had been motoring in his new car. What else was I to say when Mr Arthur saw us all sneaking in the back entrance of the hotel? I never told anyone about Tempe disappearing into the jungle with Mr Tolego, not even Lizzie. It was when Flora sucked her thumb and said she was afraid of tigers that Mr Arthur turned on Tempe.

Lizzie said it was a good thing that Tempe and Clarissa were being sent home. She said they were poisoning the troupe, making everyone turn on Mr Arthur, and that he'd only done his duty. But Miss Thrupp and Mr Milligan the electrician had gone cold on him. You could see the frosty expressions on their faces when he spoke to them, you could sense their disapproval. You could hear them muttering about not being paid enough and how the tour would end in tears.

But it wasn't Mr Arthur's fault that the audiences were thin and so many of the children were falling ill. First it was Daisy and then Valentine's little sister, Iris.

The day after Valentine and the others were put on board a steamer to Australia, Iris collapsed on stage. It was our last night in Penang and she'd been playing Winifred, the lead in *A Runaway Girl*. As soon as the curtain fell, her eyes rolled back in her head and she crumpled in a heap. Luckily, Lionel was close enough to catch her. Miss Thrupp and Lo bundled her into the dressing room and stripped off her costume, which was drenched in sweat. The rest of us had to wait in the wings.

Iris had been sick ever since we left Kuala Lumpur but no one had wanted to admit it, least of all Iris herself. She'd pretended to be too ill to see Valentine off the day she left, so it was odd that she wasn't too ill to sing and dance.

Mr Milligan pushed his way through the crowd of Lilliputians that stood grumbling outside the dressing room. He put his head around the door and gestured for Miss Thrupp to come and talk to him. Just before he pulled the door shut again, I heard him say, "He's going to kill one of the kiddies before too long if he keeps this up, and if you won't speak to him, then I will!"

I hurried down to where Lizzie was folding costumes into a trunk.

"I think Mr Milligan is going to have words with Mr Arthur," I whispered.

Lizzie dropped the costume and put her hands on my shoulders. "You were with Iris before she went on stage, weren't you, Poesy? What was she like?"

I tipped my head to one side. "She said she wanted to go on. Though she looked peculiar. Her eyes were all shiny, in the wrong way. And Miss Thrupp said she had a fever, like the one Daisy had in Kuala Lumpur."

"And Lo said she shouldn't go on, didn't she? Lo told her she was going to take her back to the hotel in a gharry, but Iris refused."

"Well, she cried when Mr Arthur said he'd give her part to someone else if she didn't buck up. If she didn't play Winifred, then Tilly would have taken her place and that would have made Iris sicker than any old fever."

Lizzie gave me a funny look and I realised something new about myself. I had sounded rather sly and unkind. But it was true. Iris would rather die than have Tilly play Winifred.

Lizzie took one of my hands and stroked it gently. "Poesy, I want you to do something for me. Not just for me but for our dear Mr Arthur. Mr Milligan will set upon Arthur if we're not careful. He's been stewing over this ever since Daisy fell ill. You know Daisy and Iris are Mr Milligan's favourites. If Mr Milligan takes it on himself to challenge Arthur, it will be bad for all of us. So I want you to go and tell Mr Milligan what you just told me."

"Why don't *you* go and talk to him?" I asked.

"Because he won't believe anything I say," she said. She turned me around and gave me a little shove in the direction of the dressing rooms.

I found Mr Milligan packing away his limelight, laying the cylinders side by side and arranging all the tanks and tubing in his special trunks. He was muttering to himself as he worked so I knew he was grumpy.

I tapped him very shyly on the shoulder and he scowled until he turned and saw it was me.

"I thought I should tell you about Iris," I said, suddenly uncertain of what exactly I was meant to be saying.

"What about the little lass, then?" he asked, looking alarmed. "She's not taken a turn for the worse?"

"No," I said, swallowing hard, hoping Iris was better and that what I was about to say wasn't really a fib. "It's that she can't be very ill because she insisted, absolutely insisted, on going on stage tonight. We were in the dressing room together and she cried when Lo, I mean Eloise, I mean Mrs Quedda, when Mrs Quedda said she should go back to the hotel."

"*Mrs* Quedda, eh?" he said, his bushy eyebrows meeting as he frowned. I knew what he meant. It was hard to believe she was a 'Mrs' anything – she didn't seem grown-up enough – but she was married and she did have a baby.

"Yes. She was very worried for Iris but Iris insisted and cried and stamped her foot." I'd exaggerated a little – she hadn't really stamped her foot but it wouldn't have been out of character for her to do it, so it was only a tiny white lie.

"What could anyone do but let Iris have her way?" I asked, turning my palms upwards in an empty gesture.

Mr Milligan took each of my hands and held them firmly in his big, warm grasp. "I'm not sure, little Poesy, why you've come to tell me this. I hope it's out of the goodness of your heart. I hope it's because you want the best for your little friend and not because some weaselly gentleman put you up to it."

I blushed and snatched my hands away from his. "Of course not. Mr Arthur would never do something like that. I simply thought you should know, because you looked so worried, I thought…"

Mr Milligan nodded and went back to disassembling the limelight. It smelled funny around him – sharp and unpleasant. Charlie had told me it was only calcium oxide, but that acrid stench mingled with my uneasy sense of guilt and seeped into my skin.

Was it wrong to want everyone to get along? Was it wrong to try pouring oil on troubled waters? I wandered back to the empty theatre and sat on the edge of the stage, dangling my feet above the disused orchestra pit. It was so melancholy without the audience. If only the show could go on forever and the curtain never fall. These days, the only time the Lilliputians seemed to be truly happy was when we were on stage, pretending we were little grown-ups. I wished we never had to take off our costumes and go back to being ourselves.

WHITE SLAVES

Tilly Sweetrick

"I sold seven portraits tonight, even though the audience was so teeny," I announced. "But beastly old Mr Arthur took all my money!"

I wasn't quite ready to call him 'Butcher' in front of everyone, especially not Eliza. Of course, she had only sold one of her portraits so she was looking particularly pouty, though the Butcher had probably let her keep her money. She pretended she hadn't heard me as we stood waiting at the stage door while the men and boys brought out the last of our trunks.

A pair of bullocks stood idling between the stocks of a wagon loaded with props and costumes. Mr Milligan strapped on the last of the portmanteaus and waved to the driver to leave. We crushed into *gharries*, four across, with Daisy and Flora on our laps. The warm evening air smelled sweet. I reached out to a cascade of white flowers tumbling over a fence as we drove past in our open carriage. The petals fell sprinkling across our skirts like tiny stars.

The steamer for India was nowhere near as nice as the *Ceylon*. It was actually a cargo vessel. We'd never had to board at night before either. Stingy Old Mr Arthur probably wanted to save on the cost of lodgings. He'd stopped giving us our pocket money in Kuala Lumpur and I'd overheard him arguing with all the grown-ups about their wages. He hadn't paid them in weeks.

Stokers moved like shadows across the deck and disappeared below to tend the furnaces. Coolies unloaded our baggage from the wagons and carried it up the gangplank on their backs and on their heads.

We were scattered higgledy-piggledy through the ship. All the middling and little girls, except Iris, were put into a long dormitory in steerage. Only Mr Arthur, Miss Thrupp, the Queddas and Eliza were given cabins. I didn't know where the boys went but I saw them being rounded up by Mr Jim and Mr Milligan. Later, I found out they'd slept in hammocks along with the crew. I wondered what little Henry Howard made of it all. He was scared of grown-up men and I could imagine how frightened he'd be if the stokers, with their black faces and coal-stained clothes, woke him during the night.

It was only when Miss Thrupp came to our dormitory to do a head count that we realised Ruby was gone. At first we thought she was somewhere on board the ship but then it became clear that no one knew where she was. We all filed up on deck and stood in line as Mr Arthur and the captain went from one child to the next, grilling them about the last moment they had seen Ruby.

When they were halfway through interrogating us, the captain turned to Mr Arthur and said, "If you cannot find her before morning, we'll have to sail without her or put you all ashore."

Mr Arthur opened his mouth to argue, but what could he

say? We were booked to appear in Calcutta and the theatre was waiting for us.

I could see Mr Arthur growing angrier, as each child denied any knowledge of where Ruby had gone. Max Kreutz stood between Poesy and me with his thumbs hooked into his braces and a scowl on his face. Poesy grabbed his arm and gave it a little shake.

"Max, you and Ruby were talking after the performance tonight. I saw you. When the other girls were getting into the carriages, you were standing beside Ruby. Did she give any hint of what she was planning?"

"If she did, I wouldn't tell you, tattler," said Max.

Poesy's face crumpled as if he had slapped her. Mr Arthur swivelled in our direction and grabbed the front of Max's shirt. "And I won't tell you, neither," said Max, looking Mr Arthur straight in the eye. He had grown so much in these past few months that he was almost as tall as a man. He jutted his chin as he spoke and held his fists tightly clenched by his sides.

A hush fell on the deck. Everyone was holding their breath. The only sounds were the cries of the coolies down on the dock and the wash of the ocean against the steamer.

Mr Arthur's face grew pale. "Do you have any idea what could happen if we don't find her before this ship sails?"

"You'll be ruined," said Max, his eyes glittering, his lips two thin, bitter lines.

Mr Arthur dragged him away and disappeared below deck. We knew Max was set for a strapping. Freddie, his twin, stood scowling at the top of the stairs. We girls formed huddles or hung over the railing staring out over the black port, wondering where in the world Ruby could be.

"She's been taken by the white slave trade," wailed Pearl.

"No, she stowed away on Tempe and Clarissa's steamer."

"She's hiding in a trunk and they'll let her out once the ship's at sea."

"But hasn't their ship already sailed?" asked Iris.

"She's run off with a stagedoor Johnny."

"She's hiding so Max will get in trouble. He fancies her and she's letting everyone know."

Then we were all silent, thinking about Max. Freddie stood by the entrance to the cabins, twisting his hands.

"Max is in big trouble, isn't he?" asked Daisy of no one in particular.

Ten minutes later, Max staggered up on deck with one hand cupped over his eye.

Mr Arthur pushed him out of the way as he strode down the gangplank and onto the docks. We saw his figure disappear into the tangle of boats, cargo and men. Eliza and Poesy stood at the rail, watching him go.

"I hope he finds her," said Eliza.

"I hope he doesn't," said Max. "I hope she gets home and tells everyone what a butcher he is and that Mr Kelly comes to fetch Beryl and Pearl. That would fix him. You know, he hasn't even been paying our ma for all the work we done? Me and Freddie got a wire from her asking where was her shillings. Then he has the cheek to strap me and his ruddy buckle cut me hard. We ain't any better than slaves. "

Eliza didn't speak straight away. I saw her watching us all closely as the shock of Max's announcement rippled through the hazy darkness. "You don't know what you're saying," she said slowly. "The Percivals often hold back our wages until well into the tour. You should remember that happened last time with Mrs Essie. No one was paid until the tour was established. Your greedy ma will get her precious shillings. But do you care about money more than Ruby? She isn't safe, Max. Mr Arthur has to make her safe. Tempe and Clarissa had an escort. If Ruby went back to Australia alone, no one will believe her. Her reputation will be in tatters."

"Like yours?" said Max, with a crooked smile. He took his hand away from his eye and we all saw the gash. A deep, dark cut above his brow, oozing blood. "He done this to me for defending Ruby's honour and not giving away her secrets. That's what my ma taught me was the genteel thing to do – keep a lady's secrets."

"How dare you! Mr Arthur is more of a gentleman than you will ever be, Max Kreutz," said Eliza.

Max laughed. "If that's what you call a gentleman, I don't want to be one."

29

ACROSS THE BAY OF BENGAL

Poesy Swift

I sat down on my bunk and banged the hard, lumpy horsehair mattress with my fist. I was terribly worried by what Max had said. Mumma was counting on those thirty shillings a month. I could only hope she wouldn't have to wait much longer. At least when the money did arrive, there would be a great wad of it and Chooky and Yada and Mumma could all go down to Swan Street for a treat of fish and chips.

The thought of fish and chips made me realise our dormitory was rather stinky. There were fifteen girls in the room and it smelled sour with coal and grease.

"Thtinky-poo," said Daisy, putting her thumb in her mouth. Her eyes looked too big for her face and her plump cheeks had hollowed out since Kuala Lumpur. "Read me a story, Poesy, please," she said, nuzzling her head against me.

"I'm too tired," I said. "We should sleep."

"I can't fweep if you bon't wead to me," said Daisy, talking with her thumb in her mouth so the words were all but incomprehensible. "Wead me Gwullfa!"

"Gulliver? Not tonight." My mind was churning with horrible images of Ruby held captive by slave traders and Mr Arthur punishing Max. All my thoughts were caught up in a whirlwind of fear and worry.

135

"I want Gull!" said Daisy, taking her thumb out to shout.

"Go on, Poesy. Don't be selfish," said Tilly. "You can't start her off on a story and then abandon her. You can't abandon people just because you're tired of them."

I wanted to cry but instead I pushed the little green book into Tilly's hands. "You read to her if it's so important."

"Did you bring this because your relative wrote it?" she asked.

"You know he's not my relative. It was a present from my granny."

Daisy climbed onto Tilly's lap and looked at the pages of the book expectantly.

"Where were you up to?" Tilly asked.

"Wapter Fix," replied Daisy, her thumb firmly back in place.

I knew she'd already heard Chapter Six but I said nothing as Tilly flipped through the pages until she found the place where Gulliver describes the way the Lilliputians raise their children.

"Their parents are suffered to see them only twice a year; the visit is to last an hour. They are allowed to kiss the child at meeting and parting but a professor, who always stands by on those occasions, will not suffer them to whisper or use any fondling expression, or bring any presents of toys, sweet-meats and the like."

"You see," said Flora, who had crept over to join Daisy. "They're like us – perhaps luckier. That's why Mr Arthur calls us Lilliputians. Read it out again."

Daisy took her thumb out of her mouth then and the two little girls listened intently as Tilly reread the passage.

"See – the Lilliputians live just like us," cried Flora. "And twice a year! They get to see their parents twice a year. Why, I only saw my mama once last year. And you know the Butcher never lets us have anything nice."

"Flora!" I cried. "Don't call Mr Arthur that awful name. Talking like that doesn't make anything better. And besides, that's only a story. We're not really Lilliputians, we're not tiny people from a strange island. We're ordinary girls."

Tilly shut the book and stroked the spine.

"Oh, let them complain," she said. "They're still little enough to be like real Lilliputians. Besides, complaining about it makes us all feel better."

"No, it makes us all feel bitter."

"Are you on his side then?" she asked. "Will you start tagging after him like Lionel?"

I punched the lumpy pillow on my bunk again but it didn't stop the tears from flowing down my cheeks. Everyone stared at me as if I was a horrible freak.

"Oh don't start blubbing," said Tilly. She shut the book and pushed the little girls off her lap. "Come with me, Poesy Swift. You and I need to have a jolly good chat."

I wasn't sure if I wanted to hear what she had to say but I wiped my eyes on my sleeve and followed her up the ladder and onto the deck. Tilly led me to the bow of the steamer and turned to face me, her hands on her hips.

"Listen, you have to stop acting like a baby," she said. "For goodness sake! You're thirteen years old. You've got nothing to sook about."

"Everyone thinks I tattled. All the girls are being beastly to me. And now Ruby has been stolen by white slave traders and it's my fault."

"Pish-posh! You need to get a few things straight. For one thing, I don't think you tattled and neither did Ruby. Tempe said it wasn't your fault, so Ruby running away is nothing to do with you. But it's no wonder she's done a runner. She's lost Tempe and Clarissa, her two best friends in the world. Mr Arthur has been a cad and you have to admit it and stop sticking up for him. You saw with your own two eyes. When he loses his temper, he behaves exactly like a butcher."

"But he won't be like that any more. I'm sure he won't. Now that Tempe is gone, things will be different. He'll make it up to Ruby. Everything will be better."

"There you go, doing it again. Jumping to his defence. You're as bad as Eliza."

I was going to say something sharp in reply but then I realised Tilly was blinking back tears.

"You used to be *my* friend, Poesy. Now the only person you care about is your Lizzie. I've lost Valentine. Do you have any idea what that means to me?"

She flung her arms around my neck and sobbed on my shoulder. I didn't know what to say. I'd never seen Tilly cry before. I stroked her hair and when her sobs had subsided I dried her cheeks with the edge of my pinafore.

"I'm sorry, Tilly. It must be awful. But you do have lots of other friends. I only have Lizzie."

She smiled, almost shyly, and took my hand. "You could be my friend again, if you wanted. If you were nice to me, all the other girls would follow my lead and everyone would like you. But there is one thing, Poesy, that I really think you have to face. You're not a little baby any more. If we are going to be friends, you do have to grow up."

After Tilly left me, I found a spot between a lifeboat and the railing and sat on a pile of rope, watching the docks, hoping to see Mr Arthur returning with Ruby on his arm. I was worn out but I knew I couldn't sleep. If thoughts could make things happen, as Yada always said, then the only thought I would hold in my mind was the one that would bring Ruby safely back to us. I watched for hours, yet I saw nothing but dark-skinned Malays moving cargo on the docks.

I woke suddenly and realised the steamer had left Georgetown. Folding my hands together, I said a little prayer that Ruby would make her way home safely. I was stiff and sore from sleeping on my rough bed of ropes. I stood up and stretched. All around lay the dark waters of the Bay of Bengal. A soft dawn light rippled on the surface of the sea.

On the other side of the bay was India. Everything would be different there. Without the big girls making trouble, Mr Arthur would be his old self. Perhaps the Indians would love the Lilliputians and there would be no more money worries. And Tilly and I would be friends again.

I took Topsy and Turvy out of my pocket and stared at their little clay faces. I'd had them since I was tiny but Tilly was right, I wasn't a baby any more. I kissed each of them on the forehead, shut my eyes and threw them over the side of the steamer. I didn't hear them splash in the water. Nor did I search for them. I kept my gaze fixed on the distant horizon.

30

BREAD AND WATER

Poesy Swift

The next day, I sat up in the bow of the steamer with Charlie and Lionel, watching the waves churn white around us. It always smelled better in the bow, away from the stink of the coal. The sea air coated our skin but it was nice to lick your lips and taste the saltiness. It made all the troubles of the night seem like a bad dream.

Charlie was practising palming a coin, turning the coppery penny between his fingers and over the back of his knuckles and then slipping it into his palm. I loved to watch the way his hands worked, the way his bones and sinews rippled with movement, the way the coin disappeared between his fingers and then reappeared again as if he really had magic in his skin.

Lionel had a deck of cards and fanned them out, fiddling with their corners.

"You shouldn't bring them up here to practise. They'll warp from the sea air," said Charlie. "Or blow away."

"They're my cards," said Lionel.

"Well, if you lose them, don't think you can borrow mine."

As if on cue, a gust of wind swept up over the bow and blasted the three of us. I held onto my skirts but Lionel lost his grip on the fanned-out playing cards and they scattered across the deck. We all dived onto our knees and started crawling about, trying to help him retrieve them, but two lifted into the air and over the railing.

"It doesn't matter," said Lionel defensively. "I can still do most of my tricks without them."

Charlie said nothing, but our eyes met and I knew that look of scorn and pity. Since the terrible show with Danny McGee, Lionel had been trying to learn Charlie's magic, but he couldn't master the sleight of hand. It was as though his man-sized, meaty fingers had grown too big to manage the deft moves.

"We should get back down to the dining hall," I said. "We'll be late for rehearsal."

"We don't need to rehearse again today," said Lionel. "Mr Arthur says we should have some lessons."

Charlie laughed. "Good, I'll teach Poesy coin tricks. That's the only lesson she's likely to get this week."

"Oh will you shut up. Mr Arthur says some nosey parker asked about our 'teacher'. So we're to have lessons."

"Who with?" asked Charlie.

"Mr Arthur himself. He says he'll teach us parsing."

"What's parsing?" asked Charlie.

"I think it's a ball game," said Lionel.

"No, it's actually something to do with grammar," I said.

Then we all fell silent, each of us pondering how long these lessons might last.

We were on our way back to the dining room when we heard Mr Arthur shouting. It ricocheted through me, bruising my heart and lungs. I couldn't bear the thought of any more trouble. He wasn't arguing with one of the girls but with a man with a strong accent. Lionel quickened his pace. Charlie and I hung back, hoping the argument would settle before we could be caught up in it.

"I will not have passengers on my ship treated as criminals," shouted the captain. "Especially not a young lady."

"She's not a young lady," said Mr Arthur. "She's a mere child. And a wretched, wilful one at that. As her guardian, I have the right to discipline her."

"Not on my ship." The captain spoke with a Dutch accent, clipping each word. "Bread and water! You give instructions to my galley to serve this girl bread and water! What sort of a pirate vessel do you think I am running?"

Charlie looked at me and raised one eyebrow.

"Ruby! She must have come back in the middle of the night," he whispered. "Who else could it be?"

I don't think I've ever felt so relieved in my life. If Mr Arthur had her locked up, at least she was safe with us again. I took Charlie by the wrist and dragged him into the hallway. I had to hear the rest.

Mr Arthur had drawn himself up to his full height but the captain towered over him. "In Penang, sir, this 'young lady' attempted to run away with the first mate of the *Tracchus*. When it became clear to her what the cost of a fare home would be, she rightly came skulking back to our troupe, her family. I am acting *in loco parentis* for the child and I believe such behaviour should be punished."

The captain pushed past him. "You are not fit to be in charge of these children," he said, his 'r's rolling out of his mouth in a garbled rage.

Mr Arthur stood by as the captain unlocked a nearby cabin door.

"Come, child."

Ruby stepped out, her eyes wild, her face gaunt and pale.

She walked past Mr Arthur as if he wasn't even there. She walked past all of us as if she were alone on the wide sea. She looked thinner, the lovely full ripeness in her cheeks gone. Her movements were odd and jerky, like those of a broken wind-up toy. She wasn't the same girl that had led the stampede on the ship in Singapore harbour. She made her way up to the upper deck, clinging to the railing on the stairs.

"You, child," called the captain, pointing at me. "Follow the girl and mind she gets some fresh air. And boy," he said, laying his hand roughly on Lionel's shoulder, "go and fetch the matron and tell her the girl has been set free."

Ruby came and slept in our dormitory, dragging her bedding from the other cabin and rolling it out on the bench beside me – the only empty space left. She had a bruise on her cheek and her eyes were flat and almost colourless. She lay with her back to me all night, but in the early dawn I was woken by the sound of her crying. I curled my body around her and drew her closer and after a while her sobbing slowed.

"You had to come back, Ruby. For Beryl and Pearl. Your sisters," I whispered. "They thought they'd lost you."

"I hate them," she said.

"Who? Not Beryl and Pearl?" I whispered, hoping that the other girls wouldn't wake.

"No, men. The Butcher and every man in the Empire."

"But Mr Arthur was so worried about you," I said.

Ruby shut her eyes. "Nobody cares about me."

I wanted to say, "I care about you," but instead I pressed my forehead against her back and held her tightly until she fell asleep.

31

Mesmerism

Tilly Sweetrick

India. The littlies fussed and fizzed at the prospect of seeing elephants and *nabobs* until I wanted to slap them. We should have been mourning the fact that we weren't arriving in America. The steamer docked at a port and then a small ferry took us upstream to Calcutta. We chugged up the Hooghly, a wide, wide river with palm trees on its banks and glistening, brown-skinned men swimming from the *ghat*s.

Calcutta wasn't what I had expected. It was beautiful and terrible with its Eden gardens, wide avenues, dilapidated mansions and piles of rotting figurines on the bank. The Butcher said they were effigies from *puja* ceremonies that the Hindus held, and he knew the names of their gods: Kali and Shiva. He made a remark about Kali being a teenage girl. As if that black-and-blue monster effigy with water washing through her was a girl. It made me shudder.

We crowded into *gharries* for the ride through the city. Somehow, I was stuck with all the Fintons. Or they were stuck with each other. You could see they were no happier about it than me. Eloise, Eunice and Eliza didn't often seek each other's company.

Charlie Byrne climbed up beside the driver and turned back to grin at us. "India," he said. "At last." He was a strange boy. He seemed to have slipped on a different skin from the moment we stepped off the ferry and onto the *ghat*s, and his green eyes had grown brighter, like shiny glass.

"Pooh, what's so special about India," said Eunice. "I don't know why we couldn't do a season in Rangoon."

"You say the stupidest things, Eunice," said Eliza. "You know Mr Arthur won't take us there."

"Why?" I asked. "Why can't we go there?"

"Because of what happened when he was tiny, only as big as Daisy. Mr Arthur's brother was murdered in Rangoon."

"No he wasn't," interjected Lo. "He shot himself."

Eliza's face grew red and splotchy. "You weren't there. Arthur was. Arthur says he was murdered. He saw Jimmy lying at the top of the stairs, dead."

"So he was murdered with his own gun and it was found under him, still clutched in his own hand?" said Lo, pursing her lips. "Mrs Essie was there too. It didn't stop her going back to Rangoon."

"Mrs Essie didn't find the corpse," said Eliza. "If I found you dead and bleeding outside my room, I would never feel the same about that place again. I would never want to go back there. What is wrong with all you people? Can't you see he's only human? He's a man and once he was a boy."

Eliza could make all the excuses she liked for the Butcher. It didn't matter what had happened to him when he was little. It was who he had become that mattered to us now.

Calcutta was white and grey – all the lovely grand buildings were streaked with stains from the monsoon. There were people in uniform everywhere, which was a good sign. I liked having soldiers in the audience.

We rode past the Victoria Memorial where white stone lay in great piles and brown men glistened with sweat, past bazaars where swarms of Indians bustled from one stall to the next, past beggars and *tea-wallahs*. Our hotel was an old building with rusting iron lacework that bled brown stains down the walls. As soon as we were through the lobby, Poesy was beside me. She came up the stairs with her arm linked through Ruby's, as if she were Ruby's new best friend. But Ruby's face looked odd and twisted and her mouth sunken, as though she'd been sucking on sour limes.

We stood out on the balcony overlooking a narrow street teeming with natives. Poesy took a deep breath and made her usual sort of remark, about how the city smelled delicious – a sweetness of milky tea and spices. She always noticed the strangest things.

"Look," she said, pointing. "Isn't it lovely." A woman stood on an opposite rooftop hanging out coloured cloths, a line of saris floating in the breeze beside her.

"That's a bad sign," I said. "We must be right on the edge of Blacktown."

"Why must you spoil it, Tilly?" said Poesy.

"The Butcher should have found us lodgings closer to the theatre."

I looked at the brilliantly coloured floating saris and then down at my day dress, looking tattier and greyer every day. It was awfully threadbare too, and I felt another surge of irritation with the Butcher. As soon as we were in our rooms, Thrupp made us take everything off, except our petticoats, to 'reduce wear and tear'. So we sat about feeling like paupers.

At breakfast the next morning, Charlie Byrne had his

Magician's Annual propped open in his lap as he spooned egg into his mouth. He always had his nose in a book, or else his hands would be flitting like wings as he practised his tricks.

"Do you ever read anything other than magic annuals?" I asked.

"'Course I do," he said.

"Well, can you lend me something then? I've read my magazines so many times I'm utterly bored. Anything will do. Anything."

So on a hot Bengal afternoon, while we lay about in our petticoats on our beds, I picked up Charlie's book and began to flick through the pages.

"Charlie's lent me this," I said, waving the book at Poesy. I rather liked that it annoyed her, even if we were pretending we were friends again. She was helping Daisy tie her curls with rags so that they wouldn't snarl while she took her afternoon nap. She pretended not to hear me but I knew her ears had pricked up. Miss Poesy thought Charlie was her special possession. She didn't like to think of any other girl owning pieces of him.

I turned back to the book and I could feel the hair on the back of my neck stand on end as I read. Mesmerism. It was a how-to book of mesmerism. I'd seen a magician do it once on stage in San Francisco. He'd made a man quack like a duck. "We should try this," I said. "Try a little experiment in mass hypnosis!"

"What?" asked Poesy.

I didn't bother to answer. I just held the book up and pointed at the title. She took a step closer.

"You shouldn't even think about it. Mesmerism is

dangerous. I saw Mrs Annie Besant do it in Melbourne and she said you could paralyse the brain with hypnosis. She says Indian magic men hypnotise everyone in their audiences to make them believe in their conjuring. But you have to know how to go about it properly. People can hurt themselves with their thoughts."

"I don't believe any of the girls in this room have a single thought inside their airy heads," I said.

"Don't be flippant, Tilly. I'm serious," she said, pouting.

"I'm serious too. A serious mesmerist."

Half an hour later, while the littlest and most of the big girls lay sleeping, I opened the door to the connecting bedrooms and ten of us gathered in the middling girls' bedroom. Ruby sat alone on a stool beside the window. Since Tempe and Clarissa had gone, she'd turned very moody. So now she sat gazing out over Calcutta, only half listening to me, as I read out the instructions for mass hypnosis.

We pushed some of the beds closer together and made everyone join in, even Ruby and Poesy, so there were four girls on each bed.

"All right, then," I said. "I will be the mesmerist and I am going to hypnotise all of you. If it works, it will be as if you were having a nap. And if it doesn't work, and you all fall asleep, then we still will be having a nap, so all will be well."

They obediently closed their eyes and listened as I chanted, "Relax and listen to the sound of my voice. There is only my voice. Relax and listen to the soothing sound of my voice. There is only my voice."

Iris giggled and I gave her an evil look so she shut her eyes again, though I was trying not to laugh myself.

"You will do what I say. You want to do what I say. You cannot keep your eyes open. They are too heavy. They must stay closed and allow you to concentrate entirely on the sound of my voice. There is nothing else. Drowsy. Sleepy. My voice. Heavy. You are growing sleepy."

I kept my voice monotonously low and soothing, describing how everyone's limbs were growing leaden as I willed them to sleep. Actually, I think I might have made a very fine mesmerist. Instinctively, I understood how to hold an audience in my thrall. Poesy opened one eye and shut it again quickly when she realised I was looking straight at her. Without stopping my monotonous drone, I tiptoed over to her and gripped her chin in my hand. Her eyes flew open in alarm but I held them in my gaze, firm and steady. I pinched her chin so hard that tears sprang to her eyes. But she didn't cry out. I had to admire her for that.

I tiptoed around the circle of girls, checking to see which ones were peeking and which were in thrall to my voice. Some of them seemed to be nodding off. Ruby sat upright with her eyes shut. There was something odd about her face. Her mouth was slack and her hands hung limply by her side. She looked like a sleepwalker. I realised I might have cracked it. I had mesmerised Ruby Kelly.

I focused all my attention on her. I felt a little shiver run up my spine. I'm not sure if it was fear or the thrill of success.

As the other girls slept on or opened their eyes to watch, I asked Ruby to raise one hand in the air. And she obeyed me. I glanced down at the blue cloth-covered book in my hand. The first thing it described was auto-suggestion, so I tried it. I didn't mean any harm.

"Now, when I say the word 'duck', I want you to say 'quack'."

When I said "duck", Ruby obediently replied with a 'quack'.

"She's faking this," whispered Iris. But I knew I'd done something extraordinary and I was determined to prove it to Iris and all the others.

"Now, Ruby, you are going to go back in time. I have the power to take you back, back, back to other times in your life. I want to take you back to when you were a little girl. Let's say your seventh birthday. You are seven years old again, Ruby. It is your birthday today. What presents did you get?"

Ruby's eyes rolled back beneath their lids. Her face twitched. For a moment she said nothing, and then she spoke in a different voice. A younger voice.

"Oh, a doll. A pretty doll. Thank you, Mama. No, I don't want to share it with Beryl. It's my doll."

Everyone snickered behind their hands. I grinned at the others, triumphant.

"Now let's take you forward again. Through the years, past all your birthdays. Don't stop at any one event. We are taking you to last week. To Georgetown. You remember when you were in Georgetown, don't you, Ruby? In Georgetown on the island of Penang?"

I saw Poesy's hands flit at me as if to signal me to stop, but it was too late. Ruby was there, back at our last day on the island of Penang. Slowly, gently I prompted her through each hour of the evening. It seemed to be going swimmingly until she began to whimper.

"And then, you walked down to the harbour," I said, keeping my voice smooth and steady, so as not to break the spell.

Ruby whimpered again. "He promised…" She stopped and a fat tear rolled down her cheek from behind her closed eyes. "I only wanted to go home. He said he'd help me. That he'd help me for free. I didn't know…"

Her voice grew more staccato, more urgent. She looked terrified and she lay back on the bed and started to writhe.

"Tell me, tell us what is happening, Ruby," I said.

Poesy jumped up and stood behind Ruby, resting one hand on her shoulder. "We don't need to know this," she hissed. Then she took Ruby's face in her hands. "Wake up, Ruby."

It had said in the book not to wake people suddenly. I tried to push Poesy away from Ruby. "Leave her. You'll ruin it."

But Ruby didn't seem to hear either of us or even notice we were there. Her face grew clouded with confusion.

"It's all right, Ruby," I said, kneeling in front of her. "It's all right. You're safe."

But Ruby wasn't listening. She started pushing away some imaginary person and crying out, "Stop, please, stop. You're hurting me." Her face turned a peculiar colour and she began to moan and cry.

"Wake her, Tilly," shrilled Poesy. "You have to wake her."

I didn't need Poesy to tell me what to do. I could see things had turned sour. I snapped my fingers. "Ruby, I command you, wake." But Ruby kept writhing and her cries grew to screams. It was as if an evil spirit had possessed her.

I grabbed the book and riffled through the pages. "It says she should wake up when I say that."

"Keep saying it, then," said Poesy.

"Wake up, Ruby. I command you, come back to the

present." I was almost shouting but still she wasn't listening. I even tried to shake her awake, but as soon as I laid hands on her, the screams grew ear-piercing.

"She's gone insane," said Iris.

"What should we do?" squeaked May.

The other girls stood in a huddle, as far from Ruby as they could. Some of them pressed their hands against their ears. They backed away and stood staring at Ruby as she fought off the invisible man while I kept searching for a solution in the pages of the blue book.

And then Poesy took charge. She had such cheek to talk to me like that. "Go and get Miss Thrupp, Tilly, quickly," she said. I was going to do that anyway but now it looked as if I couldn't think for myself.

I dropped the book and ran from the room.

By the time I returned with Miss Thrupp, Ruby was sitting up, her head in her hands. Beryl and Pearl sat on either side of her rubbing her back. Something had shifted.

"We could hear her cries all over the hotel," said Miss Thrupp. "What will the servants make of it? They'll think you're a pack of savages."

What could *she* have been thinking, to not have come running until I fetched her myself?

"It was only a game," I said, "but it went wrong."

"Indeed it did," said Miss Thrupp. "The games you girls play. Not girls at all. Savages…" I heard her voice trailing off as she led Ruby from the room. Suddenly, I was shivering. I lay down on my bed and hugged myself. It hadn't been a kids' game. We were playing with the grown-ups now.

32

A MOMENT IN TIME

Poesy Swift

The morning after Tilly's awful mesmerism fiasco, we were bundled out of the hotel door and into carriages. It was a relief to be doing something other than lying on our beds in our underclothes. We'd been in Calcutta nearly a week but we hadn't done a single show. Something had gone wrong with our booking at the Opera House. Mr Arthur reassured us that any moment we'd be on stage again. In the meantime, we were all going to have photographic portraits made of each of us. I'd never had my picture taken. Once a man came to the door of Willow Lane and offered to take a photograph of us and our house but we had nothing to pay him with except the milkman's money. Now I was to have fifty photos of myself.

All the Lilliputians who had come on the last tour had a bundle of portraits. After every show they would wander through the audience, selling them to anyone who would part with a coin. Daisy and Flora had sold all their pictures in Singapore and some of the other children had run out as well. Only Lionel and a couple of the older girls still had any left. It was terrible when people didn't want your picture. I was torn about whether I wanted to sell my portrait to strangers. But sometimes the children were allowed to keep the money and I did like the idea of having a few coins. It was almost too much to believe that anyone would give me a whole rupee in exchange for my picture.

An oxen cart followed our carriages through the streets of Calcutta and then coolies carted our costume trunks up narrow flights of stairs to the photographer's studio.

"He shouldn't have brought us down here," said Tilly, glancing nervously along the laneway. "We're practically in the heart of Blacktown. It's bad enough that our hotel is so close. Surely he could have found someone other than this *babu* to do the pictures."

"What's a *babu*?"

"Don't listen to her," said Charlie. "A *babu* is an Indian gentleman, a perfectly respectable gentleman."

Tilly rolled her eyes. "Charlie's turning into a right little *sahib*, aren't you, Chaz?"

Charlie shrugged and pushed past us, taking the creaky stairs two at a time. He never paid attention when Tilly tried to bait him.

The photographer's studio was made up of two rooms on the second floor of an old building. It was very plain, almost shabby, and the hallway where we waited our turn had a funny, oily smell. I don't know what I expected but I'd always thought that having my picture taken would be a little more glamorous. When I was finally allowed inside, I found there was a fake curtain hanging at one end of the room and a chaise longue with a small marble table beside it. As I drew closer, I realised the flowers that stood on the table were all made of paper and covered in a fine layer of dust.

Mr Arthur said Lionel and Lizzie should be in a photo

together to try to help Lionel sell more pictures. Lionel had to wear a three-quarter-length coat, a cap with a red band and a pair of military trousers with a red stripe down the leg. He knelt in front of Lizzie as if he were her beau. She wore a pale blue dress with lamb-chop sleeves and a striped underskirt. On her lovely dark curls was a wide-brimmed bonnet with ostrich feathers that fell forward as she offered her white hand to Lionel.

I wished I could look like Lizzie, so full and soft and deliciously plump. But did I really want a boy to look at me the way Lionel mooned over Lizzie? I suppose he was only acting but it made me feel itchy to think of him looking at me like that. Then I imagined Charlie on bended knee and smiled. Perhaps it depended on the boy.

When it came to my turn, I looked in the mirror and knew it would be hard for me to sell my pictures too. I was dressed as a gypsy girl, dancing with a tambourine above my head, and my elbows looked horribly sharp as they stuck out from the puffy short sleeves. The full skirt billowed out when I twirled in a circle and the little bells along the hem rang merrily, but when the photographer made me stand with my hands stretched high, it only made me look skinnier than ever.

After me, the Kreutz brothers had their picture taken together, each in silly costume as Tweedledee and Tweedledum in battle. "Ours sell like nobody's business," they said as they whacked each other over the head with rubber batons.

Then, as I was changing out of my gypsy costume, Flora stepped in front of the camera. She was dressed in a miniature full-length gown with shoestring shoulder straps and jewel-encrusted dropped straps as well. She had a silver belt around her waist and a crown of stars on her head – stars so big she almost looked like a tiny Statue of Liberty. She held a handful of the skirt fabric in her fat little fist to stop it dragging along the floor. When she raised one small hand in a regal wave everyone laughed, but you knew why Mr Arthur would order at least a hundred copies of the image.

Everything seemed to be going smoothly until Lizzie stepped forward for her solo photo as a geisha girl. She wore a heavily embroidered kimono and flowers and pearls in her hair, and her eyebrows were elaborately pencilled in a faux oriental style. She raised an ivory fan and fluttered it gracefully beneath her chin. Lionel stood beside me and stared, slack-jawed. Mr Arthur was watching too. His face changed.

"Who chose that costume, Eliza?"

"I did. I thought you'd like it," she said. "I'm a geisha, like Madame Butterfly."

Mr Arthur blanched.

"Don't be ridiculous! You are not and never will be a geisha. Go and change. I'll not have you selling images of yourself dressed like that."

He mopped his brow with his handkerchief and whispered something to the photographer and then barked rudely at Lizzie to hurry up and change her outfit. She lowered her fan and sighed with disappointment but did as she was told.

Later, as we sat waiting on the stairs for the others to finish, I asked Lizzie, "Did you mind Mr Arthur snapping at you like that? Even Lionel thought he was rude."

Lizzie sighed and tucked one of her curls behind her ear. "It's not his fault," she said.

"You never think anything is his fault. Why do you always take his side? He was mean to you, Lizzie."

"It's not easy being in charge. And Calcutta is full of sad memories for poor Mr Arthur. He came here after his brother died in Rangoon, and his father fell ill and died not long after when he was still only a tiny boy. He's had such a hard life."

"Lizzie, do you have a crush on Mr Arthur? Is that why you always take his side? I know you say he's your friend as well as your employer, but you're simply friends, aren't you, nothing else?" I held my breath. I almost didn't want to hear the answer.

Lizzie took my face in her hands and stroked my cheeks with her thumbs. Her hands were smooth and silky soft. "Poesy, you are a funny little creature. Of course I don't have a 'crush' on Mr Arthur."

I shut my eyes and took a deep breath, inhaling the lovely scent of Lizzie. She smelled of lavender and rosewater and soft powder. A sweet relief washed over me. I took Lizzie's hand and kissed the back of it.

"That's the truth, isn't it?" I asked, needing to be sure.

"Why would I lie to you, Poesy Swift?"

33

SWADESHI

Tilly Sweetrick

When we finally began our season at the Minerva Theatre, the stalls were only half full and there was no one in the galleries. The Butcher tried to blame Mr Shrouts for not doing his job properly but it wasn't Mr Shrouts who was in charge. There was only one person to blame.

The morning after opening night, Lionel sat with the newspaper spread out across his knees. I picked at my breakfast. I didn't really like the sort of food they served us. The fruit made my mouth sting and there were bits of old fish in our breakfast rice.

"It ain't going to be a good season," said Lionel.

I swear, that lumpy boy is simply the Prince of Gloom.

"Since that Alipore bombing, people aren't keen to come out at night. Didn't you notice? Even the *babu*s and *nabob*s and *boxwallah*s, all those rich Indians, the ones who would have come ordinarily, even they stayed away."

"A bombing!" exclaimed Poesy.

"Didn't you know?" said Lionel. "Two ladies had a bomb thrown into their carriage and they were both blown to smithereens."

"They didn't mean to kill the women," interrupted Charlie. "They were trying to blow up a judge or someone important."

"Not very good shots, were they?" said Lionel, snickering. Awful boy. How could he snicker about people dying!

"Would you please explain what you are talking about!" I said, feeling rather cross.

"The natives blew up two English women last year," said Lionel, rather full of himself. "The bombers are on trial right now, right here in Calcutta. They've already hanged one of them and the other shot himself rather than get caught. They've got a third one, this Ghosh fellow, he's in prison and they want to hang him too. He's a right stirrer."

I must have looked a little confused because Charlie said, "They want independence."

"Independence from what?"

"Crikey, Tilly, don't you know anything!" said Lionel. "Britain, of course."

I would have rather liked to slap him. Instead I squashed a piece of fruit onto my plate and let him prattle. "They say this Ghosh is being painted as a freedom fighter or something ridiculous like that."

He shook out the newspaper. "Listen, this is what the *babu* lawyer said: "Long after he is dead and gone, his words will be echoed and re-echoed, not only in India but across distant seas and lands. Therefore, I say that the man in his position is not only standing before the bar of this court, but before the bar of the High Court of History." What a lot of twaddle. High Court of History!"

Charlie looked uncomfortable, pushed his chair away from the table and left the room.

I took the paper from Lionel and read and reread the article about the nationalists, trying to understand it. Then my eye drifted down the page to the theatre section and I felt an electric shock. There was a review of the Lilliputians, a rather mixed one, I might add. But it was the interview with the Butcher on the same page that made my flesh creep. He talked about how 'closely guarded' he kept us 'to make sure we stayed ordinary, quiet, well-behaved kiddies'.

Though I snorted at the Butcher talking about us as if we were babies, it was when the reporter commented that the lyrics of our songs were rather suggestive that I really sat up. I could almost hear the Butcher's voice as I read his remarks. He claimed we had no idea what the words meant. I thought of Iris and how the reviewers in Penang had said she was quite the coquette when she sang 'Teach Me How to Love'. We knew exactly what we were doing, exactly what those songs meant. If he thought we were stupid little kiddies, he didn't have the measure of any of us.

Later, as we left the hotel, the streets seemed ominously quiet. We rode through the rising heat to the theatre for morning rehearsals. As I walked past the Butcher and onto the stage I heard him swear, "Damn this Swadeshi business." As if that was the only reason things were turning sour.

"What's Swadeshi?" asked Poesy. I swear that child drifts around in a cloud of not-seeing.

"They're boycotting British goods," I told her. "Anything British, for that matter. They think if none of the Indians buy British things or come and see our shows, that it will drive the Britishers out of the country. Daft, if you ask me."

"But we're not really British," said Poesy. "Maybe we should make sure everyone knows we're Australian."

"We are loyal citizens of the British Empire," said Lionel.

"Well, the loyal citizens of the British Empire won't be staying here in Bengal much longer," I said. "It said in the paper that they're going to move the government to New Delhi. We'll have no audiences while the Indians are marching up and down the streets, protesting. I don't like it one little bit."

"You've been swotting up on the newspapers then, have you?" said Lionel, condescending prig.

"Is it because of this Swadeshi business that we're not getting many people in the audience?" asked Poesy.

I hadn't noticed the Butcher sneak up behind us. "No," he barked. "It's because you lot aren't working hard enough. You're like a line of bloody limp rags."

"That's not true," I said. "You know that's not true." It felt good to talk back. It was the first time I'd tried it and it was simply wonderful.

The Butcher looked at me blankly. "Mind your tongue, Tilly," was all he said. I was surprised he didn't box my ears. I almost wished he had. I knew Mr Milligan was watching from backstage. There was plenty going on for Mr Milligan to worry about.

That night, Iris Usher looked positively peaky when she stepped out of the changing rooms. You could see sweat glistening on her neck and brow, no matter how much powder she'd dabbed on it to hide the fact that she was feverish again, just as in Georgetown. She had too much rouge on and her eye make-up was a little smudged. I could see her trembling as she reached down to buckle her shoe.

By the time Mr Arthur came into the dressing room for the first call, Iris could barely stand. He knew exactly what was wrong. He even asked her if she was all right and this time, unlike the last, she opened her little mouth and said, "I don't think I can go on. I feel too shaky."

I felt my heart make a tiny jump. It should have been my moment. I could sing Iris's role. The Butcher knew I could. But he knelt down in front of Iris and gazed into her face, feigning concern. "A trooper like you doesn't throw in the towel, does she?"

"I feel all wobbly, Mr Arthur," she said.

"Do you want Tilly to sing your part?"

It was a terrible thing to ask. He knew perfectly well it would make Iris steel herself. I willed her to crumple and watched as her face grew pinched with worry. Then she took a deep breath.

"I suppose I could try," she said, her eyes flitting in my direction and then back to the Butcher.

"Good girl," he said. "That's the spirit."

Iris struggled through every song and had barely finished singing 'The Lazy Town is Dreaming' when she stepped into the wings and her knees buckled under her. She simply folded up like a rag doll. Mr Milligan abandoned his post in the lighting booth and scooped her into his arms. As soon as they'd stripped off her costume and wrapped her in a dressing gown, she was bundled into a *gharry* with Miss Thrupp and taken back to the hotel.

I gathered up her damp costume from the floor and struggled into it, even though it really was too small for me.

"Quick, help me fasten the stays," I said to Myrtle. "If we hurry, I'll be able to sing 'When the Little Pigs Begin to Fly' before anyone notices a lapse."

Myrtle had just finished lacing up my costume when the Butcher dragged Poesy into the dressing room.

"Get out of that costume, Tilly," he said. "Poesy will sing Winifred for the rest of the show."

I stared at him in disbelief. "Poesy! You can't be serious. I can sing Winifred far better than Poesy."

"They've already seen you sing Carmenita. They'll recognise you instantly. Poesy has only been in the chorus. And look at you, you great lump of a girl, you're straining the seams. You can't possibly wear that costume. Get out of that dress this instant and give it to Poesy."

He flicked his ugly hands at Myrtle and pushed Poesy towards me.

"Strip her," he barked. "Poesy, you have three minutes to get back on stage."

I choked down my rage as Myrtle and Poesy meekly began unlacing the stays on the costume. I was numb with humiliation. To be upstaged by Poesy Swift, by a girl who was only in the troupe because I'd encouraged her, was simply too awful. If he'd let me go on as Winifred from the start, everything would have been all right. The Butcher, the Butcher, the Butcher.

We sat down for supper after midnight but I couldn't touch a bite. I went up to my room instead and wrote a letter to my mother. It was the very first time I'd written to her and I told her everything that had happened to Ruby and Tempe and said the tour was a terrible flop. She'd be sorry to lose all the shillings the Percivals owed her but she simply had to send for me. When I'd finished, I realised I didn't have a stamp, nor a single coin with which to buy one.

The next morning, I knocked on Miss Thrupp's door to hand her the letter, knowing that it might never reach its destination if the Butcher saw it first.

"What is it, Matilda?" she asked.

I could hear her baby mewling in the background and she turned away from me to speak to the Indian *ayah* who had been hired to care for him. On the spur of the moment, I changed my plan.

"I only wondered if you could advance me a rupee, against my pocket money."

She had taken little Timmy from the *ayah* and was jigging the poor squalling creature up and down on her hip. "It's because it's that time of the month," I said. "And I have women's troubles. I don't like to bother Mr Arthur with the details, but the *dhobi* hasn't come back with the laundry. If I had a few *pice* to tip the housemaid, she said she'd hurry him along."

It wasn't a very good lie and I was half supposing she'd see through it, but Timmy started screaming so loudly that I think he deafened her common sense. She fumbled for the little purse she wore at her waist and handed me a whole rupee without any further argument.

It was still early and there was no one about in the lobby. The hotel had a drowsy feel to it. Even the concierge looked more asleep than awake. I wasn't sure I wanted to trust him with my letter. As I was agonising over whether to brave asking him to sell me a stamp, I noticed Charlie Byrne sneaking through a doorway. I nearly jumped out of my skin with surprise. Charlie raised a finger to his lips.

It wasn't the simple fact that he was about so early that

startled me. It was what he was wearing. He was dressed like a low-caste boy, a street-sweeper, with a raggedy piece of fabric tied at his waist, an old, loosely woven shirt and a strip of cloth wound around his head.

"Charlie!" I mouthed, without saying the word aloud.

He eyed the concierge warily and then crooked his finger at me.

"Don't tell anyone, Tilly, please," he whispered.

"My lips are sealed, if you'll do me one little favour."

I held up my envelope and then pressed the rupee into his hand.

"Post it," I said.

He grinned, took my letter and then slipped out of the side doorway again, into the morning streets of Calcutta.

34

WAYS OF SEEING

Poesy Swift

I lay under a tree in the Maidan as tiny yellow and orange petals fell on my face. Charlie lay beside me, and we watched as the Lilliputians picnicked on the grass. The warmth of a lazy afternoon made me feel far away from my body. I listened to the sounds of bells and people's voices speaking words I couldn't understand. Somewhere a man was singing, but it was more like a wail, not a song, at least not one I had ever heard before. I didn't have a name for his song, or for anything in the park. Everything was familiar yet strange – the trees, the birds, the flowers, even the people. It was as if I would need a whole new language to describe India, not just words.

"What are those birds called?" I asked Charlie. "Those blue-black ones that are everywhere and the bigger, raggedy ones that circle over the zoo and the gardens. And the tiny little squirrels – they must be Indian squirrels. They don't look anything like Squirrel Nutkin in the story. I thought squirrels were very English animals."

"Maybe those birds are vultures," said Charlie. "There are so many vultures in India that the Parsees put their dead on towers and then the vultures eat them. It only takes minutes. But I don't think there are many Parsees in Calcutta. When we get to Bombay, we can go and see one of their towers."

I didn't tell him this made me feel squeamish. I simply stared at him.

"You don't believe me?"

"Of course I believe you," I said.

"It's true, you know. I've learned a lot about India. They have real magicians here, not just ones that do card tricks, but ones who do real magic. Snake charmers and snake jugglers and avatars and *sadhus*. I'm going to find one, a genuine *fakir*, who can show me how to grow a mango tree in an instant and conjure a rope that I can climb until I disappear, and get him to teach me everything he knows. You wait and see. By the time we leave India, I'll be a sorcerer, not simply a boy magician."

"I heard Mrs Besant talk about seeing that rope trick here in India. She said the *fakir*s were mesmerists. I'm sure they'd do a better job of it than Tilly but I suppose I'll never get a chance to find out. We can never see *anything* when we're only going back and forth from the theatre, and half the time that's in the dark."

"You only have to look around you. I've seen plenty. Yesterday, I saw a *fakir* sitting on a bed of nails. There are always *fakir*s in the marketplaces. They're amazing. I saw one that had kept his hand above his head for years and it was all shrivelled, like a little wizened stick."

I screwed up my nose. I didn't like to even think of them, these people with all their bits missing or mangled.

"Don't be like that, Poesy," said Charlie.

"Like what?"

"Afraid."

"I'm not afraid. I feel for them. Tilly says they're not like us but I don't think she's right. I think they're probably exactly like us, Charlie. When I see them hurting, then I hurt too."

Charlie looked offended and took his hand away from where it had been resting on my arm. I could feel my skin cool where his hand had lain.

"I know that, and that's why I like them. You say you want to see things but then you only look at the squirrels and the birds and the buildings. You ask questions but they're the wrong questions. You don't look at the people."

"I do!"

"You mean the audiences? They're mostly *sahib*s – white people, just like at home. But when you go into Blacktown, you see India."

It made my heart sink when Charlie talked like that.

"You haven't been into Blacktown, have you, Charlie?"

He fiddled with a blade of grass.

"You know it's not safe," I said. "With all the protestors everywhere. They've come from all over the countryside, those ones that were marching in the protests."

"There are lots of boys about. No one pays me any mind. I only go exploring to find the magic men. Sometimes I slip out during the afternoon when we're meant to be resting or if I'm feeling game, I go at night when everyone's asleep."

"Charlie!"

"It's my secret. You're not going to tattle, are you?" It was the first time I'd heard Charlie use that loathsome word.

"You know I wouldn't," I said, pulling up a flower and picking off its petals.

"You don't have to worry about me, Poesy. I can take care

of myself. But I can't have your Eliza finding out. Or Lionel. Nobody knows except you and Tilly." Then he smiled a little smile that made me imagine he was thinking of Tilly.

"Oh, Tilly," I said, spitting her name out. I didn't mean to sound so snitty when I spoke but it simply bubbled out of me. "You be careful of her. You should never have lent her your book about mesmerism. She made such a mess of things and got Ruby into trouble."

"Ruby gets herself into trouble."

"It's not her fault. She can't help how she is. If it wasn't for her sisters, she would have gone home with Tempe and Clarissa. I'm worried about Ruby, Charlie. She's been acting very oddly. She said she wouldn't set foot on the train tomorrow unless it was going straight to Flinders Street Station! She can't seem to think about anything but going home."

"She'll be right," said Charlie, standing up and dusting his trousers.

I gazed up at him, with the blue Indian sky behind him, and wished I could be so sure. I wished I could be exactly like Charlie. There were so many things boys could do that I longed for: to be carefree and confident, to be able to go on adventures and not worry about what anyone thought, to be able to shrug your shoulders and say, "She'll be right." But then, Charlie was wrong. There was nothing right about what Ruby did next.

35

THE STREETS OF CALCUTTA

Poesy Swift

The Mussalman's early morning call to prayer woke me at first light. Every other morning I'd tried to go back to sleep, but this morning I listened. It was while I was lying very still and thinking of India that I realised Ruby was gone. Her bed by the window was empty. I stared at the crumpled sheets in dismay, and my skin prickled with alarm. I slipped out of bed and padded down the hall to check if she was with any of the other girls. Finally, I knocked on the door of the boys' room.

Max opened it a crack and glared at me as he rubbed sleep from his eyes. "What do you want, tattler?" he said. Then he snickered because I was dressed only in my slip.

"I have to talk to Charlie."

I pushed Max out of the way and stepped into the room. The little boys were still asleep but Charlie sat up as soon as I came into the room.

"Your sweetheart's here to see you," whispered Max.

I elbowed him hard in his tummy and ran to Charlie's bedside.

"Come outside. I need to talk to you."

I grabbed him by his arm and dragged him into the hall.

"Poesy, what is it?"

"You can't tell anyone about this. Not even Lionel. You mustn't or he'll go straight to Mr Arthur. Ruby has run away again. Last night she said that she'd met someone, another sailor, who promised her a berth back home. But she's crazy. She's not right in her head. She's in so much trouble, Charlie. And I don't know who else to tell. You're the only one that knows how to go out and about. I wouldn't know which way to turn."

Charlie ran his hand through his dark hair, frowned and sighed. "Get dressed and tie your hair up in a scarf so you're not so obvious. I'll meet you at the top of the stairs in five minutes."

Charlie took me through a small doorway that led to the kitchens and we left the building through the tradesman's entrance.

The steamy city was beginning to wake, with wreaths of mist rising off the pavements. I followed Charlie into the streets, and even though I was ill with worry for Ruby, a tiny thrill shot through me to simply be out without a grown-up. Charlie walked quickly and with such certainty that no one would dream of asking us if we were lost.

We hurried past a long line of jennyrickshaws with all their coolie drivers asleep inside. We saw pariah dogs sniffing among the refuse behind a hotel and we stepped over the sleeping bodies of beggars curled around their begging bowls. I wanted to stop at a wayside shrine and stare at the tiny blue figure of a woman wearing a necklace of skulls but Charlie made me keep moving. We passed the stall of a sweetmeat-seller who had just lit the fire beneath a big black pan, and the scent of the warming oil was thick in the morning air. We turned into a street that was suddenly crowded with people walking in a procession around a cart decked with yellow flowers, and Charlie grabbed my wrist and wove a path around the crowd and into a laneway where a Brahmini bull stared, blinked his long lashes at us and then disappeared through the wooden gates of a tiny courtyard.

We walked and walked and walked, and I began to wonder if Charlie had any idea where we were going, for there was no sign of Ruby. As if he sensed my doubt, he said, "We're going down to the riverbank, to where the ferries dock. Ruby would have headed that way."

"How do you know she'd take a ferry? Maybe she took the train."

"Trains won't take her back to Australia. If she wants to go home, she'll have to get to the deepwater port."

When we reached the river, Charlie headed down the winding path that led to the ferry terminal on the Hooghly. There were very few white people about and the Indian people gazed at us with curiosity as we scanned the crowds and waterways.

"This is hopeless, Charlie," I said. "We won't find her like this."

Suddenly Charlie pointed. "Look, on that dock over there," he said.

I followed the direction of his hand to where a lone figure sat on a bollard.

Ruby was watching the children swimming in the wide river. A small brown boy jumped off a rock and silvery flecks of water flew up around him. Ruby seemed mesmerised by the boy. I tried to see him through her eyes, and for a fleeting moment I remembered picnics at home on the Yarra River, taking off my stockings and putting my feet into the cold water at Dights Falls. It was almost like something I'd dreamed, something that had happened to someone else in another lifetime. I couldn't imagine wanting to go back to it but I could see the shape of Ruby's longing.

We had to climb up and down rickety stairs, past the *tea-wallah* and the hawkers who lined the path to the ferries. I was about to cry out to Ruby when Charlie grabbed my wrist. "Shhh," he said. "You'll scare her off."

We approached her slowly, as if she were a frightened, lost animal. "Ruby," I said softly. "Ruby, we've been looking all along the *ghat*s for you." I moved closer and picked up one of her hands. "Come back with us."

"I want to go home," she said, and tears washed down her pale face.

"No, you want to come with us."

Ruby's eyes grew narrow. "Why should you care?"

"Because you're my friend and we have to help each other."

Charlie stepped forward. "C'mon, Ruby," he said gently, hooking an arm around her waist and bringing her to her feet.

I put my arm around her. She slumped against me and put her head on my shoulder. "I'm so tired," she said.

Charlie led the way back up from the jetty. I kept talking to Ruby in a low, soothing voice, the way I did for Yada when she was coming out of one of her fits. I know that Ruby wasn't troubled in that way, but trouble is trouble and when people get broken you have to hold them together gently, not try to ram the pieces back together.

When we reached the road again, Charlie walked up and down a line of waiting jennyrickshaws, haggling with the coolies about how much it would cost to take us back to the hotel. I knew he didn't have very much money but somehow he managed to find a coolie who agreed to take us back to the hotel for a few *anna*s.

Ruby sat between us, her head on my shoulder, her eyes shut as if she were asleep. I kept my arm firmly around her but I couldn't take my eyes off the back of the coolie who was pulling our jennyrickshaw. He was such a skinny, wiry man that I could see his shoulderblades pushing through the thin fabric of his shirt. Strands of black hair that had slipped out from his turban lay wet and shiny with sweat against his dark skin. Charlie had been right. Too often, I didn't look. I didn't see.

The rickshaw passed beneath the spreading branches of giant banyan trees, and sunlight dappled our clothes. Ruby stretched one hand into the air, as if she could catch the shadows like raindrops. "I never wanted to come to India," she said. "I never wanted any of this."

I looked at Charlie, hoping to catch his eye, but his gaze was on the wide Calcutta street.

"You'll feel differently about it soon," I said, taking Ruby's hand in mine. "When we really start to see India, everything will be different."

"Everything changes," said Ruby. "Whether we want it or not. Everything."

36

UNDER THE SEATS

Tilly Sweetrick

On the day we left Calcutta, *gharries* and oxen carts lined the street outside our hotel. I wasn't the least bit sorry to be leaving, though I was disappointed Ma still hadn't sent a wire insisting I be shipped back to Melbourne. We were harried and shoved into carriages and taken straight down to the Armenian Ghats, from where a steamer ferry carried us across the Hooghly to Howrah Railway Station.

Trains puffed steam into the morning air and the platform echoed with the babble of voices. We had to stand like a flock of sheep while the Butcher ticked our names off on his list as if we were simply baggage. Porters vied for our trunks and Mr Milligan looked flustered as he tried to direct them to handle the lighting equipment with care. A tall, skinny native wound a red rag in a circle on his head and then popped one of our portmanteaus on top. I watched it bobbing its way down the platform.

Miss Thrupp and Lo shepherded everyone into a group. They seemed to think it would be easy to lose one of us in that vast building but of course we stuck out like sore thumbs: eighteen girls in white frocks and straw hats and eight boys in sailor suits aren't easily lost among soldiers, government officials, fat businessmen, hawkers and porters.

Max and Freddie broke away from our group and started jumping up and down on the platform, trying to see in through the windows of the carriages.

"First class, that's the way to travel," they said. "You should see what the gents in first class get."

"Won't we be going first class?" asked Daisy.

"Don't be stupid, Bubs. As if there's money for that," said Max, laughing at her. "At least we don't have to travel like that lot." He waved his thumb at the Indians who were crowding behind railings, eating tiffin from baskets and waiting to be let onto the platform. As soon as the station guard flung the gates open, the Indians raced at the third-class carriage and dived in through windows and doors, scrambling to find a seat. We watched with our mouths open.

We were bundled into a carriage and sat wedged close together on uncomfortable benches. This definitely wasn't first class. As we travelled deeper into the country, I stared out at the passing landscape – houses with whitewashed walls, brown coconut-palm huts clustered together like a herd of small, leafy elephants. We crossed a wide river full of jagged rocks. A brightly coloured sari lay out on a stone, drying in the hot afternoon sun.

It was hundreds and hundreds of miles from Calcutta to Allahabad and after a while we fell asleep upon each other's laps, a tangle of limbs and sweaty petticoats. We were halfway across a long, dry stretch of country when the Butcher came into the carriage and counted us.

"Quickly, Daisy, Flora," he said, dragging the little girls up by their arms. "Under the seats."

We barely had time to grasp what was happening. Flora

squawked loudly and Daisy began to cry.

"Get under the seat, I tell you," he said, with an urgency that frightened all of us.

He knelt down on the dusty floor and forced the girls onto their backs, one little body under each of the long benches.

"Now sit up, you lot. Sit up straight and spread your skirts so Daisy and Flora are hidden and make sure they don't make a peep. The ticket inspector is coming along the carriages, and when he gets to this compartment I don't want to have him chase me down because you girls have made a hash of things. He'll throw us all from the train, each and every one of us." He handed a clutch of tickets to Myrtle, who was sitting nearest the door, and then hurried into the next carriage.

"There are only ten tickets for this compartment," said Myrtle. She counted us again to be sure: with Flora and Daisy there were twelve of us. Why the Butcher thought she was the one he should trot out as our teacher beggared belief. She could barely count. It was another sign of how hopeless he was at managing the troupe.

"I suppose he's going to make Henry and Billy crawl under the seats in the boys' compartment too," I said. Myrtle looked at me blankly. I swear, I have never seen a girl with such blank, expressionless features.

"Are you all right down there?" asked Poesy, leaning over and lifting her skirt a little so we could all see Flora's pouting face. The tot was trying hard not to cry. "Don't worry, darling. It won't be long."

That's Poesy for you – making things worse by comforting everyone all the time. It would have been a fine thing if Flora had screamed her head off and we'd all been thrown from the train. It would have saved us from what was to come later.

The afternoon sun grew hazy and the shadows cast by the palms were long across the landscape before the ticket inspector came into our compartment. He was a plump Indian in a too-tight uniform and we all watched as he fanned the tickets out and then clipped them, looking up to match a girl to each ticket. We held our breath, hoping that neither of the little ones would call out in loud complaint as they had been doing for the past hour.

Then, as the inspector turned to leave, Flora sneezed. Quickly, as if we had staged it, every girl in the carriage covered their mouth with their hand, and when the inspector turned about we must have looked a pretty sight; ten girls coughing and spluttering as if his presence had precipitated an allergic reaction.

His beetle-black eyebrows rose and he shook his head but he didn't speak. When we were sure he was gone and Myrtle had checked the passage, we flipped up our skirts and pulled the little girls out. Flora jumped onto Poesy's lap and burst into tears.

"There's cobwebs down there and it's horrible and dusty," she wept.

Daisy sat on Ruby's lap and popped her thumb in her mouth. She looked out of the window and frowned. "And I fink Fwowa fwarted and it fwelt awful."

Ruby laughed, and though it was good to see her showing a touch of her old self, I did feel sorry for the poor babies. It would be a long journey across India if they had to spend most of it under the seats.

We reached Allahabad early the next morning. We were all hungry, for although Lo and Miss Thrupp had come up and down the carriages with food that they'd bought from station hawkers, there hadn't been enough to go around.

We did three shows at the Allahabad Railway Theatre across the road from the station. Considering what happened there, those days should be etched into my memory. But all I can recall is the sound of Miss Thrupp weeping in her room, each and every night that we were in town. In a way, her sobs were the last we heard of Miss Thrupp, even though she would travel with us for another seven months. In Allahabad, Miss Thrupp became invisible.

37

DEATH AND THE INVISIBLE RIVER

Poesy Swift

Allahabad smelled of death. I woke up on the first morning we were there and even though the air was cool and crisp I could smell sadness.

In Allahabad, two rivers meet – the Ganges and the Yamuna. The Indians think they're holy rivers. They even believe that a magic, invisible river called the Sarasvati joins them. Further up the river, at Benares, Indian people make pilgrimages to die. Charlie went down to the riverbank and brought a jar of water back with him. He wanted to test it, to see if there was any magic swirling inside. He said the Indians threw the ashes of thousands of bodies into the Ganges and maybe there were spirits in the water. I wouldn't drink anything but cocoa for the rest of the time we were in Allahabad.

When my father died, we weren't allowed to see him laid out because the accident had made such a mess. The first dead body I ever laid eyes on was the sailor on the *Ceylon*. The second was little Timmy Thrupp. And I didn't even realise he was dead. That was the shame of it.

We had been rehearsing all morning and Mr Arthur wouldn't let us go until everything was running smoothly. As I was only in the chorus, I could be spared. Miss Thrupp sent me to ask the *ayah* to bring Timmy and Lo's baby Bertie across the road to the theatre. I heard Bertie wailing long before I reached the hotel room. He was standing up in his cot, his face scarlet from crying. The *ayah* was nowhere in sight and Timmy was lying peacefully in his cradle on the other side of the room. I picked up Bertie and comforted him until his cries turned to hiccups. He sucked on his fist and buried his face against my neck. Then I tiptoed over to Timmy's cot, as if my footsteps might wake him, though he had slept through all Bertie's wailing. Timmy's face was pinched and sunken. He was so still I thought he must be in a deep, deep sleep. He looked like a little wax dolly.

I shifted Bertie onto my hip and took him down the stairs and across to the theatre, where I handed him to Lo.

"Where's Timmy?" asked Miss Thrupp.

"The *ayah* wasn't there to help me carry him so I left him asleep in his cot."

Alarm flickered across Miss Thrupp's face and she ran from the theatre. I remember her white skirts disappearing through the theatre door. The next time I saw her, she was a different person.

Whatever horrible things people say about Mr Arthur, when Timmy died he was kind to Miss Thrupp. He paid for the funeral and he didn't ask anything of her. He told us that we weren't to bother Miss Thrupp with any of our needs but to come to him or Eddie or Lo if we had a problem. Then again, there wasn't much point trying to talk to Miss Thrupp. The way she grieved made me think perhaps Ruby was right: Timmy had been her son, not her nephew. She lay curled on her bed like a crumpled paper doll. She couldn't even feed herself, let alone see to any of the Lilliputians' needs. She seemed to shrink before our eyes, growing smaller and older in a matter of hours.

The funeral was held the evening of the day Timmy died. It seemed too soon to lay him beneath the earth but Mr Arthur said that in India people always buried the bodies quickly because of the heat. We travelled in *gharries* to the cemetery at Kydganj, on the banks of the river Yamuna. Lo stayed back at the hotel with the younger children, but all the gentlemen came and some of us girls and Charlie and Lionel too. I shut my eyes as they lowered the tiny box into the ground and tried to imagine Timmy travelling down the invisible river that flowed into the Yamuna.

The cemetery was lush and green, and as we walked between the tombstones and read the sad stories I realised it was years since anyone had been buried there. Most of the graves were dated 1857, the year of the Indian Mutiny. It was odd to have little Timmy Thrupp lying among the fallen from such a terrible time.

"The local people call this cemetery 'Gora Qabristan' and it means 'Grave of the Fair'," I told Charlie. I thought he'd be pleased I'd found out something about the place.

Charlie winced and then scratched his head. "I heard it only means Grave of the White People. And you know why there are so many Britishers buried here, don't you?"

"Because of the invisible river? Or because of the Mutiny?"

"They don't call it the Mutiny. The Indians call it the Uprising."

"But it was a mutiny," I said, thinking of what I'd read. "The British are in charge, after all."

"India isn't a ship."

"I don't understand you sometimes, Charlie."

"Look, if we decided that Old Man Percy was doing a bad job of running the troupe and we decided to leave, would it be a mutiny or an uprising?"

He was watching me very intently with his green eyes.

"But we wouldn't do that, would we?" I countered. "And if we did, how would we ever get home?"

As we walked through the gates of the cemetery, following the grown-ups, we could hear the sound of drumming from the village. It made the cooling night air throb.

Mr Arthur took Miss Thrupp back to the hotel in a *gharry* but the rest of us walked through the town as evening fell. Lionel pointed out the first lamp and then suddenly they were everywhere – tiny little heart-shaped earthenware lamps burning brightly in the soft evening light. People had lined them up along the roofs and windowsills. Servants knelt outside every house to set lamps on the steps and at the gateways, filling them with oil and touching a flame to the wick until the streets glowed with flickering light.

For a moment, I wondered if all this was because of Timmy's funeral. Had the natives seen us passing by with his tiny body on the way to the cemetery? Perhaps they were lighting candles for his soul. But Charlie turned to Lionel and said, "It's Divali. It's the Indians' festival of lights. Later, there'll be fireworks. Like Guy Fawkes Night at home. We could sneak out and watch."

"I don't think Mr Arthur would like that," said Lionel, "even if he has cancelled this evening's show."

Charlie said nothing further and I wondered if Lionel

knew how often his brother broke the rules and disappeared into the night.

From a turn in the road, we could see lights burning all along the river, on rafts and boats, on rooftops and glowing from laneways. It was so beautiful, all the tiny pinpoints like stars, it made me catch my breath. I hoped Miss Thrupp didn't know about Divali, I hoped she thought they were all for Timmy, whose little light had been extinguished.

38

SWEET SIXTEEN

Tilly Sweetrick

On our first night in Lucknow we were squashed into a tiny annexe of the local clubhouse. There really wasn't enough room for everyone. All the grown-ups except the Butcher stayed at another hotel. Even Miss Thrupp was sent away. Me, Poesy, Ruby, Eliza and po-faced Myrtle were all muddled into a room together. It was the first time I'd shared with Eliza since we'd left Melbourne and I remembered why once upon a time I'd rather liked her. Even if she did slip out for her 'supper' with the Butcher, she seemed perfectly sweet when we were together, like the old Eliza who had been my friend on my first American tour. For a few weeks, it was just like old times. Until she showed her true colours.

We opened the Lucknow season with a performance at the Mohamed Bagh Theatre. Like the clubhouse, it was too small and we were constantly bumping into each other backstage. Freddie and Max took up far too much space for a pair of fourteen-year-old boys. Once they were all kitted out for their onstage boxing scene they started taking swings at each other.

"Watch out," said Lionel, trying to edge past them and not be hit by a flying boxing glove. When Freddie caught Lionel with a left hook to the side of his face, the Butcher grabbed poor Freddie and boxed his ears so hard that his eyes rolled back in his head.

"Watch yourself, Kreutz," he growled. "If I catch you lashing out at young Lionel again, you'll answer to me. I won't be so gentle next time."

Lionel tried to hide his glee. Disgusting little Butcher's boy. He knew Freddie had only cuffed him by accident.

For all the problems with cramped lodgings and fraying tempers, at Lucknow every show was a hit. When Flora minced about the stage as Fifi Fricot in *The Belle of New York* and wiggled her hips like a little coquette, the audience roared, but when I transformed myself from ordinary Violet the Salvation Army girl to outrageous Violet the showgirl, I nearly brought down the house.

I loved my costume for 'At Ze Naughty Folies Bergère'. The tiara, the black velvet collar with the white silk rose and my silver dancing shoes with the big diamanté buckles were delicious. But the low-cut pale green satin dress that was nipped so neatly at the waist showed off my figure to perfection. The layers of luscious tulle petticoats were so easy to angle I could show just a little bit of lace garter at exactly the right moments.

The audiences ate me up with their eyes. They laughed at every trick and joke and wept at the least little sentiment. They treated us all like stars. Lionel tried to spoil things by saying it was only because so few touring companies visited Lucknow that the audiences were utterly grateful to the Lilliputians. But I didn't see what their terrible history had to do with me. It was simple. They loved us. The Butcher must have been raking in money and I began to see why some people rather fancied India. The audiences were hungry for us in a way I'd never felt before. Perhaps it helped that we'd escaped the heat. Now that we were further north, the days were bright and clear and the nights cool enough for us all to sleep. My blood had flowed like treacle in my veins all the time we'd been travelling through the Dutch colonies and Malaya and even in Calcutta, but in Lucknow it was as if my heart quickened and my skin sparkled with a new surge of life.

The Butcher still refused to pay us any pocket money and Miss Thrupp still moped around, a ghost on the edge of our days, but I started to feel differently about India. I began to feel differently about everything. In Lucknow, I became myself. And it was because of George. Lieutenant George Madden.

Somehow, the Butcher had managed to secure the Chattar Manzil Palace for a performance. The palace was like something I'd dreamed about, something you could only imagine reading about in a picture book. It was nearly a hundred years old but it felt timeless. The locals called it the Umbrella Palace, and its roofs spread above us like heaven. The walls and ceilings were decorated with plates of silver and the audience looked just as grand as the palace itself. There was even a maharajah, dressed in a blue military uniform embroidered with gold. He wore an utterly magnificent diamond aigrette in his turban and a gold sword with a diamond hilt slung from his sword belt. There were dozens of men in his retinue, but no women. There were generals and beautiful ladies and scores of soldiers in lovely crisp uniforms.

We performed *The Girl from Paris* in the palace hall to a huge audience. It was a perfect moonlit night. The Gomti River shone like silver and our voices rose up into the turrets and minarets and echoed through the antechambers. After the show, as we stood waiting for carriages to take us back to the hotel, the air seemed to shimmer with magic. There were men down by the water and I heard one cry out, and even though he was a native his voice sounded beautiful on the cool evening air. I turned to ask one of the other girls if they'd heard it too, the cry of the boatman, and that was the first time I saw Lieutenant Madden. He was standing quite still, like a part of the grand picture, in the silvery moonlight on the steps outside the Palace. His brass buttons gleamed and his eyes were bright. Bright when he looked at me.

We took a train trip to Cawnpore the next morning and the Lieutenant was there too. After Cawnpore, we went to Meerut where there was a cantonment station and the headquarters of a division of the army, and that's when I realised Lieutenant Madden was following me. At first, I wondered if it was simply a coincidence. I didn't want it to be a coincidence.

I'd never seen so many soldiers in one place as there were at Meerut. Their faces glowed with rapt attention as they watched every turn, every flounce, every gesture I made. I knew it was what I was born for, to be admired in that way. It made me long to dance at the Tivoli, to sing vaudeville, or at the very least perform upon a stage where I'd be seen as a real actress, not simply a Lilliputian.

Some of the soldiers were only a few years older than we were and I don't think they thought of me as a child. I'm sure George didn't. When he looked at me, I could see that I was a woman in his eyes. When he smiled at me, his smile was for me alone. He came to every show. The first night in Meerut, when I saw him in the audience, I felt a throbbing in my temples, as if my heart was beating furiously and my blood bubbling like champagne.

It was in Meerut that George finally spoke to me.

Meerut was a city of canvas, with streets lit by electric light. The tents were unimaginably elegant. They had carpets, dressing tables and armchairs, as if they were real rooms, and in some of them the walls were lined with pretty patterned material.

It was cold at night in Meerut, and though the days were bright we had to bundle up snugly in our beds. We slept under lovely *razais*, thick quilts made in Jaipur. It's funny to think that you can feel more like a princess in a tent than in a hotel.

On our last night in Meerut, as we strolled back through the city of canvas, a great crowd of girls, I looked over my shoulder and saw Lieutenant Madden following us. I shivered. Once he knew I'd seen him, he walked more briskly, catching up with us in a moment. He wore a woollen greatcoat to keep the cold at bay and he looked so dashing I was dizzy with pleasure at the sight of him.

"Excuse me, Miss Sweetrick," he said, his voice deliciously mellow and gentle. The other girls stopped too, their faces alive with curiosity.

He took a step closer to me and I shivered again. "I'm sorry to keep you, but I was wondering if you would autograph your portrait for me."

All the girls had sold dozens of photos at the end of the Meerut performance. There was no shortage of young men keen to own an image of us. George had been dumbstruck when I walked through the audience at the close of the performance that evening. He hadn't uttered a word. He had simply taken one of my portraits and given me two rupees in exchange. Now it was my turn to be rendered mute.

"You look cold, Miss Sweetrick."

He swept off his coat and draped it around my shoulders. The other girls laughed and George smiled at them as he handed me his pen and my portrait. "I'm sorry I only have one coat to share, ladies," he said to them. Then he lowered his tone so it was warm and husky. "Miss Sweetrick," he said, "I will treasure this image all the more if it bears your signature."

Finally, I found my voice. "To whom should I inscribe it?"

"To Lieutenant George Madden," he said, leaning over me to watch as I signed my name across the bottom of the photograph.

When I handed back his pen, our hands touched briefly and the warmth of his skin sent a charge of heat through me. I reached to take his coat off, to return it to him, but he raised his hands. "No, Miss Sweetrick. I'll send my batman to collect it in the morning."

That's when I knew he was a gentleman. Not only had he let me wear his coat, but he was important enough to have his own batman. I think I was walking on air for the rest of the short trip to our quarters. That night, in our tent, I spread his coat across the end of my bed so I could snuggle my toes beneath it, and I said his name over and over. It tasted honey-sweet on my lips.

Eliza was in the bed closest to me, and as I savoured my moment with George, I did something I've regretted ever since. I turned to her and asked, "What does it feel like to be in love, Liz?"

"It's wonderful and it's terrible and it changes everything," she said.

I wanted everything to change. I believed it would once we were in Delhi. In Delhi, I turned sixteen. Sweet sixteen.

As we drove through the wide streets, past heathen buildings with their strange towers and ramshackle bazaars crowded with Indians, on our way to the Rama Theatre, all I could think of was George. That first night he wasn't in the audience. I thought he would be at our show at Ludlow Castle, because he simply had to be a member of the Delhi Club. But he wasn't there either. I couldn't understand it. I knew, in my heart, that he wanted me.

We stayed at the Maidens Hotel in Delhi, and while the others were napping, I wandered the long colonnaded foyer, gazing out into the gardens, trying to will Lieutenant Madden into being, trying to make him appear through the sheer strength of my longing. I still had the note he'd given me, the one his batman had delivered when he'd come to collect his greatcoat. He'd said it wasn't very far from Meerut to Delhi, closer than Cawnpore had been to Meerut, and that he would be there to see me sing. He hoped I would sing Violet Gray again in *The Belle of New York*, and he loved it when I sang 'I Do, So There'. There was nothing improper in the note, but beneath the words I could sense something special.

It was still warm in the late afternoon, before the cool night air began to fall. I was dressed in my best fine white linens but as the heat subsided, I found a cane armchair and arranged myself to appear dainty. I was taut with anticipation, expecting to see George saunter into the foyer at any moment. That's probably why my hearing was attuned to every passing conversation.

When I heard Eliza and the Butcher chatting as they settled themselves at a table in the tearooms I didn't alert them to my presence. They were so close to me, just the other side of the potted ferns, and I could hear every word of their conversation. Every poisonous little word.

"He turned out to be a gentleman when I confronted him," said the Butcher. "But what cheek, really, thinking because he's an officer that he's less of a stagedoor Johnny."

"She was thinking very fondly of him."

"Which you know leads to nothing but trouble. Why, she's not sixteen yet, is she?"

"Oh Arthur, you forget everyone's birthdays. It was yesterday. Besides, sixteen is quite old enough to know your own heart. I was not sixteen when we began," said Eliza, disgustingly coquettish.

"But you, my dear, are altogether a different character to Tilly Sweetrick, as the child calls herself." And then he had the temerity to laugh.

It was like a lead weight dropping through my body, the moment of realisation. Eliza had betrayed me. The past few days, when I'd thought we were almost back to our old friendship, had been an illusion. Even as I sat beside her in railway carriages and we held hands, as we pretended to find our way back to that easy companionship we'd shared in America, she was conspiring against me.

Between them, Eliza and the Butcher had broken my heart. Eliza said love changes everything. So does betrayal.

39

STRANGERS ON A TRAIN

Poesy Swift

From Allahabad to Delhi, Tilly, Ruby and Lizzie sat side by side in the same compartment. They said they felt sick if they couldn't face the same direction as the engine and I didn't mind sitting opposite them. It was simply a relief to see everyone getting along so nicely at last. Ruby was starting to laugh again and it almost looked as though Lizzie and Tilly had begun to like each other. It wasn't until we left Delhi that I realised those weeks of happiness had been nothing but the calm before the storm.

The train from Delhi to Bombay was going to take two days and two nights. I'd imagined we would all be great chums on the long trip. But Tilly was determined to change everything. When Mr Arthur left our compartment for a moment, she grabbed Ruby's hand and then mine and dragged us out into the corridor.

"Where are you going?" called Lizzie, putting her head out of the door.

"Only to the lavatory," replied Tilly, as we hurried along the carriage.

"Where *are* we going?" I asked, trying not to sound too much like Lizzie's echo.

"Exploring. We are going exploring because if I have to sit

next to Eliza Finton for one more minute I'll explode."

Ruby laughed but I felt a little shiver course through me. What had happened to spoil everything?

We sat in a booth in the dining compartment and ordered the cheapest thing on the menu. It was while the three of us were sipping on a single plain soda that we met Mr Barton and his wife. There were lots of Britishers returning from Patiala, in the north, where they'd been for the races. Mr Barton said he'd been a jockey once. He was no taller than I was and his ears stuck out like jug handles, but he had become a trainer and then a horse owner and he'd even run horses that had won a place in the Melbourne Cup. How could we not be impressed? He had been in Patiala racing one of his own horses and giving advice to the Maharajah.

Mr Barton had grand stories about Patiala race week. He told us about beautiful rows of marquees and tents in the park surrounding the palace, and special performances by a famous magician in the palace theatre. The Maharajah's *zenana* had come in 'purdah', every inch of their bodies covered with cloth, and watched the magician through veils. But some of the audience had been very alarmed by his tricks and decided he was under the influence of 'the evil one'.

We all laughed at that.

"Charlie Byrne, a boy in our troupe, he's a wonderful magician," I told the Bartons.

"But if you come to see us, you won't actually get to see him perform his mischief," said Tilly. "Conjurers play with people's minds, whereas we girls, we play with their hearts."

"We're musical theatre artistes, actually," said Ruby. "When we return to Australia, I'll be eighteen and then I'm going to join the vaudeville circuit or maybe go to London and perform in the West End."

"My word," said Mrs Barton, "we'll have to see the young ladies perform if they come to London."

"You can come and see us in Bombay," said Tilly.

The next thing I knew, Tilly and Ruby and the Bartons were as thick as thieves and we were all strolling up to first class to visit them in their private compartment.

In first class, the seats were three feet wide and the padding was so thick and comfortable you could bounce on your bottom on the smooth leather and not even feel the springs beneath. There were lovely blue glass shutters, and a small window slid open so that the passengers could give instructions to the 'boy' on the other side, who sat in the small servant's compartment. He wasn't really a boy at all but a very old man who smiled at us with rheumy eyes when Mr Barton ordered him to fetch sweet lime sodas for all the young ladies.

The seats were long enough for the Bartons to take one each and recline full length, and they told us that at night their *nowker* made up the bed with a *razai* quilt and sheets. I thought of how we all fell asleep across each other's laps, a tangle of limbs and skirts, and felt a pinch of shame.

I knew we shouldn't have stayed so long, but first class was so deliciously cool. They had an air-cooling gadget in the wall, a kind of fan made of rushes and a wheel with the bottom half set in water. Tilly and Ruby stood in front of the machine while I turned the wheel and they squealed as cool air made their hair ripple out behind them.

Mr Barton laughed. "Here, we'll get our *nowker* to do

that for ye," he said. He went to slide the little window that looked into the servant's room, but before he could speak there was a knock at the door of the compartment. It was Lionel.

"Excuse me, sir," he said, polite as you please. "Mr Arthur Percival, our manager, wants the young ladies to return to their seats."

I saw a cloud pass across Tilly's face but then she was all charm and smiles again.

"Thank you so much for your hospitality, dear Mr and Mrs Barton," she said. "We've had a lovely time."

"Well, we hope to see you again, Miss Sweetrick, and your little friends. We must come along to that show of yours in Bombay."

It was only when we were out in the corridor that Tilly turned on Lionel. "You really have turned into the Butcher's lackey, haven't you? The Butcher's boy, running all his odious little errands."

Lionel blushed and I did feel sorry for him.

"You can tell him from me that we're not going back to his compartment."

"You can't do that!" said Lionel.

"Yes we can. We're going to sit in the littlies' compartment. I'm not putting up with Eliza Finton for a minute longer."

"I don't want to change," I said, alarmed.

Ruby turned on me, her eyes flashing. "You're such a turncoat, Poesy. First you were Tilly's friend, then Eliza's, then you made all that fuss about me, and now you want to climb back into Eliza's pocket."

"I didn't..." I sputtered.

"Oh, that's right," said Tilly slyly. She could be so cruelly sly. "You want everyone to believe we're just one big happy family. You want everyone to like you, don't you, Poesy? But when you've pried out all our secrets, you'll scuttle back to Eliza, won't you? Maybe you and Lionel are two peas in a pod. Maybe we should call you Lizzie's lackey."

I stood with my mouth open, staring at Tilly and Ruby in mute disbelief. I could barely recognise the laughing girls that I'd sat with in the dining compartment. They were like strangers. How could they both turn on me so quickly! Then I felt a lurching stab of guilt. Had I said something to Lizzie that I shouldn't? We'd talked about Tilly and George but all the girls knew about their romance and I'd not breathed a word to Mr Arthur. And Ruby knew I'd never told anyone about her running away the second time. I looked at Ruby pleadingly but she simply flicked her hair and said, "Make up your mind. Whose side are you on?"

"Why do there have to be sides? Why can't we all be friends?"

"Because sometimes you have to choose," said Tilly.

I bit my lip and thought of how Tilly twisted everything I'd said, how Ruby was turning back to her old, troublesome self. "Then I choose the truth." I turned to Lionel and said, "Let them sit with the babies. Why should anyone care? I'll sit next to Lizzie."

I didn't look back as I followed Lionel through the rattling carriages, back to Lizzie and Mr Arthur.

40

Naked Truths

Poesy Swift

I tried to keep my distance from Tilly and Ruby as we sat on our trunks in the cool dawn, waiting for Mr Arthur and the men to organise bullock carts for the sets and costumes and carriages for us. Bombay Railway Station was the grandest we'd seen yet, more a palace than a place where trains came and went, but I was so miserable it might just as well have been a slum.

When we walked into the foyer of Watson's Hotel I wandered away from everyone, into the hotel's grand atrium. Guests were seated at little tables, enjoying tea and tiffin, and gazing up at the Indian sky. When I was called back to the group, I realised I should have stayed with Lizzie. Mr Arthur had lumped me back in with Ruby and Tilly, along with Iris, Daisy and Flora. I dragged my feet as we trudged upstairs to our room. The others flung themselves on their beds but I went straight to the big French doors that opened onto lacy cast-iron balconies. I stood outside, feeling the morning breeze drift up from the water.

Even though I was cross with her, I know what happened next wasn't Tilly's fault. Mr Arthur was very pale when he came and ordered Tilly, Ruby and me to come to his room. For a moment I thought it was because of what had happened between us on the train but then Mr Arthur pulled up a seat in front of us and his face grew very serious.

"Now, my dear girls," he began, "I know this has not been the easiest of tours. I know there have been moments where some of you", and here he looked pointedly at Ruby, "have wished to go home. But I also believe you are serious young actresses who are committed to your craft."

We looked at each other, mystified. What on earth had happened?

"Downstairs, in the dining room, the Police Commissioner is waiting to interview you. He asked specifically for you three girls. Apparently, someone in Melbourne wrote to the Police Commissioner saying that he should investigate the troupe and that 'acts of cruelty' have been perpetrated against you and mentioned each of your names.

"I know there have been times when you have deemed me harsh, but I have always acted in your best interests. And I expect you to act with the best interests of the troupe at heart and defend our integrity. If the Police Commissioner feels there are grounds for it, he will end our season. And here we are in the best hotel in Bombay with heavy bookings for all of this week's performances. You simply cannot let the other children down and deny them this, and you cannot let yourselves down either, especially you, Ruby."

Tilly and I both looked at Ruby.

"If it comes out what you did in Penang, running away with a sailor, it is not the Lilliputians who will be judged, it is you, your decency and your moral integrity."

Ruby looked down at her skirt and picked at a loose thread.

"Is that understood?" asked Mr Arthur. "By each one of you?"

We nodded mutely and followed him down the wide staircase. I could feel my heart racing, pounding against my chest like a frightened bird, as if at any moment my ribs would break and the bird would fly out into the hot Bombay street.

Mr Arthur left us standing in the foyer while he went to speak with the Police Commissioner.

"What am I going to do?" said Ruby. "If my father finds out about what happened in Georgetown, he'll kill me! Tilly, you mustn't breathe a word. We have to put a good face on it. Even if it means covering up for that sneaking ass of a Butcher."

"I hope this isn't because of the letter I wrote to Ma," said Tilly. "I told her how badly the Butcher was treating you and asked her to send for me, but I never heard from her. She was probably so sozzled when she read the letter that she simply forgot she'd received it. You know what she's like."

"You didn't tell her about Penang?" asked Ruby, distraught.

"No, of course I didn't. Maybe Max and Freddie's ma wrote. She's got a fine temper and she'd be furious that she hasn't been getting her sixty shillings."

"Then why aren't Max and Freddie here? Why does the Commissioner want to speak to me?" I asked.

They both looked at me as if they had forgotten I was there.

Tilly grabbed my hands. "It doesn't matter why they've asked you along. You've simply got to help. For Ruby's sake. I'm sorry if you think we were beastly to you on the train," she added, more as an afterthought than because she meant it. "But it's time to stick together."

I drew a deep breath and looked from one to the other. "All right, for Ruby's sake," I said.

By the time we were all sitting before the Police Commissioner and his secretary, I had to fold my hands, one over the other, to stop them from trembling. Mr Arthur stood behind us, listening to every word we spoke. I didn't want to tell a lie but I didn't want to betray Mr Arthur and the troupe either or get Ruby into trouble. I didn't know then that lying is easier than truth-telling.

I watched Tilly and Ruby transform themselves into different people when they spoke to the Commissioner. That's when I knew they were real actresses and that perhaps I'd never be very good at performing. When the Commissioner asked them if they were happy with the way they were treated they simply crooned with satisfaction. You would have thought they'd never had a troubled moment in their lives.

But when he turned to me, I fumbled for words.

"I'm not sure why you wanted to see me, sir," I said, my voice no more than a whisper. "Mr Arthur has shown me nothing but kindness."

"Miss Swift," said the Police Commissioner. "This letter, accusing your manager of mistreatment, is from Mrs Agnes Niall. She is extremely concerned for your welfare."

For a split second, I couldn't think who he was talking about. And then it hit me, as if I'd been slapped. Yada. How could she!

I saw the look of shock on Tilly's face. Her mother hadn't

bothered to write at all but she must have told Yada what Tilly had written. Ruby was staring so hard at me I could feel her fear. I didn't want her to think I had told Yada about her troubles. I took a deep breath, as if I was relieved, and then I laughed.

"Oh my granny," I said breathlessly. "She's such a silly old thing! She has fits, you see, where she's not quite right in the head. She gets ideas about things and won't let them go. Oh, and she can have such an evil temper. She is a trial to my mother, I assure you, sir. Mother knew coming away with the Lilliputians was a great opportunity for me but Yada got in a fuddle about it all. She's simply not right in the head."

The Police Commissioner looked taken aback by how quickly the words tumbled out of me. He glanced down at the letter before him again.

"Your grandmother writes with great clarity," he said, "saying she has heard from a most reliable informant that the children in the troupe have been subjected to cruel and unnecessary punishments. She particularly mentions Miss Sweeney and Miss Kelly."

"I don't know what she's talking about," I said. "It's typical of her to take a perfectly innocent remark from one of the other girls' mothers and grow completely muddled. She is not to be relied upon. My mother knows what a fine thing it is for all of us to be travelling the world and learning a trade."

I could feel my cheeks grow flushed as my mock outrage grew.

"Why, this is a terrible thing my granny has done, to trouble responsible people like yourselves. I shall go upstairs and write to Mumma immediately and tell her exactly how meddlesome my granny has been!"

"And may I suggest, Miss Sweeney and Miss Kelly," said the Police Commissioner, obviously annoyed that his time had been wasted, "that you also write to your mothers and reassure them that you are being well treated by your employer."

"I'm not sure…" began Tilly, but I interrupted her. I could see her having second thoughts.

"What she means is that she's sure that Mrs Sweeney isn't worried. If she was, she would have written to you herself, wouldn't she?"

As we farewelled the Police Commissioner in the foyer of the hotel and turned to walk up the stairs, Mr Arthur pinched my cheek playfully.

"You were wonderful, little Poesy," he said. "You have saved the day."

Tilly and Ruby walked ahead of us and I slowed my pace so that Mr Arthur and I fell further behind them.

"I think you deserve a reward for your loyalty, young lady. What say you to coming out on a little shopping expedition with Miss Eliza and myself this afternoon? I believe a new hat to cover your fair hair from this south Indian sun is just the ticket."

At the landing, Tilly and Ruby turned to stare at me and I felt the heat of all the lies I'd told rush to my head. I felt the shame of speaking badly of Yada and all the loving concern that must have gone into her letter, but I held my head up high and turned to Mr Arthur. "That would be lovely, Mr Arthur, thank you."

Back in our room, Tilly slammed the door and made

Daisy and Flora jump with fright.

"We just made a terrible mistake," she said.

"You had to help me," said Ruby.

"The truth would have helped all of us. Can't you see? The Butcher will blackmail you forever if you let him."

Ruby burst into tears and flung herself onto her bed.

"He wasn't blackmailing Ruby," I said, "he was trying to protect her."

Tilly stomped across the room and kicked the French doors to the balcony wide open. "We should have dobbed him in," she said. She scowled at the busy street below. "He's been a beast and we sat there and lied through our teeth to protect him. We should have told the truth and been done with all this."

"I was protecting Ruby," I said softly. "And besides, Mr Arthur hasn't been that beastly. Only when we misbehave."

"Now that's rich. You've become such a fine liar you can lie to yourself as well. Or perhaps you knew your lies would buy you a new hat?"

Her words flew into me like sharp little darts.

"You should have told him about the trains," said Daisy, adding her bit. "It wasn't very nice that Mr Arthur made me hide under the seats on the way to Allahabad. The policeman should have punished him for that."

"And it wasn't nice that he wouldn't buy us new clothes," said Flora. "Poesy's getting a new hat but we haven't had any pretty new dresses, only everyone's old hand-me-downs."

Suddenly, Tilly turned around and her face grew very sly and catlike. "It's too hot for clothes anyway. You don't want to nap in those old shifts, do you, little darlings?"

That's the last thing I heard her say before I left the room to meet up with Lizzie and Mr Arthur. So although I don't blame Tilly for the Police Commissioner coming to see us, I don't doubt for an instant that Tilly was behind Flora and Daisy's shamelessness.

Mr Arthur, Lizzie and I were crossing the Esplanade after a lovely afternoon of shopping and icecream treats when we heard a faint childish song drifting on the air. There they were, Flora and Daisy, on the third floor above the street, dancing as naked as two little birds. They'd not a stitch on their plump white bodies. The balcony was their own tiny stage and everyone in the street below was frozen in surprise, faces turned upwards to watch the spectacle. Even the coolies stopped their jennyrickshaws and the *dhobi*s put down their loads of laundry. Motorcars, carriages, *gharries*, bullock carts and every person perambulating along the Esplanade stopped in their tracks. Everyone watched.

Suddenly the breeze brought the song down to the ears of the audience. Daisy and Flora sang at the top of their voices, "Old man Percival lived in a shoe, he had so many children he didn't know what to do, he gave them all broth without any bread, then whipped them all soundly and sent them to bed." They wiggled their chubby bottoms at the crowd below and hooted with laughter.

Mr Arthur turned bright red and shoved the hatbox he was carrying into Lizzie's hands. Then he ran. Lizzie turned to me and covered her mouth with her hand. We knew we should both be scandalised but we had to fight the urge to giggle. Later that evening, I realised there was nothing to laugh about.

41

BETWEEN THE CRACKS

Poesy Swift

The little ones were hysterical when Mr Arthur threatened to cut off all their hair, and Daisy wet her bloomers. When he threatened the same to Tilly, she kept that catlike smirk on her face the whole time.

"Even if he shaved my head, it would be worth it," she said, as we headed out to the theatre that night. "Of course, he's only bluffing. We'd look so wretched bald it would ruin the show and he knows it."

"Oh Tilly," said Ruby, laughing. "You are such a devil."

Tilly grew even more cheerful when she spotted the Bartons in the audience that night. They had brought a party of friends and they sat in a booth to the right of the stage. We performed *The Belle of New York* and Tilly played the lead, Violet Gray. It was a lovely role because you had the chance to be nice, naughty and noble, changing from one moment to the next.

In the first act, we dressed as Salvation Army girls while Tilly led us in 'They All Follow Me'. And it was true. We did follow her. She was especially good when she sang 'At Ze Naughty Folies Bergère'. She could be so wickedly grown-up when she flashed her ankles. When we came to the finale, Tilly turned towards the Bartons' booth and curtseyed for them, as if they were royalty.

Mr Arthur was incensed. He came into our change rooms before we had time to take off our costumes and shouted at Tilly. I was alarmed to smell a faint whiff of whisky on his breath. In Malaya he used to take a nip after supper, but now it seemed that he'd started drinking early in the evening.

"What do you think you were doing, making a fuss over those people in the booth? It was disgusting, unprofessional behaviour for an actress. You behaved like a common prostitute." He spluttered a spray of spit onto Tilly's costume as he leaned close and wagged his finger. "You had better not be starting up another flirtation, Matilda Sweeney, because I will not stand for any more of your scurrilous behaviour."

Tilly smiled a secret, knowing smile guaranteed to send Mr Arthur into a rage. "They're a very respectable married couple and they are my friends. Lieutenant Madden was my friend too, nothing more. It was you who poisoned him against me by suggesting there was something improper in our friendship. As to the Bartons, they've come down from Malabar Hill especially to see the Lilliputians and they've brought paying customers with them. I should think you'd be pleased."

Mr Arthur frowned, as if suddenly flummoxed by her coolness.

"Well, you mind yourself, Miss Sweeney. You mind yourself because I am watching every move you make."

On the way home in the carriage, all hell broke loose. And Mr Arthur wasn't even there to trigger the explosion. It was as if Tilly had been bottling up so much poison in her that once the clock struck midnight it would have to explode outwards. There were only three of us in the *gharry*: me, Tilly and Lizzie. There couldn't have been a worse combination.

"I don't know how you put up with him, Lizzie," said Tilly, taking out her hatpin and stuffing her worn straw hat in her lap. Maybe it was the comparison with the lovely new linen hats that Mr Arthur had bought us that set her off.

"You know he is doing his best, Tilly," said Lizzie softly.

"Do you call stringing you along with all those empty promises his best?"

"Stop it, Tilly. Not in front of Poesy."

"Oh, don't worry, Lizzie. Poesy is your own little shadow. She won't believe me anyway. She thinks the sun shines out of your bottom."

It was the last straw. I'd swallowed my pride and forgiven Tilly too many times that week. "Why should I believe you, Tilly!" I shouted. "You lie about everything. You say we're friends and then you're horrid to me. You call Mr Arthur a butcher but then you tell the police everything is perfect. You lie and lie and lie."

"You're a fine one to talk. You're just like one of those stupid little trio of monkeys they sell at the bazaars. You keep your eyes and ears covered and yet you open your big mouth and spew lies. How can you not see what's going on around you?"

"I don't know what you're talking about," I said.

"Well, you don't keep your mouth shut, do you? All those little lies you set about spinning this afternoon – all for the Butcher's sake."

"They weren't lies!"

"No? All that twaddle about your grandmother being potty and meddlesome when in truth she treats you like a princess and everyone in Richmond knows she's the soul of honesty with her 'Hold the right thought' and 'Love governs'. How you can be her granddaughter when you can't tell the difference between a lie and a half-truth beggars belief."

I started to sob then and Lizzie put her arm around me protectively.

"Leave her alone, Tilly. She's still only little."

"Not like you and me, Liz. We're grown-ups now, aren't we? But how grown-up will you be when Percival goes back to his wife and leaves you high and dry at the end of this tour?"

"He's not going back to her. I told you that," Lizzie said between gritted teeth.

"Why are you tormenting us?" I sobbed. "I was only trying to protect us all."

"If you want to protect anyone, you should be protecting your precious Lizzie. Because Percival will chew her up and spit her out before this tour is over."

"Stop it, Tilly. Stop speaking like that!" cried Lizzie.

"Yes, stop it," I wept. "Mr Arthur would never hurt Lizzie."

"She's his mistress, Poesy. How can you not know that? What do you think she does in his room while the rest of us are sleeping in the afternoons? Why do you think they have supper together with only Lionel for company?"

"But I've had supper with them too," I stammered through my tears. "It's all perfectly proper. They're only friendly. He is a friend to Lizzie and to Lionel."

"But not to you, Poesy. He is not a true friend to you. He only wants to use you to cover his tracks because he knows you're so innocent you don't see what's right in front of you. And he hates me because I know and I understand. He hates us all except Lionel, his little Butcher's boy, and Lizzie, his little whore."

I'd been sitting between them until that moment, but with a great cry of rage Lizzie pushed me aside and wedged herself next to Tilly. She tore at Tilly's hair and snatched at her hatpin, as if she would stab her through the heart.

The driver glanced back at us in alarm and then whipped his poor little pony so he could rid his *gharry* of its load of banshees. I wanted to leap out right then, to run and hide from them both, but there was nowhere to run and nowhere to hide. I covered my ears so I couldn't hear them scream at each other.

We tumbled out of the *gharry* and into the gutter outside Watson's Hotel. If it hadn't been for the terrible coincidence of the Bartons appearing before us, perhaps everything would have been all right, but when Tilly saw them stepping through the doors of Watson's, she almost fell into Mrs Barton's arms. I don't know what she said to them. Lizzie and I kept our distance, waiting for their conversation to finish.

But when Lionel and Mr Arthur climbed out of the next carriage, Lizzie ran to him.

"You have to stop her, Arthur," said Lizzie. "She's conspiring with those Barton people. She's determined to make trouble. It was Tilly who put the little girls up to that spectacle this afternoon. And those people are disgraceful. Why, he's in the racing industry and that woman he calls his wife, she's probably no such thing."

I'd never seen Lizzie so furious, never seen her beautiful face so distorted with rage.

"Punish her, Arthur. Punish her or there will be no end to her mischief."

Mr Arthur stood stock still, waiting for his moment. It was as if half the players in the terrible scene were frozen in time. Another carriage arrived and a load of weary girls disgorged onto the sidewalk. I watched, trembling with anticipation as the Bartons climbed into their car and waved goodbye. If Tilly had known what was good for her, she would have hurried into the hotel with the last of the troupe. But she stood in the street, farewelling the Bartons' car until it turned the corner.

The moment the Bartons were out of sight, Mr Arthur seized her by both arms. "What have you said! What lies have you been telling those people?"

Tilly didn't speak for a long moment while she looked Mr Arthur up and down with disdain. "I should have told them that you are a sneaking cad, a dirty ruffian and a bully."

He pushed her away from him and then his cane flew so swiftly that none of us saw it cutting the night air until Tilly let out a cry, a long scream of rage and pain, and bent to clasp her calf. I looked at Lizzie and saw a fierce, angry joy in her face. Mr Arthur raised his cane in the air again, to bring it down across Tilly's back. I couldn't let it happen. I had to stop him. I ran across the road and dived between them, throwing my arms around Tilly's body to shield her from the blow. Mr Arthur's arm quivered in midair, hesitating. That moment of hesitancy was all we needed to escape.

I pushed Tilly towards the entrance. "Quick, quick," I cried, grabbing her wrist and running with her into the safety of Watson's Hotel. We ran across the tiled floor, past the quiet shops and the sleepy doormen, as a sharp crescent moon glittered on the black glass above us.

Later, in our room, Tilly showed me the welt, four inches long and throbbing, where Mr Arthur's blow had fallen. It was red and angry, destined to make a long bruise.

"I was only thanking the Bartons for coming to the show. And there was no conspiracy. They were only at Watson's to drop off some friends. I wasn't telling them to fetch the Police Commissioner, but the Butcher is so guilty he assumes the worst. Now I can't walk properly," she complained.

I shut my eyes and replayed every horrid moment of the fight in the carriage, every terrible word that Tilly had spoken, each accusation reverberating in my ears. "Mr Arthur and Lizzie…" I began. But I couldn't finish the question. I didn't want to hear Tilly tell me the answer. Perhaps I'd always known but had never wanted to believe. Tilly was right. I had been like the Three Monkeys, not wanting to hear or see or speak of the evil in our midst, but now I would uncover my ears. Now, I would see for myself.

That night, long after everyone had gone to sleep, I pushed aside the mosquito netting and climbed out of bed. There was a narrow ray of light shining through the crack between the folding doors at the end of the room. Our bedroom had once been part of a suite linked to the room next door. Now the folding doors that opened onto Mr Arthur's room were held shut with long, looping chains and a thick padlock. If I stood close, I could see straight into it. And I saw that Eliza was stretched out on the bed. Lionel was sitting on a chair in the corner, practising a card trick. But where was Mr Arthur?

When he finally came into the room, Lionel looked up and nodded. Then he left the room. Lizzie and Mr Arthur were alone, alone while the fans spun above their heads and the French doors stood open onto the cast-iron balcony.

Sometimes I pretend to myself that I saw nothing, that I covered my eyes at the very moment the truth was revealed. But I didn't. I saw it all. The curve of her hip, as she opened her kimono, the way he covered her body with his own, the way she pulled the white shirt from his back. My heart beat so loudly that I could hear it inside my own head. I tried to tell myself that he was drunk. There could be no other excuse. But deep inside, I knew there was another truth. The truth that I had ignored from the first moment I'd stood shivering outside our cabin door on board the *Ceylon*. The truth that I had pushed away whenever it crept close to me. The terrible, ugly truth.

42

KISS MISS 1909

Tilly Sweetrick

'Kiss Miss'. It was on everyone's lips. Whenever I heard someone say it, I remembered George. I would never know the sweetness of his kiss. That thought twisted in my heart like a knot of pain. But of course 'Kiss Miss' was only what the Indians called Christmas.

Kiss Miss, Burra Din, no matter what they called it, Christmas 1909 was the worst of my life. The grand dining room at Watson's was decorated with paper streamers and lanterns and there were three sorts of roast meat and fish and lobsters and far too many peculiar Indian dishes, but I couldn't eat a thing. I picked at the food and rolled the soft core of my bread into tiny lumps. Perhaps that's what gave Max the idea. He picked up a little ball of squashed bread and flicked it across the table at Freddie.

"Pelleting," said Freddie. "See, I've heard of it. The Britishers used to reckon it was great sport. Let's have a go."

When Freddie kept landing perfect shots in the faces of the boys on the other side, Max picked up a whole bread roll and flung it across the room. It hit the cream pudding, and then the table erupted. Everyone started flinging things: bits of meat, potatoes, handfuls of pie and pudding. Daisy threw a chicken drumstick at Flora. The *khitmungars* scurried about, scraping the food from the floor and looking completely alarmed. Freddie knocked one of their turbans right off and we all screamed with laughter.

The Butcher leaped up from his table and raced at the Kreutz twins, dragging the pair of them out of the dining room by their collars. The fury on his face was enough to subdue all of us. Daisy began to cry as Lo furiously wiped a blob of gravy from the front of her dress and picked a handful of peas from her hair. As fast as the frenzy had erupted, it settled again and most of us were sent to our rooms to change our clothes so they could be given to the *dhobis* to wash. But that meant we spent all of Christmas afternoon sitting on our beds in our underwear. I simmered with rage against the injustice of being treated like a child.

We weren't allowed down to the dining room for breakfast the next day and waiters brought us trays of *chota hazri* in our room, as if we were little children. I picked at the grapes and watched the other girls, each looking thoroughly sorry for herself. Poesy was the most sullen. Since the night Lizzie had tried to stab me with my own hatpin, Poesy had barely said boo to anyone except Charlie Byrne. Sometimes, I wondered if she actually fancied him. For a little boy he was rather sweet, but he was still only thirteen. What was she thinking?

On the evening of Boxing Day we performed *La Poupée* to a full house. It's such an awful show. The only decent role in it for a girl is Alesia, who pretends to be a doll and gets the prettiest costume. The rest of us mostly clump around the stage in monks' habits, and I never like having to play the boy roles.

For some reason, the Butcher decided to cast Poesy as

Alesia. Maybe he was trying to get her back on side by giving her a big role opposite Lionel, who played the romantic lead, Lancelot. As irritating as Lionel could be, he did sing nicely, but Poesy really wasn't up to it. She jerked her way gracelessly across the boards and sang upstage so her voice didn't carry into the theatre. It was almost as if she were *trying* to ruin the show. She was so awful that the Butcher had Iris take her place in the second act. Poesy's face was smudged with tears as she wiped away her make-up and changed into a monk's cowl. When Lizzie tried to comfort her, she gave her the cold shoulder. It was the only satisfying moment across two horrible days.

One disaster led to another and when Eddie Quedda made a hash of arranging the flats and brought out a castle backdrop from *Cloches de Corneville* instead of the monastery, and then forgot to cue Max and Freddie, the twins had a go at him as soon as they stepped backstage. "Even little Daisy could do a better job of stage-managing than you, Eddie," said Max. "You're not worth a brass razoo."

"Watch your tongue, Max," said Eddie. "Or I'll cut it out of your nasty little mouth. And I'm Mr Eddie to you." He actually brandished a knife that he had been using to cut the canvas.

"Don't you wave that knife around at my brother," snarled Freddie. "You were one of us a couple of years ago, mate. Remember when our big brother Louis knocked you senseless for giving him cheek?"

Eddie threw his knife into the stage boards at Freddie's feet and boxed Max's ears so hard that Max yelped aloud. You could probably hear him from the audience.

The Butcher suddenly appeared, his face livid. He stepped between Max and Eddie and pushed them apart, as if they were two warring boys.

"It's not your place to discipline the kids, Eddie," said the Butcher. "Mark my words, if you hit any one of them again, I will thrash you. It's not so long since I turned you over my knee, and if you behave like a child I'll treat you like one."

"He insulted my professionalism," said Eddie.

"No, he told the truth," said the Butcher, his eyes narrow and steely. "You're hopeless. When we get back to Melbourne, go back to juggling, Quedda. There's no place for you in management."

There was no time to continue the argument. The children were streaming into the wings, ready for the next costume change, and men and boys raced onto the stage to shift the backdrop for the next act.

Late that night, as we wiped away our make-up and changed back into our street clothes, I saw the Butcher sitting on a stool by the stage door swigging whisky from a silver flask and cursing the entire troupe. No one had sold very many portraits that night and there were no stagedoor Johnnies for him to shoo away, but he sat there anyway. Mr Milligan took his chance to corner the Butcher.

"We're running low on hydrogen," said Mr Milligan, "And I haven't been able to find a supplier here in Bombay. Calcium oxide and oxygen, they're not a problem, but if I can't refill the hydrogen cylinders before we leave we'll not make Colombo."

"Surely some of the other theatres are using it. Cadge some from an electrician at one of them."

"You're living in the past. Most of the theatres here don't need limelight. They have electricity and use arc lighting. The only way I can source hydrogen is to pay triple the going rate. And I can't see how you can cover that when you haven't paid my wages since Calcutta."

"Look, Milligan. You know the season's been a poor one. What do you expect of me? Eddie Quedda is incompetent, Miss Thrupp is a broken woman, and those minxes Tilly and Ruby have been trying to undermine my discipline at every turn. It was Tilly who put the little ones up to making that spectacle on the balconies at Watson's. She was behind the Police Commissioner's visit, the riot on Christmas Day, and Lord knows what mischief she's planning now. Since Lucknow, Tilly has been behind every bit of trouble that has beset this troupe. That girl will be the death of me."

I stepped out of the shadows and looked the Butcher straight in the eye. He didn't even blush.

"No stagedoor Johnnies for you tonight, Matilda," he said with a smirk.

My mind seethed with sharp replies, but the stinging pain in my leg made me swallow my rage. He'd said I'd be the death of him. I could only hope it was true.

43

LA POUPÉE

Poesy Swift

I couldn't bear to be near her. Every time Lizzie tried to talk to me I felt my stomach churn. I couldn't stand the smell, the touch, the very sight of her. I had loved Lizzie too much. I had been blind.

When Mr Arthur told me I could play Alesia opposite Lionel in *La Poupée* I should have been thrilled. Instead, I simply felt numb. Once, I'd rather liked the story of the puppetmaster's daughter who tricks the shy monk, Lancelot, into marrying her. It had seemed terribly romantic. Now it felt like a litany of lies. I wasn't sorry when I was told Iris was to take my role in the second act. I didn't want to pretend I loved anyone. I had played a puppet for too long.

As we filed out into the Bombay street after the show, the Butcher announced that he hadn't been able to arrange enough carriages to take us home. Lo pushed me towards the vehicles but when I saw Lizzie sitting in the *gharry* looking at me expectantly, I turned away. Ruby and Tilly were standing on the pavement with the boys – they were the only two girls who were forced to walk back to the hotel. I ran to join them.

"I don't mind walking too," I said.

Ruby and Tilly didn't seem to notice me. They hooked

arms with the twins and strode across the street while I fell into step with Charlie. The little boys, Henry Howard and Billy Waters, ran ahead but suddenly, as they passed a carved temple wall, a giant wild animal leaped out of the darkness. Henry screamed "Lion!" and turned in his tracks. Charlie caught him and held him fast. "Don't be stupid. There are no lions in Bombay!"

"Tiger!" screamed Billy. Then we all saw the creature properly and everyone began screaming. Mr Arthur raised his cane in the air. "Keep back!" he shouted, pretending to defend us. But the beast didn't charge him, it started dancing and shrieking like a lunatic, and I realised it was only a man dressed in a bizarre costume, rather like a giant monkey. Charlie darted forward and grabbed the Butcher's wrist.

"He won't hurt you, Mr Arthur. Don't mind him. He's only a street performer. He's dressed as the monkey god and he goes about collecting alms for the Hanuman temple."

We all stood staring in surprise, feeling shaken, while Charlie took a step closer to the monkey beggar and held out a tiny coin. The monkey man made a hooting noise and jumped around Charlie. The whites of his eyes gleamed in his dark, painted face and he bared his teeth like a real monkey. Then he laughed, a high, cackling sort of howl, before he raced away and scrambled up a wall further along the street.

Mr Arthur took another surreptitious swig from his flask, and I noticed his hands were shaking. Coward. Charlie was twice the man. I touched Charlie's arm lightly as he fell back into step with me. "There was nothing to be afraid of," he said.

"I know," I said. "I don't feel afraid of anything when I'm

with you."

Behind us, Mr Arthur spread his arms wide, herding everyone along the pavement as if we were his pets and needed to be harried to keep pace. He waved his cane at the back of the boys' legs and I could feel the swish of the wood as it swept past my skirts.

"You know, Lionel, old boy," he said, his voice drunkenly slurring, "I definitely prefer to keep my monkeys on a string."

Charlie and I quickened our pace, catching up with Ruby, Tilly and the twins.

"We'll show him," said Tilly, glancing back at Mr Arthur. "We're not his puppets, his *poupées* or his little monkeys on a string. We're like that wild man monkey, aren't we, boys?"

The twins grinned at her, their faces alight with wickedness. "How's that, Tilly?" said Max. "You planning something cheeky?"

Tilly glanced back at Mr Arthur swinging his cane in the air and laughing with Lionel. "I'll give him more than cheek, one day," she said. "I'll make him wish he'd never been born."

Charlie put his hand on my elbow. "C'mon," he whispered. "We don't want to listen to this lot." He broke into a run, leaping off the pavement and racing down the wide, dusty street.

I ran too, my legs flashing out from beneath my skirt, my heart pounding, past the sleeping houses, past the ornate temples, away from the ghastly intrigues of the Lilliputians and into the darkness of the Bombay night.

44

COUNCIL OF WAR

Tilly Sweetrick

Daisy wouldn't stop crying. "The mosquitoes are as big as chickens," she sobbed. "There's a hole in the net and they keep eating me up!"

"Oh come here, you baby," I called to her. "Come and jump in with me."

She fumbled her way out of the mosquito netting and crossed the bare floor on her tiptoes. She started to cry again when I put my arms around her.

"Mr Arthur was horrible to me today," she sobbed. "He smacked me. He said I was being naughty because I couldn't remember my song. But he'd changed the way we always sing it. He never used to smack me."

"It's all right, sweetie," I said, stroking her hair. "Things will be better soon."

"I don't like it here in Poona," she said, as she snuggled up against me and fell asleep.

I stared into the high arc of the mosquito net and wanted to weep. I didn't like Poona either but not because of the mosquitoes. Poona made my heart ache for George. Every night, soldiers from the cantonment filled our audience. I knew I'd never see George again but the idea of him, of what might have been between us, haunted me. Burning in the wake of my grief came rage against the Butcher. Three of his sisters had met their husbands in India when they were no older than me, including Mrs Essie. I was sixteen years old, for goodness sake. Old enough to know my own heart.

As Daisy began to snore softly, I found myself thinking of all the things I could have done differently in Bombay. I wished I'd asked the Bartons for more help. Giving them another letter to post to my mother was a useless gesture. She was thousands of miles away and she hadn't even bothered to do anything about the last one. I had to find someone closer to rescue me. Like the Monkey Man, I would have to beg for alms.

When we arrived in Bangalore, I knew I had a better chance. It was a lovely city of parks and spreading trees and we stayed at the Cubbon Hotel in proper rooms. There was a military cantonment in Bangalore as well as a constant flow of Britishers to the goldfields at Kolar.

On our first free afternoon, when we'd been sent back to the hotel for a rest before the evening show, Iris spread her scrapbook out on the table and started trimming a postcard.

"There's not much point in sending it home, is there?" she said. "If I write anything true on it, the Butcher will put it in the rubbish and Mama will never see it. You know, this morning he hurt my arm when he dragged me out of bed. I didn't mean to sleep in. It's just I'm tired all the time."

I was glad that even Iris had taken to calling him the Butcher. She sat tracing her fingers around the edge of the postcard. A small breeze blew in through the high windows and she tipped herself back in the cane chair.

"It's not fair. Valentine is always the lucky one. I want to go home too," she said in a wistful voice.

I walked over to her chair and whispered in her ear. "We could all be home. Soon. Or at least sooner than was planned."

It was the first time I'd floated the idea of taking charge of our own destinies to any of the girls, and all of a sudden the air felt electric. Iris looked up at me as if I'd said something extraordinary. For the longest time, she simply stared at me. Then she changed the subject. "Look," she said, pointing to a picture in her scrapbook. "That's a picture of Mr Arthur with us in Manila. That was a lovely tour, wasn't it? Maybe it's not Mr Arthur's fault. Maybe it will be better when we leave India."

I was disappointed but not surprised. I would have to bide my time before I won her over. But I would win in the end. I was determined to win each and every child in the troupe.

Poesy looked up from her book as if I'd called her, as if she heard my thoughts. "How could we be home any sooner?" she asked.

"Put your hat on and come with me if you want to find out. I'm meeting Freddie and Max for a walk in Cubbon Gardens."

As soon as we were well clear of the hotel, Max pulled a little tin of tobacco from his pocket and rolled a cigarette for himself and Freddie. Poesy Goody-two-shoes trailed behind us. I picked a cassia flower and tucked it behind my ear and Freddie beamed at me with a sloppy, puppy-dog look. It was sweet, but I hoped he wasn't getting ideas.

We sat on the steps of the bandstand, us girls on the top steps and the boys one beneath, and I explained everything to Poesy. It was a risk to include her, but it was time to start taking risks. "But that's mutiny!" exclaimed Poesy, her mouth falling open in surprise.

"No it's not," said Freddie, blowing a stream of smoke into the air. "It's a strike. We're workers, he's the boss and we're going on strike. That's all. It's a worker's right, least that's what my old man says."

"How can you think such a thing would work? Where would we go? Who would take care of us?"

Freddie took one last drag on his cigarette. "Me and Max can take care of ourselves," he said. Then he stubbed his cigarette out on the edge of the rotunda and threw the butt into the bushes. I felt quite irritated by him trying to act the man.

"No you can't, Freddie," I said. "None of us can do this alone. We must find people to help us. If I'd had my wits about me in Bombay, I would have asked the Bartons.

"The thing is, Poesy, we need everyone on side or it simply won't work. We can't ask Eliza, she's not going to turn on her lover, even if he is a lying old beast. And we'll never win Lionel over, the Butcher pays him two rupees a week to keep him on side, but if we can get Charlie then we'll have all the other boys. Which is why you are so important. Because you and Charlie Byrne are friends, aren't you? He's sweet on you. Everyone knows that."

Poesy pretended to be surprised and blushed. "But what about Myrtle and Rosie and Amy and Lulu? And the middling girls too! Do they know what you're planning?"

"Not yet. But don't you worry," I said, "Ruby and I can sort them. It's Charlie I'm worried about."

"What about Eunice and Lo?"

"Haven't you noticed that Eunice can barely stand to speak to the Butcher? And Lo is furious with him because he hasn't paid her or Eddie in weeks. The Fintons aren't going to be a problem. They hate the Butcher for ruining their sister."

Poesy hung her head and knotted her fingers. "I can't believe I didn't see. I thought he was being kind because Lizzie was so lovely. I can't believe how she lied to me." A fat tear dropped from the end of her nose.

"Then you're in?"

Poesy wiped her tears away with the back of her hand and nodded fiercely. "What do we have to do?"

45

SERENADING THE SAHIBS

Tilly Sweetrick

We were billeted in ordinary people's houses in Kolar because there wasn't a hotel big enough to take us all. It was perfect. The audiences were hungry for us.

The lovely thing about performing in out-of-the-way places is that everyone thinks you're something special. Even though no one used limelight in Melbourne any more, even though the musicals we performed were out of fashion, the audiences ate us up with their eyes.

Our train arrived at Ooorganin station at Marikuppau and a tall, balding man took off his *topee* and waved. Who would have thought that someone as ordinary as Mr Ruse could change our lives? His bald head glinted with sweat and his pale face shone as we lined up before him. It was such luck we were in his carriage on the road to Kolar. I watched Mr Ruse carefully as he explained he was an engineer on the new Kolar railway extension. Huge amounts of gold were pouring out of the mines, but the town was full of mud and dust so he was very pleased he'd been able to help organise our accommodation. He simply loved musical theatre.

Mr Ruse lived in a steep-roofed European bungalow with a long, low-ceilinged verandah that was screened from the road by trellis. There were pots of ferns and small palms on green shelves, and as we climbed up the steps the house felt cool and welcoming.

A funny old butler wearing a sash and a turban directed the porters to bring our trunks inside. Another servant brought out a tray of lemonade and a dish of marzipan, toffee fudge and chocolate creams.

It was the first time we'd been in a real person's house since arriving in India, and it made me feel oddly homesick. I'd never thought I would long for Richmond or that any place in India could remind me of home, but there was something strangely comforting about Mr Ruse's house. The living room was full of deep armchairs and there was a piano in the corner. I couldn't help but wander over to it and rest my hands on the keys. On top of the piano, in a lovely silver frame, was a picture of two little girls with fair ringlets. Their photograph was tinted so the girls' hair shone and their cheeks glowed with just the right hint of pink.

"Those are my daughters," said Mr Ruse, lifting the photograph from its place with great care.

"We look forward to meeting them, sir," said Poesy, peering over his elbow.

Mr Ruse put the photo back on the piano tenderly. "Oh, you won't meet Alice and Emma. They've gone home to England. All the children go home."

"Don't the Britishers like to keep their children in India? Is that why we don't see many white children in our audiences?" asked Poesy. "Because they've been sent away?"

Mr Ruse looked embarrassed. I was close enough to Poesy to take hold of her hand and give her a little pinch without anyone noticing. Really, someone had to let that child know when she was rude.

"We send the children home so they can have a proper education," said Mr Ruse. "I hear you lucky children travel with a teacher provided by the Australian government."

I pinched Poesy even harder then, in case she started saying that Myrtle was a teacher, which is what we were meant to tell strangers. She tried to jerk her arm away but I squeezed her hand even tighter.

"Not exactly, Mr Ruse," I said, sad and soulful. "Mr Percival tells people that we have a teacher but Myrtle is only a year older than I, and though she writes her name very nicely she can't really teach us anything. I do worry about the younger girls. They can barely write their names. Ruby and I try to help them when we can. But Mr Percival…"

I broke off, leaving the Butcher's name hanging. I didn't want it all to come out in a rush. We couldn't be sure of Mr Ruse yet.

Mr Ruse frowned.

"I'm sorry to hear that, Miss Tilly. This was not my understanding of your situation."

"You mustn't mind us, sir." I took a step closer and rested my hand on his arm. "We're very grateful to you for taking us in. It's so lovely to be in a real home. We're tired of hotels."

Mr Ruse pulled out a handkerchief, dabbed his face and stepped away from me. Perhaps I'd moved too quickly. Then I heard the click of the beaded curtains parting and Mrs Ruse swept into the room.

"Welcome, children. But my goodness, you are big girls, aren't you?" she said uneasily. Somehow I didn't think we'd find our rescuers in Kolar.

That evening, the Dorgaum Theatre was full to bursting. Mr and Mrs Ruse had front-row seats and I noticed Mr Ruse's grey eyes grow misty when Daisy sang 'Rainbow'. At the end of the show, I led Daisy up to meet the Ruses and I could tell they were both moved by her baby sweetness.

"People have been so kind here," I said. "Daisy wishes we could stay in Kolar longer, don't you, darling."

"Oh yes, I don't like going on the trains," she said.

"Why's that?" asked Mr Ruse. "I thought all little children were fond of trains. Our girls used to love riding down to Bangalore."

I looked at Daisy and winked. She knew what to do. She lowered her voice until it was a husky whisper. "Because sometimes Mr Arthur makes me lie *under* the seats with all the spiders and dust. That way he doesn't have to buy me a ticket. But sometimes I gets scared and sometimes I cry and pinch the big girls' legs, but they're not allowed to let me out." She pouted and pushed her face into my hip so I could give her a cuddle.

"Why, you poor little tot! That's disgraceful," said Mr Ruse.

I glanced over my shoulder to check for the Butcher and then nodded solemnly. "We're not supposed to talk about it," I said, my voice hushed.

There was an awkward silence when the Butcher approached the Ruses to thank them for accommodating us. I saw his confusion at the coolness of his reception and I wanted to laugh out loud.

Next morning, as we were climbing back into the carriages to leave for the station, Mr Ruse took my hand.

"Don't worry, Miss Tilly," he said. "You and all the other

children have friends. I've spoken to my associates in the Society for the Prevention of Cruelty to Children and we're keeping an eye on you and the other Lilliputians. You are not alone."

Ruby whooped with glee when I repeated what he'd said, but Poesy fell silent. I wondered if we could trust her.

At the next show in Bangalore, Mr Ruse sat in the third row from the front with a group of men. I saw him direct their gaze to Daisy and they whispered among themselves as the curtain fell for a change of scene.

After the show, the gentlemen gathered in the bar, drinking whisky and sodas. As I passed by the doorway, Mr Ruse came out to speak with me.

"We're very worried about your case, Miss Tilly," he said. "Many of the other gentlemen here tonight are members of the SPCC. We're most concerned by the allegations you have made against Mr Percival. It's not appropriate for us to intervene at this juncture but if you and some of the other girls could write to the British Resident in Mysore, who represents the government here, and to the Commissioner of Police in Bangalore outlining your predicament, either one of them might be able to approve an intervention."

I was terribly disappointed – I'd rather wished one of the gentlemen would march up to the Butcher and punch him on the nose – but at least there was hope.

It was after midnight when we got back to our rooms, and I sat up writing into the night. I was careful to tell the truth and not embellish the facts too much. I wrote to the Resident and the Commissioner, as Mr Ruse had instructed. I even wrote to the Maharani of Mysore because even if she was a native she was a woman and a queen and perhaps she could do something too.

It must have been three in the morning by the time I tiptoed down the hallway and slipped my letters under Mr Ruse's door. I trembled with every step, terrified someone would see me in nothing but my nightgown and kimono wrap, wandering the corridors of the Cubbon Hotel. I dreaded to think what the Butcher would make of it if I were caught.

The room was bright and hot but I couldn't wake up. Someone shook me but I pulled the sheets up and pushed their hand away. I only wanted to stay in bed for another ten minutes, only another ten minutes of sweet slumber.

"Get out of bed, Matilda Sweeney," growled the Butcher. "Get out before I drag you out by your hair."

"What's the time?" I asked, still groggy with sleep.

"It's nine-thirty."

I turned my back to him and pulled the sheets over my head.

"This is the last straw, Matilda."

"Go away," I muttered, suddenly terrified that someone had seen me at Mr Ruse's door and reported it.

The Butcher stripped the sheet from me, grabbed my wrist and wrenched me out of bed.

"You hurt me!" I exclaimed, rubbing the skin on my arm where his horrid paws had touched me.

"We've been waiting for you in the foyer for the last half hour. But that's the least of your offences, girl. Do you have any idea the damage you are doing to our season here with your idle gossip?"

"I don't know what you're talking about," I said, turning my back on him and storming into the bathroom. I tried to shut the door in his face but he put his fat boot in the way and forced it open. It was indecent of him to shout at me when I was still in my nightgown.

"Do you take me for an utter fool?" he shouted. "I know you've been spreading your poison through the troupe. You've poisoned that sweet little Poesy Swift against Lizzie. You're a viper in our midst. But poisoning the other children against me won't get you home. Your mother signed a contract, and she can send all the telegrams she likes but I am under no obligation to send you back to her until July next year."

I turned and stared at him. "Ma sent a telegram?"

He laughed, that horrible laugh that made his face twist into an even more brutal expression. "Yes, it's incredible, isn't it, that she could find the shillings to cover the cost of the wire. She'll have to do without her toddies this week."

I hated him. I hated the way he thought our families were gutter trash. I hated his sneering face. If he thought he had me trapped, he had another thing coming.

"And you'll have to do without me," I said. "Without all of us. I've written to the Police Commissioner in Bangalore. I've written to the Resident here too and told them how you cut me with your cane. I've talked to the SPCC. Everyone hates you. Everyone."

"How dare you! You vixen!" His eyes blazed and I thought he was going to hit me again, but he only took a step closer, his breath hot in my face. "It won't do you any good. Tomorrow we'll be in the Presidency of Madras and out of Mysore, out of their jurisdiction."

"Then I shall do the same in Madras. Everywhere we go. Everywhere! And the world will know what a vile bully you are!" My voice roared up from the pit of my stomach, shrill with rage.

"Stop it this instant!" he shouted, boxing my ears so hard my head felt it was going to explode. I tried to push him away and escape but he blocked the doorway.

I didn't care that I was cornered. I hated him. "Next time I'll tell them everything," I shrieked. "I'll tell them about you and Lizzie too. I'll tell them what happens after supper every night."

His face flushed a peculiar shade of purple and then he grabbed me by my hair and bashed my head against the wall. I screamed and stumbled backwards against the *almirah*. He came at me again.

If it hadn't been for Poesy, I believe he would have killed me. Her face must have blanched at the sight of us: the Butcher, his hands in my hair, pulling my head back and forth and beating it against the cupboard; me, spewing out my fury and pain.

She screamed and screamed and screamed. The Butcher let go and I slid down the wall, to lie limp on the cool tiles. In an instant, Poesy was in the bathroom, kneeling beside me. She put her arms around my shoulders and looked up at the Butcher, her eyes blazing. "What have you done, Mr Arthur!"

A second later I heard his footsteps going out of the door and away down the passage. Away from us.

"Tilly, Tilly," said Poesy, her cool hand against my cheek.

"Are you all right?"

I sat up slowly. My ears were ringing and I couldn't stop my body shaking but my thoughts were as sharp as a knife. He would pay for this.

"Help me to the bed and bring me some water," I said.

Poesy wept, silently, as she tended me. "I'm sorry, Tilly," she said. "I'll do anything you say. Anything. We have to stop him."

Even though it made my head ache even more, I smiled.

On the train to Madras, coconut palms, lush green paddocks and then dry, dusty red plains flashed past. If I looked at the landscape with squeezy eyes, I could almost imagine I was back in Australia. But then I saw a family of native women with pots and bundles on their heads walking beside a field of sugarcane, and a dark-skinned man on a bicycle riding along a dusty red road. The illusion shattered. I was a long way from home.

The other girls in the carriage were asleep, their heads lolling against each other's shoulders. The Butcher had made us help with the costumes as we bumped out of the theatre the night before, just to save paying a few *annas* to a native, and it was after two in the morning when we finally crawled into bed. Everyone was exhausted.

I was too disappointed for sleep. Mr Ruse hadn't turned up at our final performance. I didn't even know if he had found my letters under his door. Everything seemed hopeless. Once we left Madras, there wouldn't be another chance of escape until we reached America. I knew I couldn't wait that long.

46

SHARED SECRETS

Poesy Swift

Tilly and I stood leaning on the balustrade, watching as all the costumes and sets were unloaded and carried inside by coolies. Flora, Daisy and the younger boys ran squealing up and down the verandahs of the Moore Park Pavilion. Mr Milligan shouted instructions, directing the crates with the flats in them in one direction, and the costumes in another.

"He's not on our side, you know," said Tilly, nodding her head towards Mr Milligan. "He's only out for himself."

"You can't know that, Tilly," I said. "He stuck up for Iris in Penang. And I'm sure he didn't like it when Mr Arthur locked Ruby in her cabin."

"But he did nothing. Him and Eddie and Lo and Jim McNulty and that cow Miss Thrupp. They take the Butcher's money and do his bidding. They never even stay in the same hotel as us any more. At least they used to be nearby. Now, there's no one between us and the Butcher."

Tilly's face was like a stone sculpture. There would be no forgiveness for anyone from her.

We couldn't open our season because the workmen hadn't finished kitting out the pavilion to transform it from a sports arena into a theatre. Instead, that evening, we watched a *fakir* perform on the long verandah of our hotel. He wore a white turban and a white *dhoti* but his chest was bare. His skin was so dark it almost merged with the shadows, as if his clothes were simply floating on air. He set up on a straw mat while the audience lounged about in cane chairs to watch.

It was the first time I'd seen the mango trick. Charlie stood close by, leaning against a verandah post, watching intently while the *fakir* placed a handful of red-brown earth in a tin and pressed a mango seed inside. Then, with his boy helper, he used four bamboo sticks and a piece of coarse muslin to make a little tent. The muslin was translucent but he lifted it at the front so we could see the tin with the mango stone inside. Then he drew another piece of cloth from his basket and tossed it over the top. Next, he put a small *chat*, or water pot, at the back of the tent to water the mango seed before he went on with his act.

No matter how hard I concentrated, I couldn't understand how he worked his magic. He asked a gentleman to put a card in an envelope, a card he couldn't possibly have seen, and yet he knew exactly what was inside without opening the envelope. He lit candles by simply snapping his fingers. Then he came and begged for rupees. I don't know where Charlie found the money, but when the *fakir* came close to him, he slipped the man a few *pice* and then edged closer to watch.

Before the *fakir* began another trick, he lifted the folds of the tent to show that the mango had begun to grow. We could all see a little green shoot poking out of the tin. Someone shouted that it was a hoax and the *fakir* tipped the seed from the tin so we could all see it was truly sprouting. Then he covered it and watered it again and went on performing other tricks. When he had finished, he lifted the folds of the

237

tent again. I couldn't believe my eyes. The little sprout had turned into a proper shrub, a tiny tree with a single golden mango hanging from its branches! Everyone clapped and gasped, except Charlie, who frowned and tipped his head to one side. Then the *fakir* covered the tree again and watered it once more, but when he whipped the cloth off, the tree had disappeared. Only the little tin can lay empty on its side, spilling red-brown earth onto the verandah.

When the magic was at an end I looked for Charlie, but he had disappeared as surely as the mango tree.

That night, my room at the Castle Hotel was steamy with heat. The other girls had collapsed into heavy, sweaty dreams, but still I couldn't sleep. Tomorrow we would be back at work, rehearsing in the mornings, taking enforced naps in the afternoon and putting on eight shows a week, if you included the matinees.

My head swirled with worries. When I shut my eyes I could see the *fakir*'s mango tree sprouting, and then suddenly, out of his little tent sprang Lizzie, as golden as if her skin were made of mangoes. I woke in tears. I hadn't spoken to Lizzie since we'd left Bombay. Despite everything, I missed her terribly, but I could never forgive her. And I would never, ever forgive Mr Arthur.

I climbed out of bed and sat on the windowsill. Then I saw him. Charlie. He was hurrying down the steps of the hotel and into the street.

The next morning, as soon as we had finished breakfast, I caught his wrist.

"I need to talk to you," I whispered. "About something important."

Charlie raised one eyebrow and smiled, the sort of smile he used when he was performing magic tricks. Before he could reply, Lionel sauntered over to join us. Neither Charlie nor I spoke another word. It wasn't safe with Lionel in earshot.

Mr Arthur worked us hard that morning, running through the schedule for the week and making all the girls block their movements on the new stage. At the end of rehearsals, Charlie picked up his *topee*, I fastened my hat in place and we strolled across the wide green lawn outside the pavilion to a line of waiting vehicles. Charlie was cunning. He picked a tiny tri-rickshaw that only the two of us could fit inside, while the others rode in *gharries* and carriages.

Before we reached the hotel, Charlie tapped the driver and we climbed out at the Elphinstone Soda Fountain.

"C'mon," he said. "Time for a private talk, you and me, without all those long ears about."

Inside the shop, jars of marshmallows, sweets and jellies were lined up on the long bar. Charlie ordered us each a soda and paid for them from his mysterious stash of coins. We sat on high bar stools and I stirred icecream into my soda and sipped the cool sweetness of it through a straw. It was exactly like the 'spiders' that you could buy in Swan Street at home. But my mind grew cloudy when I thought of Melbourne. If Tilly's plan worked, we would be in Melbourne in a matter of weeks. I couldn't imagine being back in our tumbledown house in Willow Lane.

Charlie watched me from over the top of his soda. "So, you and Ruby and Tilly are up to mischief. Ever since Kolar, you've been planning something, haven't you?"

"You're the one with the secrets. Where did you go

last night?"

Charlie stirred his soda so that it frothed up to the lip of the glass and said, "You tell first."

"If I do tell, you mustn't breathe a word to Lionel," I said. "Because if you tell him, he'll ruin everything."

"I have my secrets from Lionel too," he said.

I scooped some froth out of my glass and sucked it off my finger. This was going to be harder than I'd imagined.

"You know, Mr Arthur has gone too far. We can't trust him any more. He's hurt too many girls."

Charlie grew still. "He's not laid a finger on you, has he, Poesy?"

"No! But that's not the point," I said hotly. "He's become worse and worse. He thrashed Tilly with his cane in Bombay and he knocked her head against an *almirah* in Bangalore."

"So what do you plan to do about it?"

"Tilly and Ruby and I have found some men who can help us stop Mr Arthur from treating us badly. We met them in Bangalore and Kolar. They're members of a society that protects children. And they have members in Madras too. Tilly says if we find SPCC men here in the audience, they'll help us get away from Mr Arthur."

"What if some don't want to get away from him?" asked Charlie. "Lionel won't turn on him and neither will Eliza."

At the mention of Lizzie, I felt my heart beat faster. "But he's been horrid! If we stop him, it could rescue Lizzie from a terrible fate."

"Lizzie won't want to be rescued by you or anyone else. Mr P. reckons he's going to marry her, soon as he gets a divorce."

"You can't know that!"

"I know Lionel wouldn't play chaperone if he thought Mr P. wasn't going to do the right thing. He's too fond of her."

"So you knew all along about Lizzie and Mr Arthur!" I said.

"Didn't everyone?" he shrugged. "I mean, you don't want to talk about it but you know it's going on. Though sometimes even Lionel likes to pretend it isn't."

I had to swallow hard to stop myself crying. I was so ashamed that it had taken me so long to face the truth. It was awful to think of myself as being just like Lionel, pretending that everything was all right when it wasn't.

"Lionel has to wake up to himself. And you have to help me save him too. We're going on strike – all of the troupe – as soon as we can. Tilly says we need to act before we leave India."

"Strike!" He laughed, as if I'd said something funny. "That's a turn-up for the books. I thought I was the one with plans. But what I'm planning won't help any of you lot get away from Mr P."

He looked down into his soda.

"What are you up to, Charlie Byrne? Why do you keep slipping out at night?"

Charlie drew a deep breath. "You mustn't share this with anyone. Not Tilly or Ruby or anyone."

I nodded and waited for him to go on.

"I'm not coming away with you all when you leave India."

I was so stunned that my mouth fell open. Before I had time to gather my wits, to fully fathom what he meant, Charlie stood up.

"Wait here," he said, leaving me with his terrible

revelation, before darting through the doorway and into the crowded street.

I saw him take a fistful of coins from his pocket and press them into the hand of a dark-skinned Indian boy. The Indian boy took something out from under his coat and handed it to Charlie. Their eyes met and they laughed at the same time as if they were old mates.

I slipped off the stool and marched out into the street. Charlie and his friend glanced up as if I'd caught them doing something very naughty indeed. The Indian boy was dressed in a dark-blue cotton school uniform and his glossy black hair was parted neatly on one side.

"This is Poesy," said Charlie. "Poesy, this is Prem."

"What did you sell him?" I asked Prem. Immediately the words were out of my mouth, I regretted them. Charlie scowled at me.

"It's very fine meeting you, Miss Poesy," said Prem, ignoring my question. He turned to Charlie and lowered his voice. "And I shall see you tonight, yes?"

Charlie nodded. He said goodbye to Prem then grabbed me by the arm before I had a chance to say anything more.

"He didn't 'sell' me anything. I asked him to buy me some things I need for my magic tricks, so he was doing me a favour. Prem's uncle is a pharmacist."

We went back to our sodas but Charlie had grown sullen. He sat sucking on his straw so furiously that the paper collapsed and went flat.

"How can you even think of staying here, Charlie?" I said, feeling tears well in my eyes. "How would you get by? Is that boy something to do with this?"

"While all you lot have been arguing with Old Man Percy and worrying about your petticoats, I've been finding out about India. I've been learning real magic."

"You mean those funny old *fakir*s?"

"No," said Charlie scathingly, "though some of them are jolly good magicians. Poesy, they have stories here, like the stories we read about Homer and the Odyssey, except it's not all ancient and dead. It's as if the people still have magic in them too. That's why there are so many holy men here. They reckon gods come down and walk around in the skins of ordinary people. This country is full of magic."

"Don't be ridiculous, Charlie. There's only one god and that's our god. The Christian God."

Charlie slumped forward and put his head in his hands. "You don't understand. There are things I need to learn. There are sorcerers here that make our stage magicians look absolutely tame and ordinary. If I could find one to take me as an apprentice…"

"It won't be allowed. You're a white boy."

"What about all those people down at the Theosophical Society? What about that Mrs Besant of yours? She thinks the Indians are onto something."

"She's not my Mrs Besant. Just because my grandmother took me to see her in Melbourne doesn't make her mine. Besides, she wouldn't approve of a thirteen-year-old boy running around India by himself."

"She might. She's adopting a boy who she says is going to be a new world leader and he's only thirteen. She found him on the banks of the Adyar River and knew he was special, some sort of great spirit. That's the sort of thing that happens here! Besides, even if a *fakir* won't apprentice me, I can still learn from watching. There are lots of *boxwallah*s down around Elephant Gate, behind Fort George, that might want a boy like me to work for them."

"Did that Prem talk you into this?"

"No," said Charlie. "Prem is going to be a lawyer, like his father. He's studying at the Christian College."

"Then how do you know him?"

"He loves magic too. It's his hobby. It used to be mine, but now I don't want it to be a hobby. I want it to be my life."

I stared into his face, so alight with earnest excitement, and my heart ached. He must have seen my lips trembling. Very gently, he rested his fingertips against my mouth, as if to silence me.

"You keep my secret and I shall keep yours."

THE GATHERING STORM

Tilly Sweetrick

Bandmann Comedy Company posters were everywhere in Madras. They were real performers from London, doing the sort of vaudeville that I knew I was simply made for. They were playing in a *real* theatre that seated at least 800 people. If the Butcher hadn't worked us so hard and kept us so poor, I would have been in the audience at Victoria Hall every night. But the Butcher was our slavedriver: each night we performed a different musical, two shows on Saturday and even a show on Sunday. The Butcher and Mr Shrouts hadn't even found us a proper theatre in Madras. The Moore Park Pavilion was more of a boxing arena than anything else.

Our supplies of limelight ran out in the first week but that wasn't such a bad thing because it meant I could make out the faces in the audience. I felt my heart leap when I finally spotted Mr Ruse. It had been hard to find ways to talk to people in Madras. The Butcher's eyes were on me whenever I wandered out to stand by the buffet at the end of the show.

After the performance, I met Mr Ruse on the balcony at the back of the pavilion, far away from the ticketing area where the Butcher was counting the evening's takings.

"Are you all right, my dear?" he asked.

I pushed a hank of my hair away from my forehead and showed him my fading bruises.

"He beat me the night before we left Bangalore. He knew I'd been talking to you."

Mr Ruse stepped away from me, and my heart sank. It was like trying to lure a frightened animal out of the forest. I had to be careful not to startle him.

"The Resident in Mysore received your letter," said Mr Ruse, his voice so low that I could barely hear him. "He's written of his concerns to the authorities in Madras."

"Is that all?" I asked.

Then he crooked his finger to indicate I should follow him and he led me to the edge of the balcony. He pointed into the crowd. "Those gentlemen down there are with the SPCC here in Madras. Mr St John, Mr Baker, and you might remember Mr Wilkes from Bangalore. They'll be coming to your performances during the week, to keep an eye on things. While you're in Madras, people will watch over you. I'm sure Mr Percival will be mindful of that."

I wanted to tell him how ridiculously useless it was to be watched while we were on stage. As if the Butcher was going to march out and beat us in public! I gritted my teeth and then took a deep breath, trying to curb my irritation.

"Mr Percival has booked our fares to Colombo," I said. "We're to go straight to the station when the curtain falls next Wednesday to take the train to Tuticorin and then the ferry across the strait to Colombo. We shan't be there long enough to convince anyone of our situation and then he's taking us to China. We'll be out of the country on the seventeenth. We'll never get home if you can't help us now," I said, letting my eyes brim with tears.

I rested my hand on his arm again and gazed pleadingly into his face. He shook himself free, little beads of sweat peppering his brow. "I will be back in Madras on Tuesday next week," he whispered. "Don't despair, Miss Tilly."

Mr Ruse didn't know me at all. I wasn't going to despair. I was going to make something happen.

The next day, Freddie, Max and I locked ourselves in the change rooms at the pavilion and came up with a new plan. We were going to force the SPCC into taking action.

That night, I told the others to be ready to work the crowd. As soon as the curtain fell, we ran among the audience, our photos sweaty in our hands. I sent Iris to talk to Mr Baker and Ruby to find someone new while I took charge of Mr Wilkes.

"Poesy, you have to work on Mr St John. You have to walk him down near the stage door so he's in place when Max does his bit."

"I can't. I don't know what to say!" said Poesy, wringing her silly little hands.

"You can't get cold feet now. Tell him Percival's a beast, that he beats us all. Tell him that the Butcher lied to our parents, as good as kidnapping us. That they all must help us before he takes us out of India."

"What if he doesn't believe me?"

"Why wouldn't he? Show him your bruise. That one on your arm."

"But you gave me that and it's only tiny."

I pushed my hair back and pointed to the welt on my forehead. "But the Butcher gave me this. You saw him do it, Poesy. And remember, you're not Lizzie's pet any more. There's no one to protect you. Next time, it could be you."

She made a little hiccupping noise of grief and then marched down into the stalls.

We'd planned for Max to stir up trouble by baiting Lionel, but the whole thing turned out better than we'd expected and the Butcher played right into our hands. As Lionel walked past Max, Max whispered under his breath, "Butcher's Boy." It was guaranteed to make Lionel mad with rage and Max knew it. Before anyone could stop them, the two boys were on the floor, punching each other furiously. The Butcher pulled them apart and dragged Max into one of the change rooms.

We all heard Max cry out. Not just a small cry of distress. He howled at the top of his voice as if the Butcher was flaying him alive. I ran to the stage door and shoved it wide open, hoping that the audience milling around on the verandah would hear Max's cries. Eddie Quedda's face lit with alarm and he hurried towards me, slamming the door in my face. I could hear him speaking outside with Mr St John. Poesy had done her duty and pointed him in the right direction.

"Who is that crying out? The boy needs assistance. What's going on back there?"

"Look, he's a troublemaker, that one," said Eddie, his voice jovial. "The boy played the fool on stage tonight, jumping around like a ruddy jumping jack, and he made trouble backstage – against the rules – so I reported him to Mr Percival. Mr P. is meting out a bit of discipline, that's all."

"I've heard reports, you know. Rumours from Bangalore…"

"They're rumours, I assure you."

"Look, young man, I'm no expert on children but I know the sound of a child in distress."

"He's an actor, sir. He's going to be louder than your average boy. Mr Percival knows how to handle him."

Mr St John didn't persist. He probably needed another whisky to get his Dutch courage up and working. But I was pleased to see there was still a crowd milling about as we left the pavilion. You could almost feel the swell of rumours, like distant thunder, gathering force and rumbling through the audience as they drifted out into the warm night.

48

DARK MAGIC

Poesy Swift

On Sunday evening, Charlie tried to slip away without me. I wouldn't let him. He'd promised to take me and I held him to his promise.

Prem was waiting for us at the back of the Castle Hotel. While Charlie slipped into the shadows to change into his street disguise, Prem handed me a cloth bag. "For you, Miss Poesy, so that you can come about with us as our sister."

I pulled the drawstring top open and peeked inside. "It's not a sari, is it?" I asked, anxiously. I had no idea how the Indian ladies stopped those long pieces of cloth from falling off.

"No, we call this costume a *salwaar kameez*," said Prem. "I have borrowed it from my sister, Meenakshi."

When I still looked hesitant, Prem reached into the bag and pulled out a corner of each of the three items inside.

"This is a *salwaar*," he said showing me some light white cotton trousers, "or this type we actually call *churidar*. And then this blue shirt, we call a *kurta* and you wear this over the top of the *churidar*. Then you must wear a *dupatta*, which is the long shawl, to cover yourself."

I nodded and took the bag back into the hotel. I couldn't possibly change in the laneway like Charlie. In the ladies room, I locked myself in one of the cubicles and struggled into the strange outfit. The light cotton pants were almost like pyjamas, with a drawstring waist. The indigo blue shirt was as light as a feather but it had long sleeves and came right down to my knees, almost like a dress. But the shawl was the piece I liked best. It was a beautiful deep peacock blue and it was so long that I could wrap it around my head to hide my blonde hair and fair skin and still have enough to cover my shoulders and drape over my wrists. At the bottom of the bag, there was a pair of worn cloth slippers that covered the whiteness of my feet.

I stuffed my day clothes into the drawstring bag and hid it on top of the cistern before sneaking out into the laneway to meet the boys. Charlie beamed at me, as if I was in the loveliest costume rather than borrowed clothes. I smoothed the *salwaar* shawl across my shoulder and smiled. It smelled faintly of attar of roses and sandalwood, and I wondered what it would be like to be Prem's sister.

We walked down to the shore first, to the wide, warm beach opposite the Senate House. Small groups of people sat watching fishermen pull their boats up onto the sand as night fell. Scattered along the shore were little stalls from which the smell of hot oil and fresh fish came wafting up the beach. Prem and Charlie wandered across to a stall where they ordered some supper. Charlie bought something called a *dosa*, which was like a great big crispy pancake, while I had some rice and curry and a tiny fried cake on a banana leaf. I wasn't very dainty at eating with my fingers. It seemed to be a terribly untidy way to go about things but Prem ate quickly, deftly, without making a mess at all.

We walked along the warm sand. There were no Britishers about and I felt oddly uncomfortable, even though it was growing too dark for anyone to see me. I wasn't afraid but I was out of my element. Charlie seemed to fit perfectly.

We came to a section of the beach where a *fakir* had set a straw mat and in the middle was a cane basket. Around the mat, flaring torches were embedded in the sand. We stood about waiting for him to begin.

His assistant stepped forward, a small, thin rag of a boy with thick black hair. At the *fakir*'s command, he climbed inside the basket and pulled the lid over his head. Then the *fakir* took out a shiny sharp sword and plunged it into the basket. From inside came a terrible wail. I clutched Charlie's arm in horror. No one in the crowd moved as the *fakir* plunged in sword after sword until blood began to flow out through the cane and the wails of the little boy stopped.

I felt quite weak at the knees. I squeezed Charlie's wrist. "Don't worry," he said. "It's only a clever trick. Watch."

Charlie and Prem acted as if it were the most ordinary thing in the world to see a little boy murdered before our very eyes.

The *fakir* began to chant and remove each of the bloodied swords. When the last sword was withdrawn, he waved his hand over the top of the basket three times and cried out something magical. Suddenly, the lid popped off and the little boy jumped out, grinning. He did a dance around the basket and the audience cheered. In the glow of the torchlight, it was clear that the child didn't have a mark on his skin and yet only moments before he had been howling in pain.

Feeling queasy, I walked away from the boys, down to the

water's edge, and stared out at the black sea. I couldn't bear to watch any more dark magic. I'd only meant to stay away for a minute, but when I turned around the *fakir* was rolling up his mat and the boys had disappeared.

I wrapped my shawl tightly about me and studied the thinning crowd with alarm. Every face seemed dark and utterly foreign. My feet sank into the deep sand and I had to carry my slippers as I ran in a panic up the beach to the boulevard. Standing on the pavement, I looked in every direction, but though there were groups of men and boys everywhere I couldn't see Prem and Charlie. I hurried back into the city, staring up at the buildings, trying to get my bearings. With horror, I realised I had no idea how to find my way back to the Castle Hotel.

I hurried through the Madras streets, self-conscious about my strange clothes, unable to speak to either Indian or Britisher. What would they make of me? A pale-skinned Australian girl dressed like a native. A group of young Indian men called out to me but I couldn't understand what they were saying and I dashed into the next street, terrified. I nearly collided with two British soldiers who came reeling through the doors of a club. I ran faster, blindly, my gaze flitting from one building to the next, hoping to recognise one that was familiar.

Then, to my horror, I saw Mr Arthur coming out of a doorway. Part of me longed to fling myself at him, to beg him to take me back to the hotel, but then I remembered what he'd done to Lizzie and I stepped into the shadows and hid myself. I could smell the rank scent of whisky as he reeled past.

I wanted to be sick. I knew I simply had to get off the street and calm myself. When I was almost at my wits' end, I turned into a wide street and saw golden light flooding out through the doors of a public hall. Both Indian and white people, ladies and gentlemen, were crowding into the hall, beneath a sign that read 'Free Lecture'. I slipped in through the doors, my head bowed, and found myself a seat on a bench in a shadowy corner of the hall. I kept my eyes down and the shawl pulled forward to hide my face.

It was a strange twist of fate to discover Mrs Besant was delivering the lecture. I remembered that the Theosophical Headquarters were somewhere in Madras. She stood in the centre of a small stage at one end of the hall. Her silvery hair was thick, like a girl's, and her eyes were bright and sharp. She wore a white satin gown with a fichu of pale brown lace at the collar. When she took off her white gloves to speak, her hands were strong and brown and sinewy. Beside her, dressed in a white jacket with tiny gold buttons, was an Indian boy. He couldn't have been more than fourteen.

Mrs Besant spread her arms wide, as if to embrace the audience. When she spoke, her voice was like a song. It rang out across the hall.

"Truth may lead me into the wilderness, yet I must follow her; she may strip me of all love, yet I must pursue her; though she slay me, yet will I trust in her; and I ask no other epitaph on my tomb but 'She tried to follow Truth'."

To follow Truth. I had no idea what that meant any more. The world was full of liars and the ground beneath my feet shifted from one day to the next.

I couldn't make sense of what Mrs Besant was trying to

explain until she turned to introduce the boy beside her. He must be the one she was adopting, the boy that Charlie had talked about. She called him Jiddu Krishnamurti. He reminded me a little of Prem but he was thinner. His eyes were like beautiful doe's eyes – brown and soft – and he looked at the audience with a strange, unboyish tenderness. "His mystical name is Alcyone," Mrs Besant announced, "but his aura is completely free of selfishness, his past lives have made him wise beyond his years."

I don't know why that was the thing that made me cry. All of a sudden, my whole body began to shake. I didn't see why anyone should be wise beyond their years. I wanted to wind back the clock and go back to being the innocent girl I'd been six months before. I wanted Mr Arthur to go back to being the kind and dashing man he'd been when I'd first met him at Balaclava Hall. I wanted Lizzie to be the lovely big sister who had held me in her arms. I wanted Tilly to be the same cheerful, whistling girl who'd come strolling down my laneway. I wanted my old life back.

People nearby turned to stare at me as my sobs grew louder. I jumped to my feet and ran out into the night. A man at the door called after me but I didn't stop. I ran and ran and just when I thought I would have to throw myself on the mercy of the next passing stranger, I found Prem.

I was so relieved to see him I almost threw myself into his arms.

"Miss Poesy!" he said. "Where have you been? Charlie and I split up to search for you. We were so worried."

"Oh Prem," I said. "I'm in a terrible muddle."

I looked into Prem's face and he was so like the boy on

stage that I wanted to ask him if he too was wise beyond his years. His skin seemed to change colour as he took a step back and the darkness rippled over his forearms like a shadow. In the soft light of the laneway, he looked as if a candle had been held against his arm, his brown skin turning to sooty darkness in the folds of his elbow, in the crease near his neck. I wanted to reach out and touch him, to see if the silky blackness would come away on my hands. But he kept me at a distance.

I felt a flood of heat from the pit of my stomach. It reached all the way to my cheeks and made them burn. I lowered my head and let the edge of my *dupatta* cast a shadow across my face.

"Come with me, Miss Poesy. I will take you to Charlie."

As we walked along Mount Road, Prem said, "Charlie will be most relieved I have found you. And I also am very relieved. For your sake and also because I must not stay out much later. My sister's groom is coming to visit tomorrow and my mother and father are very anxious that everything be perfect, so I must not be too late tonight."

"How old is your sister?" I asked, looking down at the tiny slippers Prem had lent me.

"Oh, she is twelve years old, Miss Poesy," said Prem.

"Twelve! That's younger than me. She can't be married yet!"

"She will be getting married in a few weeks, when the date and the time is more auspicious," said Prem. "Twelve is not so young. My own wife is eleven years old but she lives still in her father's house. Our families agreed she must stay with her parents for a few more years."

I stopped in my tracks and gazed at Prem in disbelief. To

think of him as someone's husband was such a topsy-turvy idea it made me dizzy.

"But do you love her?"

Prem laughed uncomfortably. "I have promised I will do so. I will be responsible for her. My parents selected her with great care. One day, when I am a lawyer like my father, we will all live together and be very happy."

It was probably rude to gawp but I couldn't help myself. We were standing stock still on the pavement, staring at each other, each of us bewildered by the other, when Charlie came running up to join us.

"Poesy!" he cried. "Where have you been?"

I turned to Charlie and touched his arm. I wanted to hug him but it didn't seem proper. Not in front of Prem.

"I'm sorry. I've been horribly lost. Please take me home, Charlie," I said. It was such a funny thing to say, because, of course, we had no home.

Back at the Castle Hotel, I changed into my old clothes and stuffed Prem's sister's things back into the drawstring bag. I gave it to Charlie before running up the stairs. On the first landing, I nearly collided head-on with Lionel.

"What are you doing up at this hour?" I asked.

"I could ask the same of you," he said.

"None of your beeswax."

I thought he'd snap back at me but he simply stepped aside and let me hurry down the hallway. It was as I turned the corner that I saw them. Lizzie and Mr Arthur. They were standing outside the room that Lionel shared with Mr Arthur.

Lizzie was dressed in nothing but her kimono with the

sash loose at her waist. Had she no shame? Mr Arthur gripped both her arms and began talking to her in a hurried undertone. I didn't know where to look.

"No, Arthur. It's too late. I waited for hours."

"Don't leave me, Lizzie, don't go back to your room. Stay with me."

"You know I can't. As if there hasn't been enough trouble. If I'm not in my bed in the morning, it will only make things worse. Besides, you can't let poor Lionel sit on the stairs all night."

But he wouldn't let her go. He pulled her close to him and squashed her face against his.

"Don't! Arthur, you're hurting me!" she said.

It was too horrible. I wanted to turn away but I stayed fixed to the spot in my shadowy alcove. Then he kissed her. He pressed his lips against her cheek and I saw her pull a face, as if it were the last thing she wanted. She tore herself away from him.

"Go to bed, Arthur," she said, and then she ran down the hall in her bare feet and disappeared into her room.

I felt sick. Sick to the pit of my stomach. How could he? She obviously didn't love him. He was hurting her. He was a drunkard, a brute and an adulterer. But Lizzie was disgraceful, shameless. She let it happen over and over again. It was disgusting. He was a monster, and if Lizzie wouldn't expose him, then someone else would have to tell the truth about Arthur Percival.

49

PROMISES AND HALF-TRUTHS

Tilly Sweetrick

Mr Wilkes wasn't exactly a stagedoor Johnny, so even though we weren't meant to have men in our rooms at the Castle Hotel, Ruby and I invited him inside. It was simply comic the way he blushed when I batted my eyes at him. His hair was silvery white, as white as the beautifully tailored suit that he wore, and he carried a natty little cane with a silver handle. He sat on one of the low bedroom chairs and rested both hands on the top of his cane.

"I want you to know, young ladies, that I am staying here at the Castle as well. I would like you to think of me as your personal protector. You may call upon me day or night should that rascal Mr Percival treat you with any cruelty."

We sat at his feet, our skirts spread around us and tried to make our gaze admiring.

"You're so kind, dear Mr Wilkes, and we feel much safer knowing you're near. But what's to become of us when we leave Madras?"

"I know," shouted Daisy, as if she had made a great discovery. She skipped across the room and shamelessly plonked herself in Mr Wilkes's lap. "Mr Wilkes can come to Colombo with us!" she said, giving his silvery goatee beard a pat.

Mr Wilkes looked like a startled rabbit. I lifted Daisy

off his knee and gave her a little tickle under her armpits to let her know I wasn't cross.

"You mustn't mind Daisy," I said apologetically. "She's only excited to find we have a friend."

Mr Wilkes's eyes grew shiny and pink and he patted my hand. "Oh my dear, yes, I would like to be your friend."

Poor old Wilkesy. We felt so sorry for him we let him spend the whole afternoon in our room. He said he was an artist and he showed us some awful drawings he'd done in his sketchbook of native girls at a well, and another of them washing their saris by a river. We posed for him so he could do awful drawings of us too and by the time Lionel banged on our door to let us know it was time to go to the Pavilion, Mr Wilkes would have followed us anywhere, even to Colombo and beyond.

As devoted as Mr Wilkes could be, I knew he wouldn't stand up to the Butcher. Mr Ruse, on the other hand, was a big, powerful man. If we could convince him to confront the Butcher, the cur would be intimidated. But we needed to up the stakes. Through Mr Wilkes, I wrote to Mr Ruse, begging him to make our situation public. On Tuesday morning, I received a note from him saying he would bring a notary to us to take formal statements against the Butcher from any child willing to put their accusations in writing. If our stories were written down, he said, the SPCC could consider further action.

On Tuesday afternoon, the day before our last performance in Madras, Mr Wilkes and Mr Ruse came to our rooms with a proper notary, Mr Bowes. He carried a big black book with him to take statements from as many of us as were willing to talk. Some of the girls panicked. Some lay on their beds and wept. Some tried to hedge their bets. In the end there were only five of us: me, Ruby, Daisy, Freddie and Poesy. While we all gathered around a table, Max stood with his back to the door, listening for the Butcher.

I thought it would be my evidence that counted for most. I thought all I needed from the others was for them to verify that I had indeed been cruelly beaten. I told the truth. Every nasty detail of it. I lifted my skirt and showed where the cane had cut and the place where my head had been bashed against the *almirah*. I left out the bit about the Butcher ruining everything between me and George Madden, and Ruby was careful to say nothing about her sailor in Penang. I'd also told Poesy not to say anything about Tempe and Clarissa. It wasn't how we wanted them to think of us. But we didn't tell any lies. At least, I didn't.

One by one we told our stories, but something happened as the notary began scribbling. As each one of us came forward, the stories grew fiercer. I could have slapped Daisy when she said that the big girls forced their toes into her mouth so she couldn't cry out while she lay under the railway seats. It was too ridiculous but the notary scratched it down in his big black book.

Freddie stretched things too, making it sound as though the Butcher boxed his ears every day. Then he rolled down his stocking and showed his shins, saying the Butcher had kicked them until they were black and blue. But Freddie's shins were always black and blue. Everyone knew perfectly well that half his bruises were of his own making and the rest were probably Max's fault.

The real surprise was when Poesy came to give her evidence. It was as if with each telling, the stakes were raised. I never would have believed she could trump us all.

She fiddled with her skirt, pinching the fabric between her fingers, and then she looked up into Mr Ruse's face, her eyes shining as if tears were only a whisper away. For a moment I thought she was going to let me down and start snivelling, but she was full of surprises. "In Bangalore," she said. "Mr Arthur kicked me too. He came to my room and demanded my pocket money – to buy whisky. When I said I needed it to buy stamps to send letters to my mother, he lost his temper. I think he'd been drinking. He smelled of whisky and smoke. And then, after he hurt me, I gave him all my savings. And then, and then…" she twisted the edge of her skirt in her hand, as if the next part of her story would have to be wrung from her. "He put his arm around me and then he…"

She stumbled again and her eyes flitted from my face to the notary's and then back to me. I nodded at her, willing her to keep going.

"He put his mouth against my cheek, and it was horrible. He tried to kiss me!"

Then she burst into tears. It was a good effect, though it was probably horror at her own lies that made her weep.

When the men left, Ruby, Daisy and I danced around the room, laughing with relief. Even Max began to giggle. Only Poesy didn't join in. She stood by the window, making little miserable sniffling noises.

"Oh buck up, Poesy," I said. "Remember, it's all for the greater good."

It was probably because of Poesy that I didn't hear the Butcher coming. He must have passed Ruse and the notary on the stairs. He burst into the room and grabbed a fistful of my hair.

"What have you done, Matilda? Will you ruin me, girl?"

I started to cry hot, angry tears that poured down my face, but not because I was afraid.

He twisted a hank of my hair around his trembling hand. "If I catch you trying to undermine me again, I'll cut all this off. I'll cut your hair to the skin of your scalp and I'll make your life a living hell, Matilda Sweeney."

I wrenched myself free and ran. Mr Ruse and Mr Bowes were standing in the foyer, waiting for the doorman to flag them a *gharry*. I cried out to Mr Ruse as I leaped down the last three steps and flung myself into his arms.

"He saw you. He knows what we've done. He says he'll cut off my hair the minute we leave Madras," I whispered, drying my tears with the back of my hand. "Please. I can't leave for Colombo with him."

Mr Ruse took the stairs two at a time with the notary hot on his heels. Mr Wilkes took my arm and tried to lead me to a chair, but I had to know what was happening. I tore myself away from the old man and followed the others up the stairs. As I stood behind Mr Ruse, I saw the colour drain out of the Butcher's face.

"You've threatened this child for the last time, Percival," said Mr Ruse. "Your jig is nearly up. We've taken statements and they will be sent to Colombo and Rangoon and Hong Kong – to every port in the Empire, so that wherever you go, your reputation will precede you. You'll be utterly disgraced.

You'll never be able to hold your head up in public again."

"You ruin me and you'll ruin these children too."

"Nevertheless, you must be held to account," said Mr Ruse.

The Butcher laughed as if he couldn't believe that Mr Ruse could be so ridiculous.

"You think I like caring for these brats? You think they're so wonderful? You try taking them in hand! I'm sick and tired of the selfish, whining lot of them. I'm sick of this whole damned business. I've done nothing but bleed money ever since we set out. If someone would pay their fares back to Australia, I'd be more than pleased to hand them over."

Mr Ruse should have called the Butcher's bluff then and there but he was afraid. He turned on his heels and shot me a look that I couldn't read. Was it an apology for his weakness or a promise of things to come?

50

STRIKE

Poesy Swift

I wished I could magic away the day I lied about Mr Arthur, make every word I'd said vanish from the pages of Mr Bowes's big black book. My mouth felt burned from the untruths. But the die was cast. There was no turning back.

Our last night in Madras we all seethed with restless energy. You could feel it like a mutinous rage rippling through the troupe. Only Tilly was possessed of an eerie calm. She said she'd met with Mr Ruse before the show and everything was under control. She glided between one group of children and the next, rehearsing each of us for the denouement.

For a while, I didn't think the men would come, that we hadn't really set anything in motion. After the show, I stayed backstage with Charlie. I had to have someone to anchor me, to stop me from feeling as though the whole world were unravelling.

It was after midnight when the men finally arrived. Most of the audience had gone and we had packed the last of our things in a desultory way. Freddie and Max seized their moment and cornered Lionel. I took hold of Charlie's wrist and held him fast, to stop him intervening. I could feel he was trembling.

Lionel was carrying Mr Arthur's cashbox in his arms so

there wasn't much he could do when Freddie swung the first punch. It was an oddly silent scuffle. In a moment, Max and Freddie had bundled Lionel into a cupboard, shoved the cashbox into his lap and told him to stay put until they came back for him or they'd beat him up again.

"I can't bear this," said Charlie, running outside.

I found him standing on the steps of the pavilion, his face in his hands while moths and insects buzzed in the light above our heads.

Then the men came out of the shadows. There were more than twenty. Their white shirts caught the light. I saw Mr St John among them and Mr Wilkes as well.

Mr Arthur had been packing up his ticket box and was carrying it along the top verandah. When he saw the men he hurried to the stairs but they surrounded him before he could reach the foyer. He backed up against the balustrade and the men closed in around him in a circle on the staircase.

"I warned you, Percival," said Mr Ruse. "You can't take the children to Colombo. We won't have it."

Mr Arthur glanced at the crowd of men who flanked Ruse and his face grew strangely vacant. I couldn't be sure if he was afraid or amused.

"This is my company, sir. These children are contracted to me. I have no idea why you suggest I cannot employ and transport them as I see fit."

"They're afraid of you, man, with good reason. And we're here to see that the children's interests are protected. They won't go any further with you. Not one step. Myself, Mr Wilkes and Mr Baker are with the SPCC."

"What's that? Saps that Persecute Commercial Companies?"

There was a mixture of laughter and outrage from the men. Some of them shouted abuse at Mr Arthur, calling him 'cur' and 'ruffian'.

"This is not a joke, Percival, I assure you," said Mr Ruse.

"I don't suppose it is," he replied. "There is nothing amusing about being responsible for twenty-six young people. But you can have them, if you want them so much. I dare you. You take responsibility and you'll find out. Feed them, dress them, pay their fares. Put up with their tantrums, their deceit, their hysteria, and then wipe their mouths when they've been sick all over you."

He glanced over the balustrade to where a group of us were standing, staring up at him. I don't know what he thought he read in our faces but it must have made him a little bolder.

"I don't believe many of them wish to go with you. I've trained these kiddies since they were infants, some of them for more than a decade. I am like a father to them. Whatever that lying little minx Sweetrick has told you, you'll find they're not all as disloyal as she."

As the argument swelled, the rest of the Lilliputian cast and crew came out of the Pavilion. They lined the balconies to watch.

"Gather the children together, Tilly," said Mr Milligan. "Each of you must make your choices."

Mr Ruse's eyes flickered over the group.

"If you move, Percival," he said, "if you so much as breathe a word of threat to any one of these innocents, it will be as much as your life is worth."

Mr Arthur grimaced and held his ground while Tilly dodged among us, checking that we all knew what to say.

When she came to me, she gave my arm a little squeeze. "You only have to tell the truth this time."

I swallowed hard, swallowed all my lies and braced myself for what lay ahead.

We were herded into a line, all twenty-five of us. At the very end of the line was Lizzie. I saw her step away, into the shadows of the Pavilion, her face pale in the darkness. It was like a mask, without expression or feeling.

Mr Arthur caught sight of her and for the first time his face twisted with grief. He turned on Mr Ruse. "You take these children by force, Ruse, and you accept responsibility for the hell they'll deliver up to you."

Mr Ruse ignored him and asked us, one after the other. "Will you go with Percival to Colombo, or will you come away?"

As a chorus, we chanted, just as Tilly had rehearsed us: "We're afraid to go with him, sir. We don't want to go any further."

Then one by one, we were marched past Mr Arthur, made to stop before him and stare straight into his frightened blue eyes.

"Will you go with Mr Percival or will you come away with us?" asked Mr Ruse.

"I'm afraid," I said. My chest hurt and I put one hand against my ribs and pressed it to still the ache. "I don't want to go with him."

I couldn't look at Mr Arthur as I denied him, but I watched Tilly as she spoke. She spat the words at him. Most of the children looked at their boots, some for fear of Mr Arthur, some for shame, but Tilly stared so hard at him that he turned away from the triumph in her gaze.

Only Lionel was absent, but that had always been part of the plan. No one asked after him. Lizzie stood back the whole time, absolutely silent. She didn't declare her loyalty. She didn't need to. No one expected her to turn on her lover.

I thought it was over, I thought we would be able to walk away at last, but Tilly rested her hand on Mr Ruse's arm and said, "Our pocket money. Don't forget our pocket money."

Mr Ruse smiled and nodded. You could tell he was feeling emboldened by his success.

"You owe these children 105 rupees in pocket money, Percival. You must pay it to them before you dare to leave the country."

We couldn't believe it. I shook my head, so sure that there would be no money to give, but Mr Arthur pulled a wad of rupees from his pocket and counted them out. Then Mr Ruse wrote out a receipt for him, while Tilly stood by his elbow, whispering urgently. Mr Ruse looked down at her and nodded.

"The children intend to raise their own money for the fares without any assistance from you," he announced. "We'll need their wardrobe, the music box and the sets as well."

"It's too late," said Mr Arthur. He ran his hand through his hair, as if now there was nothing left but to accept his utter defeat. "Most of the sets, the music box and the costumes were sent ahead days ago. Last night's and tonight's have already gone to the station. You can't have them."

"We'll pay the necessary railway charges for the return of the trunks."

Mr Arthur rustled in his pocket and pulled out a railway

receipt for the baggage and scribbled something on it so that Mr Ruse had permission to take the goods. "Good luck and be damned," he muttered.

As the *gharry* with Mr St John and a group of us girls drove away, I saw Eliza standing alone in the street outside the pavilion, watching us leave. Her face was whiter than her dress. She looked like a ghost, her eyes dark, her hair coming loose.

For a moment, I wanted to run back to her, to beg her to come away with us, but then Mr Arthur stepped into the road. Slowly she walked towards a *gharry* with Lionel and Mr Arthur on either side of her. They each held one of her elbows, as if she were about to collapse or take flight, like a broken butterfly.

51

RISING STARS

Tilly Sweetrick

We drove to the Castle Hotel in triumph, only to find all our things had been sent to the station and our rooms assigned to new customers. It was terribly annoying. We decided to eat at the Castle anyway because at least they were used to serving us after midnight. Normally we would have had supper in our rooms, but this time we ate in the dining room and Ruby and I sat either side of Mr Ruse to discuss what lay ahead.

Some of the younger girls put their heads on the table and were asleep before supper arrived. It was nearly two in the morning but I felt fresh as the day. It was the loveliest feeling, to know we were free.

Then the most appalling thing happened. Mr Ruse spotted the Butcher. He was walking up the stairs with Eliza and Lionel, like three beaten curs with their tails between their legs. I don't know what came over Mr Ruse. He simply couldn't seem to accept that Lionel and Lizzie were happy to stay with the Butcher. He chased them up the stairs and we could hear him arguing with Lionel, who obviously didn't want to join us in the dining room.

Then Charlie, who had looked black as thunder all evening, went racing up the stairs too and then Poesy after Charlie. What could I do but run after them?

By the time we reached the second floor, Mr Ruse was dusting his hands, as if he'd just completed a rather dirty job.

"I've locked him in. I've locked him in and I'm sending for the police. He's a moral outrage and the girl and boy should be taken from him by force."

"Eliza is eighteen years old, Mr Ruse. I don't think the police can take her against her will."

"But they can take the boy," said Mr Ruse, looking a little hurt that I wasn't pleased.

Charlie was standing by the door with his ear pressed against it, listening to Lionel who was shouting through the keyhole. Then he turned to us and his mouth trembled.

"Old Man Percy, he's got a gun. He's got a gun and he says he's going to use it on someone if we don't all come back to him."

Mr Ruse was so shocked that he stumbled backwards and then fled down the stairs, calling to the hotel staff for aid.

I felt strangely calm, despite everything. When Lizzie came bursting into the hall from another doorway, I didn't feel the least surprised.

She stopped, suddenly embarrassed at the sight of us all, standing like characters in a melodrama. She didn't speak to me. I might as well have been invisible. It was Poesy and Charlie she directed her sad little speech towards.

"I came through the connecting bathroom. He doesn't know I'm gone. You must get the door open. You simply must get the door open and tell him you'll come back to him."

It was Charlie who solved it all too quickly. Charlie and his sneaky magic. He pulled a little pocketknife from his jacket, fiddled with the lock, and in a moment he had the door open.

"Come away, Poesy, Charlie. Come away from there this instant," I said crossly.

I backed down the stairs, ready to run the minute the Butcher came into view. But when the door opened there was only Lionel there, his face drawn, and in the background, we could see a figure hunched in a chair, sobbing. I could hardly believe it was the Butcher. He was crying like a baby.

"It's all right now, Lizzie," said Lionel. "I've hidden the pistol. He won't harm himself."

He stared at Charlie as if he were a stranger. "Go on, you lot, bugger off. Why are you standing around gawking? It's not a sideshow. You're not wanted here."

Poesy cried all the way to Mr St John's house.

"Do stop, Poesy," I said, trying to contain my irritation. Mr St John was looking distinctly embarrassed. We all knew Poesy was his favourite. Most of the children had been taken away from the Castle Hotel because of the trouble with the Butcher, and Mr St John had been happy to have a group of us as long as Poesy was included. We could have stayed at the hotel, because the Butcher, his lackey and his lover had been thrown out into the street by the manager, but Mr Ruse was determined to send the girls away.

"I can't stop thinking about Lionel and Eliza," Poesy sobbed. I knew she had almost added "and Mr Arthur" because, I swear, that girl was part chameleon. She could change her colours more times in an evening than there were hours in a day.

"Don't you worry about them," I said. "They'll probably spend the night at the train station, sleeping in a carriage. Or take it all the way to Tuticorin. And we shouldn't mind. What they do from now on is their business. Our business is to earn our fares home."

Mr St John's bungalow wasn't quite as luxurious as I'd hoped and we were all put in one room together, but in the end it didn't matter. I didn't sleep all night. I felt strange and new-made and as if all the world was mine.

We were back at the Castle Hotel within a day and I was rather pleased to have the run of the place again. Ruby and I had a room to ourselves and we organised all the younger girls into new groups while Max and Freddie took charge of the boys.

The papers were full of the story of our strike. All of a sudden, people from all over Madras turned up at the hotel wanting to meet us and hear our story, people who hadn't even bothered to come to our performances. Which was lucky, because we needed to do a whole new season of shows to earn enough for our fares home.

I wanted to secure the Lyric Theatre on the corner of Ellis Road, but when Mr Giacomo d'Angeli, a darling Corsican, announced himself at the Castle, we were glad of his offer of a venue. We were dependent on the kindness of strangers.

Two days later our very first show was held on the Parisian rooftop garden of Mr d'Angeli's hotel. The terrace glowed with electric light and he had to turn people away at the door, the publicity had been so extravagant.

Before the show began, Ruby and I stood at the parapet, our arms around each other's waists. The city stretched beneath us, with its wide boulevards and grand old houses, the crowded bazaars and in the distance the shimmering sea. Though the day had been unbearable in its heat, the evening was as warm as a sweet embrace. Ruby turned to me and kissed my cheek.

"You have saved us all, Tilly. You have saved me especially and I will never, ever forget."

We watched the evening star rise up from the sea and waited for our audience.

52

Taking Charge

Tilly Sweetrick

Everybody wanted us. They flocked to the Castle Hotel to make proposals to me and Ruby. There were so many offers of venues that it was hard for us to decide where to go next. We did another show at d'Angeli's before moving on to the first floor of Misquith's Music Shop. It was after our third successful show that the trouble started.

Eddie and Lo and little Bertie, Mr Milligan, Jimmy and Miss Thrupp had gone to the Commercial Hotel on the night of the strike but eventually the lot of them turned up at the Castle, looking very sorry for themselves. Ruby and I were eating breakfast when Eddie Quedda came simpering into the dining room while the rest of them waited in the foyer.

Eddie sat down at our table, bobbing his head. "Girls, it's good to see you all looking so well. You know, me and Lo and the others, we've been worried about you lot."

"You weren't very worried about us when the Butcher was knocking us about," said Ruby tersely.

Eddie looked to the foyer where Lo was bouncing the baby on her knee. "I got a family to support, girls. You got to see things from my point of view. That Mr Ruse of yours, he won't let us work with you," he said, his voice almost wheedling. "Mr Arthur has left us in the lurch. We don't have our fares home and we don't have much to live on neither."

"Pish-posh," I said, "I saw the Butcher hand you a big wad of cash the night we went on strike. Have you spent it already?"

"But you didn't see what he gave me, did you?" Eddie slapped a couple of funny old Java notes onto the table. "They're worth almost nothing here. It's rupees we need."

"I don't see why we should help you," I said. "I know you told the Butcher if he'd pay you, you'd work for him again."

"Business is business, Tilly. When we're back in Melbourne, we've got to find work again, just like you. Be fair."

"You're the one that's not being fair. You never stuck up for us. Why should we stick up for you? Your 'business' is with the Butcher, not us. We don't owe you a fig. If you want to harass someone, go and sue the pants off Mr Arthur Percival."

Eddie slunk away then and I was glad to see the back of him. We thought we had washed our hands of him. Little did we know! Eddie marched straight down to the Police Courts and filed a case against the Butcher, setting in chain events that the newspapers would feed upon for months to come. I was to become famous, but not in the way I'd always imagined.

A week later, we fled Madras in a flurry of confusion. Mr Arthur had filed a case against both Mr Ruse and Mr Wilkes in the Police Court, accusing them of kidnapping. Within hours we were on a train heading west. We had to leave the Presidency of Madras before the morning was out.

By late afternoon, we were in Bangalore, where we were greeted by crowds of admirers and members of the press.

I kept our story clear and simple, though I knew it was being reported as an international scandal.

I had far too many other things to worry about. The shows in Bangalore were dreadful. After the last awful production of *Florodora* in Kolar where everyone missed their cues, Ruby and I called a meeting. We weren't going to attempt the musicals any more. We were only going to do revues. Ruby and I made everyone perform their best pieces in front of a panel of me, Ruby, Myrtle and the Kreutz twins. At the end of the auditions, I stood up and made an announcement.

"I have two pieces of news, one rather lovely and one a bit awful. Firstly, we've received an invitation from the Maharajah of Mysore to perform at his palace."

When the flurry of excited chatter had settled, I went on, "Secondly, Eddie Quedda has won his case and the Butcher has produced rather a lot of money to prevent himself being thrown into jail."

Everyone cheered, which was quite stupid of them.

"Stop it! There's nothing to cheer about. Eddie winning is not particularly good news for us. As you know, the Butcher has been scribbling nasty letters to the press from his hidey hole in Pondicherry and has filed that ridiculous case against Mr Ruse and Mr Wilkes as kidnappers that led to us having to leave the Presidency. Of course he also said we are in breach of our contracts. Now, the magistrate in the Police Court has let Wilkesy off but Mr Ruse has lost his defence against the Butcher. The case is going to be heard in the High Court. The wretched magistrate thought Mr Ruse has a kidnapping case to answer. We all have to return to Madras to give evidence."

"But that's stupid," said Ruby. "He didn't kidnap us. We couldn't run away fast enough."

"Of course it's stupid," I said. "You might just as well say *we* kidnapped Mr Ruse! The thing is we are in breach of our contracts because we're not meant to perform unless the Butcher agrees. So now the Butcher is going to try to sue Mr Ruse for more than sixty thousand rupees!"

A murmur went through the troupe. It was such a vast sum of money it made everyone shiver to think of what would happen to poor Mr Ruse if he lost the case. I put my hands up to quieten them all.

"Now it's our turn to help Mr Ruse. After everything he's done for us, it's only decent that we go back to Madras and get him off the hook."

I wasn't afraid of the court. I wanted to march straight up to the bench and give that judge a piece of my mind. I had truth on my side.

Poesy had grown white as a ghost. You could smell her fear. But what did she expect? Every folly comes back to you. Now Poesy Swift would have to swear under oath, to swear on the Bible, that Mr Arthur Percival had tried to kiss her.

53

THE CAGED BIRD'S SONG

Poesy Swift

As we passed under the arches of Bangalore Railway Station, I felt my heart sink into my boots. It seemed we were travelling backwards, into the dark.

There had been something sad and meagre about our performances in Bangalore and Kolar. We didn't have Mr Milligan and Jimmy to arrange the sets, nor Miss Thrupp and Lo to help us with our costumes. We didn't even have the music box to accompany our songs. We had only two sets that we didn't know how to assemble, and an assortment of costumes from two shows. Mr Ruse didn't understand that without the music box that had been sent on to Colombo or Eddie to play the piano, or Mr Arthur to cue us on and decide upon the blocking in each venue, the performances were going to be nothing less than shoddy.

Every evening, as the audience applauded Daisy's last song, Mr Ruse stepped forward and told the same tired story about Mr Arthur cheating on the railway fare and then he would bow out and let Daisy tell the story herself. Daisy held the audience in thrall, as she had at every show we'd done since the strike. It was a good performance. You could see the women's faces melt with sympathy when she lisped her way through the description of lying under the seats on the trains, among all the spiders and cobwebs, of how she had to stay for such a long time even when she pinched the other girls' legs to beg if she might come out. Why did people like to hear of little girls being treated badly? Wouldn't it have been better if we'd told a story about how grateful we would be if they could help us to go home? Why did everyone want to feed on the miserable account of little children betrayed?

At night we tramped back to wherever we were staying, having to smile until our faces hurt to show our gratitude to our hosts.

We should have felt breathless with excitement about performing in Mysore. The Maharajah was one of the great maharajahs of India, one of only three for whom the army performed a twenty-one-gun salute. But every face on the train to Mysore was tense with worry.

All the splendour of the Maharajah's palace, with its murals and gold leaf and all the elaborate tiling and fretwork, couldn't distract me from misery. He was building another palace too, a palace that everyone said would be one of the grandest in all India. We were taken to see the elephants at work as they carried great loads of timber and dragged pallets piled high with stones.

The worst of being in Mysore was that the boys were taken away from us to stay in a hotel while we girls were taken to the old Maharani's palace. I didn't like being separated from Charlie. He was feeling so low about Lionel that I was worried he might go back to his original plans of becoming a sorcerer's apprentice and simply disappear into the night.

On the morning after our performance, I woke early to the sound of bird cry. No one else was awake and I slipped from our room without the other girls noticing. I stood, very quietly, in the courtyard of the palace, looking at the columns stretching upwards, their carved rosewood dark and glossy in the morning light. I heard a door shut somewhere further away in the palace. How could one princess have so much to herself?

I liked this palace much better than the gaudy, cluttered rajah's palace we'd performed at the night before. The coloured mosaic of tiles was cool beneath my feet as I walked back to my room.

It was as I crossed from the cool dark into a patch of sunlight that Richmond came jumbling back into my mind. It was like a fever that grew in my brain until I was back in our little terrace in Willow Lane, then walking in Studley Park on a Sunday to catch yabbies and tadpoles, past the Chinese market gardens, the Yarra Bend Asylum – and all the time Chooky was running ahead of me. The Salvos played on the corner of Coppin Street and Bridge Road, and my hands were sticky with fairy floss or greasy from fish and chips wrapped in white paper and layers of newspaper. The rabbito was coming along the street with his handcart and wild rabbits hanging all around it. I picked one out and watched him skin and gut it and I took it in to Mumma on an enamel plate, then I rode the rabbito's cart to the end of the street. But suddenly it wasn't the rabbito's cart at all but the back of a grey elephant and then I was trapped inside a red *howdah* as the elephant charged into the jungle. The rabbito turned and scowled and it was Mr Arthur and he lifted a spiked *ankus* and shook it at me as

I shrank down into a corner of the *howdah*.

I woke on the cool tiles. For a moment, I thought it was Lizzie's hand on my brow, just as when we'd slept side by side in the little bunk sailing across the Surabaya Straits. But when I looked up, it was a beautiful Indian woman in a green-and-gold sari. Her hands were soft and smooth and she murmured gentle-sounding words that I couldn't understand. Then in English, she whispered, "May I suffer instead of you, child." It made me weep, to hear a stranger speak like that to me.

A servant came and picked me up from the floor, and the Maharani had me laid on a long couch beneath a high window. They brought me sherbet and bathed me with cool cloths and the Maharani came back to me later in the morning, when my fever had abated.

"I have a small gift for you, little songbird," she said. "You sang so sweetly for us last night, I want you to have this to remember your time in Mysore."

She took my hand and in it laid a small silver brooch. At first I thought it was the symbol of the royal family, the Wodeyar's two-headed eagle. But then I realised it was something much smaller, a tiny bird with its throat stretching up, its beak open as if it were in song.

"It is a nightingale, little one."

I fell asleep again with the tiny brooch in my hand and dreamed of rivers and palaces, of dusky red plains and cool green gardens, and when I woke I was myself once more.

I didn't see the Maharani again. I might have dreamed her visit but for the fact that when we climbed onto the train I still held the silver brooch in my hand.

The nightingale is such a small bird that you'd almost overlook it but for its lovely voice. I had heard them singing from a cage in the palace courtyard. And now I was about to go back to my cage and sing. I felt so hollowed out that I could ring like a bell. I clutched the brooch tightly in my hand. The tail feathers felt as sharp as pins.

54

Happy Ever After

Poesy Swift

I walked up the steps of the Elphinstone Hotel, almost hoping that Lizzie wouldn't be there. I'd watched the hotel from a distance, waiting until I saw Lionel and Mr Arthur leave. I hadn't told anyone what I was planning, not even Charlie. But ever since that fleeting moment in Mysore when I had mistaken the Maharani for Lizzie, I hadn't been able to get Lizzie out of my mind. I dreamed of her every night. It was as if she were haunting me.

You'd have thought that after all the publicity the clerk at reception would have been wary of handing out her room number, but he didn't bat an eye when I asked him which room Miss Finton was staying in.

She opened the door dressed in nothing but her kimono. I could tell she was expecting Mr Arthur or Lionel. Anyone but me. Her mouth went slack and she pushed her hair away from her face.

"What do you want?" she said wearily.

"Lizzie, I only wanted to see you. To see that you're all right."

Her mouth twisted downwards and she clutched the front of her kimono. I thought she was going to shout at me, to tell me to leave her alone, but she pushed the door open even wider and drifted over to her bed where she lay down and burst into tears.

I shut the door and sat down beside her. Her body heaved and shuddered as she sobbed. Very gently, I began to stroke her long, dark hair.

"Hush, don't cry, Lizzie. Everything will be all right."

She sat up and looked at me, her face a portrait of misery. "No it won't, Poesy. It will only get worse. Arthur is mad, determined that he's going to win, but how can he?"

"It's not about winning or losing. He only has to let us go."

"Is that what you came for? To ask me to take your side?"

"No, I came to see if you were all right. I've missed you. I've missed you ever since Bombay."

She wiped her face dry with her hands. "It's been awful. Simply awful. Pondicherry was a nightmare. Arthur made us travel in a bullock cart because he'd lost so much of his money. It was vile. Hours and hours of hot and dusty travel. And then when we got there, no one spoke English, only French or all those different mumbly-jumbly Indian languages. It was simply me and Lionel and Arthur. And Lionel was there constantly or I was all alone. We stayed in a horrible little guesthouse and everything was broken. I cut myself…"

Her face grew clouded. I took her hand and saw where a wound was healing across her palm.

"How did you get that?" I asked, touching the red line very tenderly.

Eliza looked confused. "We were having an argument. I can't remember what we were arguing about. Everything and nothing. And then I smashed the lamp. I couldn't stay in the room a minute longer. My hand throbbed and I ran to the beach.

"I stood on the sand and there were black rocks and a black, black horizon and I stared out across the water. That's all that's between us and home, you know. That water. I tried to push down my sobs but the hot air seemed to feed them, I felt I was suffocating. I was choking on the heat, on the loneliness.

"Everything has changed. Everything and everyone is awful. The people in Pondicherry didn't know any better but they kept calling me Madame Percival, as if I were Arthur's wife."

"But you will be, won't you?"

Lizzie looked at me and her blue eyes grew hard. "How can I know? If 'she' won't divorce him, how can I ever be his wife?"

"Perhaps you don't want to be," I said. Because despite everything, despite all the proof of her actions, I couldn't believe she loved him. I had to hear her say it myself.

"It's all I want," she said flatly. "It's all I've ever wanted."

55

SORCERER'S APPRENTICE

Poesy Swift

Reporters came and went from the Castle Hotel. We weren't meant to talk to them, though they sat at the back of the court day in, day out, writing down every word that was said. I tried not to meet their eyes. I was frightened they might look into my heart and see my terrible confusion.

The worst thing about those long weeks in Madras was not being able to perform. I kept thinking if only we could sing, if only we could be in front of an audience that looked at us with pleasure, rather than the busybodies and reporters that flocked to the trial. Mr St John had tried to secure us a performance at the Madras Club in Mount Road where he was a member, but it was a stuffy old men's club where children weren't welcome. Finally, his wife arranged an invitation for us to perform a 'benefit' at the Adyar Club. It was a clever way of getting around the fact that we weren't allowed to sell tickets to shows because of the court case.

We were lounging about on the verandah of the Castle Hotel when Ruby and Tilly decided we should keep on with a different version of the revue and try to make it more like vaudeville.

"Here's your chance, Charlie," said Tilly. "You can do your magic."

Charlie sat in a cane chair, flicking through a magic catalogue. He looked up at Tilly briefly and then back at the catalogue.

"Perhaps," he said.

Tilly rolled her eyes. Charlie had become so morose, no one could talk to him. As the court case dragged on, he grew more and more miserable. I knew he was thinking of Lionel.

"C'mon," I said, pulling him out of his chair. "We're going for a soda."

It was the best thing about not having Mr Arthur around. No one was paying attention to our comings and goings, nobody watched over us.

I was glad to see Prem sitting at the Elphinstone Soda Fountain. He lit up when he spotted Charlie, though he was still rather shy of me. We sat in a booth together and ordered a soda each.

"Charlie's going to do a magic show. At the Adyar Club," I told him.

"No I'm not," said Charlie. "I can't do a show without Lionel. I don't have an assistant."

I bit my lip. "I could be your assistant."

"Oh yes, Miss Poesy," said Prem. "You would be a most fine assistant."

"See," I said. "Prem thinks it's a good idea."

Charlie looked up uncertainly.

"I suppose if it's at night, I could do some tricks with fire."

"That would be a very excellent way to begin," said Prem encouragingly. "I could obtain some white phosphorus and some carbon disulphide for you."

Charlie started to smile. "If you could get me some phosphorated ether too, I could do fire on the waves."

"Certainly," said Prem eagerly. "You must do fire on the waves. Do you need me to procure some sugar cubes also?"

"No, they have them in the dining room of the hotel."

I was so relieved to see Charlie animated, I held my breath for fear the spell would break.

"Maybe I should do second sight too," he said. "It makes it look as though I know things in advance. You'll have to be in the audience, Poesy, while I'm on stage. You go down among the crowd and let someone pick a card."

He reached into his pocket and pulled out a deck of cards, fanning out a selection before me. "You offer them out, like this."

I pulled out a Queen of Hearts and held it close to my chest.

"Now, as you hand it to Prem, take note of which card it is and I'll know exactly what it is by the way you question me. See, if you say "*What* suit?" then I'll know it's Clubs. If you say "*The* suit?", that means Spades. "*Which* suit?" is for Diamonds and if you simply say "Suit?" then I'll know it's Hearts."

The catch was to only offer the audience face cards so there weren't too many choices. In the next hour we practised the trick over and over, using the same system for the value of the card as well. Charlie could tell which card it was by how I framed the questions. Finally, I swapped sides in the booth and sat next to Prem so we could use him as our practice audience. I saw Mr Dorai, the owner of the soda fountain, glance in our direction. He was smiling as if he thought we were terribly funny.

When I fanned the cards out for Prem, I held them under

the table and for a minute our hands touched as he picked out the Knave of Hearts. I couldn't help smiling. We did make an odd threesome.

On Saturday evening our carriages trundled down Boat Club Road, through dappled sunlight, and turned into the gates of the Adyar Club. It was the loveliest club we'd visited the whole time we'd been in India, with tennis courts, a golf link and a smooth green croquet lawn. Mr St John said it was the best club in Madras for music because it was actually a ladies' club.

As we strolled across the lawns, Tilly and Ruby were almost drooling at the clothes the ladies wore. "Look over there," said Tilly, "the lady in the blouse that's simply dripping with lace jabots. She must have mohair pads to plump her bosom and backside. See how snugly that bertha fits her? I love how she's nipped in at the waist."

"I'm surprised she can breathe in this heat," I said.

"Sometimes you have to suffer for beauty's sake," said Tilly.

Everywhere I looked, there were women in lovely costumes. There were even some who'd come in low-cut evening dresses and white kid gloves with little pearl buttons. We were glad to be in our *Florodora* costumes and not our day clothes. It made us feel less like charity children.

We thought we'd perform on the terrace as there were people milling all over the lawns, but Mrs St John hooked her arm through Ruby's and Tilly's and led them down to the water. I followed behind. All along the water's edge, chairs and long benches were arranged as seating.

"We thought a water fete would be just the thing on a night like tonight. When you've won your case against that wretched man, you'll be able to think of Madras fondly, as a city that treated you with care."

All along the river, boats were hung with lanterns. The soft light shimmered on the river's surface. Twenty feet from the shore, festooned with garlands of flowers and hung with lamps, was a wide raft set up as a stage. *Lascar*s stood waiting beside little rowboats to take us out to the floating stage. Two hundred people sat on the lawns watching as twelve of us climbed out of the boats as elegantly as possible.

I stood on the edge of the floating stage and stared at our faint reflections rippling on the surface of the river. We seemed very insubstantial – six girls in lacy petticoats, six boys in oversized dress coats and top hats. The stage was moored so it didn't move at all but I felt as though I had lost my anchor. For the first time, I felt a terrible stage fright. I was glad to be at a distance from the audience, the men smelling of gorgonzola cheese, relish and spirits, the women stinky with perfume that only faintly masked the ammonia they had dabbed beneath their arms to prevent sweat stains.

Once we started singing 'Tell Me, Pretty Maiden' I became myself again. When I sat on Charlie's knee and sang 'If I lov'd you, Would you tell me what I ought to do, To keep you all mine alone' he didn't look at me but at the audience.

I knew he was waiting for the song to be over so he could do his magic, so I didn't mind. As soon as we'd finished, the *lascar*s rowed the five other boys and all us girls back to shore while Charlie stayed behind. This was Charlie's moment. He stood alone in the centre of the floating stage, surrounded by a circle of unlit candles.

He set up a tiny folding card table beside him and on it placed three glasses of water. Then he stretched his arms wide. "Before I came to India, I imagined it a country of darkness. But in India I have found friendship and I have found light."

As he snapped his fingers, one by one the circle of candles magically lit themselves.

"And in the light of India I have found the sweetness of fire."

He held up two tiny white cubes beneath the glow of the lanterns so everyone could see that they were sugar lumps. Then he put one into the first glass. Instantly fire appeared on its surface. Charlie held the glass up and it glowed a strange blue against the dark river. Gently, he blew on the glass until the flames looked like waves. Then he did the same with the other two glasses. And as he blew, first on one and then the other, the blue flames rose out of the glasses like waves. Then he flung the water onto the surface of the river where it flared for a moment before disappearing.

"In India, my mind has become lit with magic," said Charlie. "There are wondrous forces at play in the subcontinent that can turn a simple boy into a master of the invisible, a reader of minds. To help me demonstrate this gift, I call upon my assistant, Miss Poesy Swift."

This was my cue to stand up and curtsey. There was a snicker from the Kreutz brothers, but the audience played along.

"Miss Swift will offer you playing cards," continued Charlie, "and through the power of magic I will enter your minds and all your choices will be revealed to me." Charlie closed his eyes and waited as I offered the fanned-out cards to a lady. She picked the Queen of Hearts.

"Suit?" I cried to Charlie. He put his fingers to his temples as if he were trying to draw the answer from the ether.

Little beads of sweat trickled down my neck, I was so nervous for him.

"Hearts," he replied at last.

The lady who'd drawn the card nodded to the audience and there was a smattering of applause.

"Value?" I cried.

"Queen," answered Charlie. "The lady has drawn the Queen of Hearts."

The woman stood up excitedly and waved the card at the audience. "That's exactly right," she cried. "Isn't he clever?" And everyone applauded.

Once we'd provided a few more demonstrations of Charlie's cleverness, he drew two doves from his sleeves and sent them winging out into the hot night air. I was so glad to see them disappear across the water. I'd been worried that they might not survive being inside his jacket for so long in the heat.

As Charlie gave a bow, the Kreutzes were rowed out to the stage for their Tweedledum and Tweedledee battle and then Daisy sang Fifi Fricot's song from *The Belle of New York*. To close the evening, the whole troupe performed 'When You Steal a Kiss'. Tilly sang the verse but everyone sang the chorus, twenty-four voices floating across the water to the crowd on the lawns. Behind the audience, the Adyar Club glowed like a temple.

I'd always thought it was a silly song but I found myself looking at Charlie every time we sang 'turtle dove'.

Words are not the only thing when you are making love,
Your eyes are always whispering "Come be my turtle dove",
Every time you take her hand she knows your love is true,
And lips are only needed when you steal a kiss or two.

Suddenly, he looked straight into my eyes, as if he'd heard my voice above all the others. I felt a strange shiver course through me as we sang the next line. It was as if, for a fleeting moment, Charlie and I were the only two people on the Adyar River, the only two people in the world.

56

BENEATH THE BANYAN

Poesy Swift

Laughing and breathless with our success, we marched up the grassy slope to the ballroom. It had a beautiful dance floor that begged our shiny black shoes to tap out a rhythm, and all the girls began to dance with each other.

I danced with Flora until I noticed something that made me feel horribly uncomfortable. They didn't have electricity at the club yet, so there were two rows of little Indian boys tugging on the ropes of the *punkah*s with a hypnotic rhythm. One of them looked like Prem. Even though I knew it wasn't him, all my cheery feelings drained out through the soles of my dancing shoes and I remembered where I was. Tomorrow, we would be back in the courtroom. Tomorrow, the barristers would call for more of the children to repeat their statements to the judge.

I left the dance floor and wandered outside. The Adyar River flowed lazily past the south verandah. I leaned against the balustrade next to Charlie, watching as two small boats rowed past the club towards the mouth of the river and the sea.

"I wish we could jump in a boat and row away like that."

"I thought you wanted to stick around to see Mr Ruse cleared and Old Percy punished."

I hung my head. "I'm so afraid, Charlie. They're going to

call Daisy tomorrow. What if they ask me to take the witness stand too? Tilly will kill me if I change my story but I think I'd rather die."

Charlie was silent for a long moment, staring out at the water. "I'd gladly run away. I hate being Lionel's brother. I hate the way everyone talks about him as if he's a sneaking ass."

"He can't hear what they say behind his back," I said.

"That doesn't make it any better."

I couldn't stop a sigh escaping from between my lips.

We both propped our chins on our elbows and stared out at the river.

"What are those lights, over there?" I asked.

"That's the Theosophical Society Headquarters," said Charlie.

"Where Mrs Besant lives?"

Charlie nodded.

"Charlie!" I cried. "That's the answer. Mrs Besant can help us. We won't have to stay with the others any more. We won't have to go to court either. And she'll know what to do. She can help you and me and Lionel. Maybe she can even help Lizzie. We have to throw ourselves on Mrs Besant's mercy."

"I don't think that's a very good idea," said Charlie.

I stepped close to him and cupped my hands, whispering hot and warm into the shell of his ear. "We can take a boat across. Please, Charlie. Please. If you won't come, I'll row myself there. Please."

He pulled my hands away and held my wrists tightly, studying my face. "You can't, Poesy," he said.

"I have to. I can't go to court tomorrow. I simply can't say those things that I said in my statement."

"What did you say, Poesy?"

I couldn't tell him. "Please come away with me, Charlie."

The Adyar Club ladies had decided to put us up at the club for the night so Charlie and I waited until after lights out and then met in the shadows of the club. We stumbled past the badminton courts until the ground grew squishy beneath us and we knew we were drawing closer to the boat ramp.

"I wish I'd thought of doing this sooner. You must know this is the right thing to do, Charlie. Mrs Besant says there is no religion higher than Truth," I said, tugging at the rope that held the rowboat. "So I'm going to tell her the truth. I'm going to confess everything."

The Adyar River was blue-black in the darkness, like a river of ink flowing down to the warm sea.

I could see the Theosophical Society, a shadowy grey building against the dark undergrowth. The moon rose over the sea and cast a blue light on the water. I flinched when a black fish jumped near the boat. Drawing closer to the southern shore, there was a dense forest of mangroves. Charlie steered us into a safe haven and climbed out first, tying the boat to the twisty root of a blackened tree.

"What if there are snakes or tigers?" I asked, suddenly fearful.

Charlie put his hand out to me. "We'll be all right."

We walked into the forest, through a tangle of banyan tree roots. There was a light on in a grand old building ahead of us, but suddenly it switched off and we were plunged into darkness. We stood among the roots of the banyan tree, holding hands. Charlie looked at me. I could see his eyes shining, as if what little light was in the forest was coming from inside him. "Poesy," was all he said, the single word an admonition.

"I know. She won't want to help us," I said. "We're actors, not Indians or avatars or anyone important. We're kids caught up in a stupid fight." I sat down in the dry grass and red dust. "I'm such an idiot."

"It was a bit of a nutty idea," said Charlie. "But you meant well. I can row us back now and no one will know. I'm glad we came. It's good to remember I can still slip away so easily."

I started to sob. It hurt my chest. It hurt every part of me.

"Oh Charlie, you can't run away. If you leave the troupe, I'll have no one. You can't stay in India, you simply can't."

"I know," he said, slumping down on the ground beside me.

The moon shone through the roots of the banyan tree and cast shadows across his body. He looked like a strange animal, crouching in the grass beside me. Suddenly, I realised he was crying too.

"I can't leave Lionel. Not now. He's trapped, and because of him I'm trapped too. Once old man Percy loses the case, and he will lose, Lionel will have to come back to the troupe. Everyone will be cruel to him and Freddie and Max will bully him. If he had to go home and face Ma alone, after all this, it would kill him. I can't abandon him."

"What are we going to do?" I said, putting my head on his shoulder.

"You have to finish what you've started and I have to stick by Lionel."

We sat for a long time beneath the banyan tree. I took Charlie's hand in mine and held it in my lap because touching him made everything seem less frightening. Then I held his hand to my face and kissed his palm. It was only a little kiss. It was only meant to be a 'thank you'. But suddenly our faces were close to each other, the warm evening air seemed to squeeze the breath from me and I pressed my lips against his. He smelled of the river, of sugar, of sulphur, of heat and dark. He was so still it was as if his body had turned to stone, but his lips were like soft, warm butter. Then he pushed my face away, very gently, and put his arms around me. He held me as if I might break, he held me as if I were made of glass.

For a long time we sat like that, fragile and silent. I wanted to kiss Charlie again but I was too afraid of what might follow. The moon rose over the river and the gardens, and the night was full of sound, of scuttling creatures and night birds, of insects and the lapping of the Adyar. Charlie and I were silent, as if we were both waiting for something so dangerous that we dared not speak its name.

Suddenly I understood. I understood why Lizzie had given up everything for Mr Arthur. I turned to Charlie and stole another kiss.

I kept my lips pressed to his until he pushed me away.

"What's wrong?" I asked.

"I forgot to breathe," he said.

Suddenly we were both laughing like little children, lying beneath the banyan tree giggling until our sides hurt, until we had forgotten our pain and our kisses.

57

THE TRIAL

Tilly Sweetrick

Every morning before we left the hotel, I inspected every Lilliputian. We had to dress carefully for court. We had to look as innocent as the day. The boys wore dark shorts, black stockings and white shoes and they'd brushed their fringes so much that the hair stuck to their foreheads. We girls wore our best dresses with black stockings and either black boots or white sandshoes to match the boys.

The High Court was grander than the Maharajah of Mysore's old palace, with its turrets and towers, and barristers in black gowns flapping across the dusty courtyards. We climbed wide stairways and walked along black-and-white tiled corridors lined with dark wood panelling to reach our courtroom.

Little squares of coloured light fell from the high windows and speckled our white dresses with patches of red and green and gold. We sat in a group, the fans spinning lazily above our heads and the polished benches growing warm beneath us, and watched our fate unfold.

Mr Ruse had organised us a most delicious barrister, Mr Browning. He and Mr Bowes found witnesses from all over Madras who spoke in our favour. The only witnesses that the Butcher had been able to find to speak on his behalf were his little *toady bacha*, Lionel, and that old *chamcha*, Mr Shrouts.

When it was finally the Butcher's turn to take the stand, after weeks of evidence, he positively writhed in the witness box.

Mr Browning tore him to shreds. Every tatty little piece of the Butcher's folly and mismanagement was brought to light and every lie exposed. When Mr Browning started to question the Butcher about our education, you could see a ripple of disgust move across the gallery. It was hilarious. The more the Butcher tried to defend himself, the deeper he dug his own grave.

"The bigger girls taught the little ones in the afternoon," he said.

Ruby and I looked at each other and smirked.

"But you claimed in an interview with a newspaper reporter in Calcutta that Myrtle Jones was a teacher registered with the Australian government."

"All right," admitted the Butcher. "I said Myrtle was a teacher for advertising purposes."

"What is that supposed to mean?" asked Mr Browning.

"When she was asked, she was to say she was a school-mistress. Look, she's not been much with the Company so she ought to be educated. I've seen her write her name – she's not a complete fool."

Myrtle looked a little hurt at this, but some of us stifled a giggle. She did have simply the worst handwriting.

"The success of the company depends on the goodwill of the public," continued the Butcher slowly, as if he were explaining something to a crowd of idiots. "Stories of gross cruelty or improper conduct on the part of a manager would affect our success, so of course I will defend our public interests. Meddlesome people have interfered but this company is of a professional standard. I've had no trouble anywhere else."

"I believe the Police Commissioner was called to investigate in Bombay?" said the lawyer.

"That was because of a meddlesome person from Melbourne. The report emanated from *Melbourne*, not Bombay. Can't you see, the girls are lying?" the Butcher almost shouted. "Ruby Kelly and Matilda Sweeney wanted to go back to Melbourne to work in the variety shows. That's all. They are lying to have their own way."

"Miss Kelly and Miss Sweetrick, whom you refer to as 'Sweeney', are not the only children who have given evidence of your immoral behaviour. Other children have said that you hit them and took their money to buy drink."

The Butcher gripped the balustrade of the witness box, trying to contain his rage. He leaned forward and spoke so slowly it seemed he was having trouble breathing.

"They are lies. None of the accusations are true."

"Are you suggesting that Miss Poesy Swift is a liar?"

I could feel Poesy stiffen in her seat beside me. Thank goodness the Butcher didn't look at her as he replied. It would have unravelled the witless girl.

"She's a lovely child," said the Butcher. "And an asset to the company."

"Can you suggest why clean-minded children should speak against you?"

Arthur looked straight at Ruse. "Some dirty-minded people set them to do it."

"Who are the dirty-minded people you refer to?"

"I can't say," said Mr Arthur, but he glared at Mr Ruse as if he wanted to set him on fire with the fury of his gaze.

"What reasons do you suggest led these people to act?"

"To get the Lilliputian Company on the cheap. To steal my company and my livelihood from me."

I wanted to yawn then. I was so sick of him. I wanted to walk right up to the witness box and yawn in his face. They were going over and over the same old thing. But then they got to the part where Iris was ill and was taken home and the Butcher shot himself in the foot. Mr Browning detailed how the Butcher carried Iris out of the theatre and put her in the *gharry*. Then he looked up and asked, "Do you often carry the girls about?"

"We carry the smaller children home on our shoulders when there is no *gharry* to take them," replied the Butcher.

"Did you ever carry Eliza Finton?" asked Mr Browning slyly.

The Butcher jumped up in his seat. "How dare you! How dare you make such a suggestion."

Mr Browning looked even slyer and foxier. "Why do you get so angry?"

"How dare you imply I would carry her in public! She is a grown woman."

"She has her hair down her back in the style of a girl. Answer the question."

"No!" shouted Mr Arthur.

The judge banged his gavel for the hundredth time that morning and ordered Mr Browning to take a different line of questioning, but Mr Browning said he was finished with the witness and would like to call Mr Ruse to the box.

When the Butcher slipped past Mr Browning's table we saw him mutter something, and then Mr Browning jumped to his feet. "As the witness passed me he called me a 'dirty ruffian'," he announced.

"I did not," said the Butcher stiffly.

There was much argument and to-ing and fro-ing and then the judge said he hadn't heard it either but he cautioned the Butcher anyway. I'd never realised how childish grown-ups could be.

It was lovely to see Mr Ruse in the witness box. He looked so much more intelligent than the Butcher. He presented his evidence in a calm, well-spoken manner and the judge nodded sagely as Mr Ruse was asked to relate the details of what happened on the night of the strike. Of course, he told the truth. But the Butcher couldn't bear to hear it. He leaped to his feet and shouted at the top of his voice, "You took them away by a show of force!"

"I never laid a finger on you," said Mr Ruse.

"As if I'd be fool enough to provoke violence when you had twenty of your cronies to back you up!"

"I am not a kidnapper. I have never heard of a more ridiculous accusation in my life."

"You've stolen those children from me. Poisoned their affections."

"You poisoned them yourself," countered Ruse in disgust.

The judge banged his gavel for order and the turbaned court officers came bustling to the front to lead the Butcher away.

I was enjoying myself immensely until I turned to look

at Poesy. I should have realised the Butcher's flattery would unhinge the child. Her eyes were brimming with tears but it wasn't because of him. She was looking straight at Eliza and Lionel, the lover and the lackey, huddled together on a bench behind the Butcher's *babu vakil*.

We were so close to victory, I couldn't bear the thought of Poesy spoiling things. For all those interminable weeks, as the weather grew hotter and hotter and Mr Ruse grew more haggard and we waited for the trial to end, we had managed to stick by our stories. If Poesy withdrew her statement now, it could make the trial drag on even longer. The Butcher would never win but we would sweat for weeks to come if she didn't keep her mouth shut.

I watched Poesy carefully as Daisy climbed into the witness box. Because Daisy had told her story so many times to so many audiences, Mr Browning had convinced the judge to allow her to give evidence before the whole court, rather than interviewing her 'in camera'. She looked so small as the little gates swung open and a court officer lifted her into the witness box. She had to stand on a chair to be seen over the railings.

When Daisy began to speak, Poesy did the most irritating thing. She covered her ears with her hands and shut her eyes, just like a wretched monkey. She couldn't have drawn more attention to herself if she'd screamed. I grabbed her arm and twisted it hard. I wouldn't allow her to spoil our triumph.

58

THE WAY BACK

Poesy Swift

Dirty-minded. Mr Arthur said dirty-minded people had made us lie, but I was the one with the dirty mind. I wanted to forget everything and everyone. I wanted to forget myself.

I'd fled from the court with no plan, no idea of where I could hide. I ran through the flower bazaar, deeper and deeper into Blacktown.

I skidded to a stop at the entrance to an old hall that had its doors flung open wide. A dark-skinned coolie carrying a hand of bananas stared at me as he trotted along the street with his load, as if I was something peculiar. An emaciated cow stopped beside me and began feeding from a pile of old flowers. I was out of place and out of time. Inside the hall, there were great crowds of women in brightly coloured saris kneeling together and men in crisp white jackets. A ceremony was in progress and two children sat beneath a canopy while a crowd of grown-ups gathered around them. Then I saw Prem and I knew that he was the one I was looking for. I knew it must be the auspicious day of his sister's wedding. I knew why I was there. It was *kismet* – my fate. I could see Prem, standing with his parents and his sister. Or was it his wife? It made my stomach do a strange turn.

I walked up the steps of the hall and stood in the doorway,

casting a white girl's shadow. A few people turned to see who the stranger was, including Prem. I think he tried not to see me but I waved frantically. He looked alarmed and excused himself from his parents. He was dressed in a beautifully tailored Indian jacket but he had some strange ritual markings on his forehead.

"Is something wrong, miss?" asked Prem.

"Don't call me 'miss'. You know I'm only Poesy."

"Miss Poesy?" said Prem. "What has happened?"

"I've run away."

"What have you run away from, Miss Poesy?"

"From myself," I said lamely.

Prem glanced over his shoulder and I knew I should let him go back to the ceremony. Growing up was too hard, too full of difficult choices, yet Prem seemed so sure of what he would do with his life. If only he would tell me what to do with mine. "I'm sorry, Miss Poesy, I have to go back to my family."

I could feel Charlie next to me before I could see him. I could sense his presence.

"Come away now, Poesy," he said. "You can't expect Prem to help you."

And of course, he was right. We weren't Lilliputians at all but wayward Gullivers, shipwrecked and dependent on the locals for our livelihood. Very soon, we would have to go home. Back to our own families.

"You're too impulsive, Poesy," said Charlie, as he led me through the twisting lanes, back to the red towers of the High Court. "You only make things worse for yourself. You can't go running around India on your own."

I stopped in my tracks and stared at him. "But you do."

"I'm a boy. The rules are different for boys."

"I wish they weren't."

"You can't wish the world into being with your thoughts, Poesy."

I watched the curve of his neck as he stomped off ahead of me. Since our night beneath the banyan tree, everything had changed. Charlie wasn't comfortable with me any more. We were still friends but something had shifted.

"I can still wish we could go back to being like we used to be," I called after him.

He came and stood in front of me, his hands in his pockets. "We can never go backwards, Poesy."

Back at the Castle Hotel, before I even began to climb the stairs, I could hear the girls hooting in the dining room, celebrating the end of the trial. No one was in any doubt as to what the judge's findings would be. I stood alone in the bedroom and looked at the detritus of our weeks there.

On the table by the window were some postcards the others had been writing home.

Dearest Mother,

A few lines to tell you everything at last. I would have told you before but feared you would fret. The company is broken up. Mr Arthur and Eliza are getting away to America. Percival has been a pig to us and the way he has banged some of us about is awful. His talk was disgusting. He mocked at us and said we couldn't

get away for two years. He behaved like a cur when the men were
about and had nothing to say. We all simply danced for joy about
it all. Mrs Quedda and Miss Thrupp the matron are now in
charge of us and they are good to us. Don't worry. I shall be with
you soon.

Your loving daughter Tilly Sweetrick

And that was the sum of it. Everything and nothing on the
back of a postcard. I read Tilly's card again and again and
realised she told no lies. The court had already appointed
Miss Thrupp as our guardian, though no one would listen to
her, and Lo was back with us again too.

I was just laying the card down when Tilly walked into
the room.

"Reading my private letters?" she said.

"I'm sorry. I didn't mean anything."

"You never seem to 'mean' half of what you do, Poesy. But
thank goodness you're back," she said tartly. "Lionel's come
back too, you know. The Butcher dumped him on the steps
of the hotel before speeding off to Pondicherry with Eliza in
a new motor. Mr Ruse says he's going to race after him, but I
can't see the point. It's not as if Eliza wants to be rescued and
that's the truth!"

I flung myself down across my bed and picked up my
book. I didn't want to listen to any more of Tilly's truths.
Inside the cover, Yada had written a note to me and I traced
her handwriting with my fingertips. *To my darling Poesy, in
the hope that after travelling the world, she will discover the
beauty of her old familiar home.*

I hadn't looked at those lines for months but suddenly I understood them. I flicked through to the final pages of *Gulliver's Travels*, searching for the bit where Dr Gulliver wrote about the end of his journey: *"Every traveller, before he were permitted to publish his voyages, should be obliged to make oath before the Lord High Chancellor, that all he intended to print was absolutely true to the best of his knowledge."*

To the best of my knowledge, the truth was twisted and tangled into knots that I could never unravel. There was only one thing of which I was certain: I was ready to go home.

59

ESCAPING LILLIPUT

Poesy Swift

I didn't fit inside my skin any more. On the outside, I looked no different to the girl who had sailed away from Port Melbourne nearly a full year earlier. Inside, I was someone else.

We spent ten days in Colombo, singing the same old songs over and over again. We'd scraped together half the fare but we were running out of audiences. Finally, a steamer company offered to let us travel with them at a discount.

When the ship passed through the heads of Port Phillip Bay, orange and blue light shimmered on the surface of the water. We all crowded onto the deck and watched the city light up as darkness fell. The great ships in the dock at Port Melbourne shone like palaces as we steamed past them. We hung over the rails, each of us anxious to be the first to see a familiar face. On the pier, a crowd of dark figures massed. Some of them sat on bollards, their bodies dim outlines, hunched with the weariness of waiting.

Above the noise of escaping steam, I heard Freddie and Max shouting triumphantly from the bow, "We're home!" Then from the stern came the cries of Daisy and Flora and the other girls. It was as though they all cried out in one voice. "Oh, my darling mummy!"

The people on the pier jumped up and down, clapped

their hands, waved handkerchiefs, brandished umbrellas and called out all at once so you couldn't know whose family they were from.

Our little black French steamer was only a shadow against the lights of the *Orvieto*, but the mothers reached out as if they could recognise their lost children in the darkness.

The girls at the stern broke into a chant, "Oh my mummy, my mummy, my mummy, my mummy," even though Daisy and Flora barely knew their mothers, Rosie and May were orphans, and Myrtle's mother beat her at the drop of a hat. Their voices wove in and out of each other, like birds swooping across the black water.

As we drew closer, we could see policemen running along the edge of the pier to prevent the mothers from falling over the side into the murky water. The women rushed along the edge as if they couldn't endure waiting any longer.

We were close enough to make out their faces now. It was easy to pick the Kreutzes standing in a family group, their broad, blonde faces staring up at the approaching steamer. The biggest Kreutz brother put his fist in the air and yelled out "Oi!" and then the whole family started shouting at the boys at once and I could make out not a word of it.

"They only charged us half third class," yelled back Max and Freddie. "And yes, we've got all our clothes."

Flora let out a squeal of excitement when she recognised her mother, who had come with a crowd of people.

"Mummy, Mummy, this is a French steamer. I can talk French now. *Passez-moi du pain*."

"Where's my mummy? Oh where's my mummy?" cried Daisy in a tearful voice.

"She's coming; she'll be here soon," shouted a voice from the pier. Suddenly, a figure pushed to the very edge of the dock, nearly tumbling into the water. A policeman held the crazy woman back and Daisy, crying and laughing called, "I thought you wasn't come. Oh, my mummy. Keep near the gangplank, or I might lose you."

I'd written to Mumma and Yada telling them not to come to meet the ship and saying that one of the adults would see me home. I didn't want my family to see me with the Lilliputians, to see what I'd become. Once, there was nothing more that I wanted to be. Now I thought of my bed in Willow Lane, of lying down to rest alone in my own room and the familiar smell of the old horsehair mattress. I imagined my old button-up boots under the bed. I would never fit into them again but I was determined to fit back into my family.

For an hour as the steamer berthed, conversations rippled up and down the pier, even when only snatches of each sentence could be heard above the noise of the port.

I found Charlie standing with Lionel on the far side, staring out to sea.

"Is there no one waiting to meet you?" I asked.

"Our Ma's probably down there somewhere, but Lionel doesn't want to bump into any of them reporters," said Charlie.

"I think I'll wait in our cabin," said Lionel, slipping away from us and into the darkness.

Charlie and I stood in silence, our arms on the rail, listening to the cries of the other children and their mothers. Slowly, he reached out and hooked his little finger through mine.

"Will we see each other again?" I asked.

"Maybe. Maybe not. Me and Leo will sign up with another touring company. We won't stay in Melbourne. What about you? Williamson's juvenile company, the pantomimes, any of that lot would have you, Poesy. You're good. You know that, don't you?"

"I'm never sure. The only thing I'm sure of is that I don't want to be an actress. I want to help people, Charlie, really help them, not just entertain them."

Charlie laughed. "I don't want to entertain the punters either. I want to fox them and astonish them and bamboozle them. That's what I want."

It was good to part with a smile, rather than tears.

As we all gathered to disembark, Tilly sidled up to me. "No one's come for you, have they, Poesy? Don't worry. I'll sort you out. You can ride with me and Ma back to Richmond."

But the last thing I wanted was for Tilly to take charge of me. I could see Mrs Sweeney, talking to a reporter and pointing at Tilly as if she were the evening star, newly risen. As Tilly waved, I slipped under her arm and made my way to the edge of the Lilliputians.

Then I saw her – a little old lady crushed at the back of the press of people had tied her handkerchief to the point of her umbrella and was running along the outskirts of the crowd, flourishing a signal of welcome. It was Yada. My wonderful, crazy Yada with her love for truth and all the right thoughts.

The regular gangway was too steep for many of the mothers so a safe passageway had to be constructed while the women cried out and shouted at the steamer. As soon as the way was clear, the families charged, pushing past the policemen and reporters.

Mrs Sweeney led Tilly and some of the other girls to talk to the men from the press but I pushed through the crowd in search of Yada. I didn't want to hear what stories Tilly would tell. Nothing anyone said would ever be the whole truth.

Between the facts of the trial, there were so many things that could have been said, so many other truths. There was a baby buried in Allahabad and two little girls dancing naked on a balcony in Bombay. Lionel with his broken puppet in Surabaya, Ruby mesmerised in Calcutta and Tilly sleeping beneath a soldier's greatcoat in Meerut. Eliza weeping in her kimono on the beach at Pondicherry and Charlie and me kissing in the darkness beneath a banyan tree in Adyar. There was more than any one of us could ever tell.

Epilogue

Poesy Swift

There are many lives I might have lived and things that might have been. I have loved and lost friends and family, but my life is not unhappy.

On a bright, clear Melbourne morning in the spring of 1926, I opened my letterbox to find a small pale pink envelope. Inside was a studio portrait of two strangers, a beautiful dark-haired woman in a simple wedding dress and a plump, weary middle-aged man with a flower in his buttonhole. At least, I thought they were strangers, until I read the card that accompanied the image.

It was from Eliza Finton. Or should I say, Eliza Percival. The photo was of her wedding and the man she had married was Mr Arthur.

The words on the card were few: *Dear Poesy, I thought you would like to know that, at last, we are truly happy ever after. Yours, Lizzie.*

I don't know how Lizzie found me. She hadn't been in touch with her own sisters in years. There were rumours that after living in Pondicherry for some months, she and Mr Arthur had fled to London to escape their debts. But then Fred Kreutz told me he'd seen them walking down a street in San Francisco during the war years.

We all grew up and became other people. Tilly signed on with J. C. Williamson for a while but then she married one of her stagedoor Johnnies – a wealthy Toorak businessman. Ruby teamed up with Tempe and Clarissa again and the three of them took to the vaudeville circuit, singing as the Trixiebelle Sisters. They signed up with an agent to tour the East, but in Singapore Ruby ran away with a ship's captain. Freddie and Max changed their name to King and went to America where they worked with the director Mack Sennett in his Keystone Kops comedies. Max came home after the war but Freddie stayed in Hollywood to become a star of silent films.

Some of the other girls became dancers at the Tivoli and little Daisy Watts outgrew her lisp and became a star. I took my daughter to see her every year in the pantomimes at the Princess Theatre.

I never returned to the stage. After the scandal, neither Mumma nor Yada wanted me near a theatre. I went to the Continuation School, became a teacher and grew to love my work. When I had my first class in a little country schoolroom, the children laughed with delight when I sang them 'Tell Me, Pretty Maiden', but I never missed the stage. I only missed Charlie.

Within weeks of coming back to Melbourne, Charlie and Lionel sailed for America with Mrs Essie. The Percivals' reputation was in tatters and they would never show their faces in Australia again. Mrs Essie toured a smaller version of the company that included Charlie, Lionel, Lo and Eddie. They travelled up and down the west coast of the United States until the war broke out and the troupe began to drift apart.

Lionel came home and signed up with the Australian Infantry. He was nineteen years old when he sailed to France. He died at Ypres. I saw his name on the lists of the fallen on the same day that we discovered Chooky had died on the Western Front.

I grew terrified that Charlie had died too. I tried to find him. I wrote to Mrs Essie but she said he had disappeared. I could find no one in Melbourne who knew what had become of Charlie.

When I married, I never told my husband about my early career on the stage. It was a box that I placed a lid upon and never opened until Eliza sent me her photo. I wrote to her. I couldn't help myself. It was a long and difficult letter. I told her I was married too and that I had a little daughter named Elsie. Elsie Charlotte Brookes. Charlotte was for Charlie.

Lizzie wrote back. A polite, brief note. She had seen Charlie in Shanghai. He was working as a magician, travelling with a White Russian theatre troupe. He was about to travel deep into China and then south, to India.

When my husband came home from work that night I told him everything, and I wept while he held me tenderly. I wept with longing for India, for the darkness, for a stolen kiss beneath a banyan tree. I wept for a girlhood lost to me too soon.

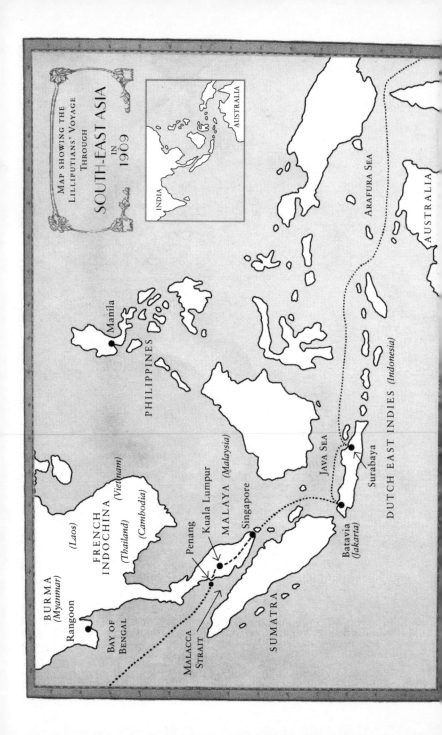

MAP SHOWING THE
LILLIPUTIANS' VOYAGE
THROUGH
SOUTH-EAST ASIA
IN
1909

INDIA

AUSTRALIA

BURMA
(Myanmar)

Rangoon

BAY OF
BENGAL

FRENCH
INDOCHINA

(Laos)

(Thailand)

(Vietnam)

(Cambodia)

Penang

Kuala Lumpur

MALAYA *(Malaysia)*

Singapore

MALACCA
STRAIT

SUMATRA

PHILIPPINES

Manila

ARAFURA SEA

AUSTRALIA

DUTCH EAST INDIES *(Indonesia)*

Surabaya

JAVA SEA

Batavia
(Jakarta)

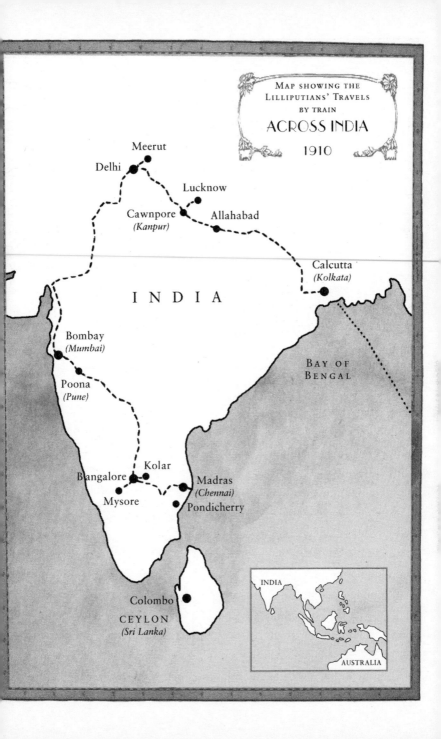

MAP SHOWING THE
LILLIPUTIANS' TRAVELS
BY TRAIN
ACROSS INDIA
1910

Meerut

Delhi

Lucknow

Cawnpore
(Kanpur)

Allahabad

Calcutta
(Kolkata)

INDIA

Bombay
(Mumbai)

BAY OF
BENGAL

Poona
(Pune)

Kolar

Bangalore

Madras
(Chennai)

Mysore

Pondicherry

Colombo

CEYLON
(Sri Lanka)

INDIA

AUSTRALIA

Author's Note

This novel is based on a true story. I hope, through fiction, that I have come as close to the truth as is possible but as Poesy says, there was more to the story than one person could ever tell. Percival's Lilliputian Opera Company is based on a real theatre troupe (Pollard's Lilliputian Opera Company) that successfully toured the world from the 1880s. Drawing from court records and newspaper reports, this novel is a reconstruction of their last, disastrous tour.

The basic facts of the events that led to the demise of the Pollard's company are indisputable. In July 1909 Arthur Pollard boarded the steam ship *Gracchus* at Port Melbourne. In his charge were twenty-nine children aged between seven and eighteen years of age who had been trained to sing and dance popular music-hall hits of the era. It was to be the beginning of a two-year world tour. Eight months later, in February 1910, the tour ended in scandal when the children walked out on their manager at the close of a performance in Madras and refused to travel any further with him. In the months that followed, the children attempted to earn their fares back to Australia while complicated legal proceedings raged in the High Court of Madras.

Although the names of the players have been changed, each fictional character is based on a member of the 1909 troupe.

The locations and physical settings I describe correspond with the troupe's itinerary and where it was not possible to determine exactly what happened I based the events on plausible constructs. Historical and political events mentioned in the novel from the employment of children in the match factories through to the Alipore bombing were the backdrop of the lives of the child performers.

Annie Besant, who is featured in a number of places in the story, was a prominent political activist, writer and orator of the Victorian and Edwardian eras. She was also President of the Theosophical Society, based in Madras, and a staunch advocate of Indian Home Rule. It is more than likely that many of the children were aware of her presence in India, and Besant's comments on truth in the lecture Poesy attends are a direct excerpt from an actual public event.

In writing *India Dark* I have attempted to detail the known facts of the case and flesh the story out to make the children's experiences as vivid and true to life as possible. What can never be known is what was in the hearts and minds of the young people caught in an impossible situation.

ANGLO-INDIAN WORDS

almirah   a word commonly used in Anglo-Indian households
for a cupboard

ankus   a goad used on elephants

anna   (Indian currency pre-1957), a coin worth $^1/_{16}$ th of a rupee

ayah   an Indian nanny or nursemaid

babu   originally a Hindu gentleman (especially a Bengali one),
but used in a pejorative way by the English

babu vakil   an Indian barrister

boxwallah   an Indian or European businessman or shopkeeper

chota hazri   light breakfast

chamcha   a stooge

dhobi   a washerman or laundryman

dhoti   an Indian loincloth

fakir   a poor Muslim or Hindu monk or ascetic

gharry   a cart or carriage

ghat   a path or stairs leading down to the river; also a quay for
a ferry

howdah   a chair or framed seat carried on the back of an
elephant

khitmungar   a male servant who waited at tables

lascar a native soldier or East Indian sailor

nabob a wealthy person

nowker (also spelt *nokar* or *naukar*) a domestic servant

pice (Indian currency pre-1957) a copper coin worth ¼ of an anna

puja any religious rite in Hinduism

punkah a large swinging fan made of cloth suspended on a frame from the ceiling and worked by a rope pulled by a *punkah-wallah*

rupee standard monetary unit of Anglo-Indian currency

sadhu a Hindu holy man

sahib a polite form of address, equivalent to 'Mr', for respected Indian and English men

Swadeshi nationalist political movement

tiffin a light snack

toady bacha a sycophant or bootlicker, literally a 'toad-eater'

topee a hat commonly worn by Anglo-Indians, especially a pith hat or sun helmet

wallah a word that is always attached to an activity to indicate someone's business, for example, a *tea-wallah* sells tea

Wodeyar the famous royal dynasty that ruled the Kingdom of Mysore for over 500 years, from 1399 to 1947

ACKNOWLEDGEMENTS

In 2001, while researching an earlier novel, *Bridie's Fire*, I interviewed Australian theatre historian Peter Freund. At the end of our interview, Peter pulled open a drawer and took out an essay he had written about the demise of Pollard's Lilliputian Opera Company. "I'm not a novelist," he said. "But someone should write a novel for kids about what happened to these children." I am deeply indebted to Peter for presenting me with that challenge.

Historical fiction requires time, patience and, if it is to have any integrity, the generous input of many people. I could not have written *India Dark* without the support and assistance of organisations and individuals in Australia, India and Indonesia.

I am grateful to the Australia Council, which provided me with a New Work grant that funded the initial period of researching and writing this novel.

I'm also indebted to the State Library of Victoria for offering me a Creative Fellowship that gave me time and space to read, dream, research and draw a thousand threads together. Thank you to Dianne Reilly, Juliet O'Conor and Dominique Dunstan of the State Library of Victoria, for their support during my Creative Fellowship and for facilitating access to the collections.

In addition to the resources of the SLV, I was fortunate to gain access to material in the Performing Arts Museum collections (Melbourne), the Nehru Memorial Library (Delhi), the Tamil

Nadu Archives (Chennai), and the British Library (London).

I'm very grateful to the many historians whose work underpinned much of my research, but especially Peter Downes, whose history *The Pollards* was invaluable and whose generosity in sharing his research was pivotal to making sense of this story.

Asialink, in conjunction with the Australia-India Council, funded my residency at the University of Madras in South India. Their support was crucial in providing me with an opportunity to discover India for myself and retrace the route that the children had taken in 1909–1910.

I had never been to India prior to tackling this story and had spent no more than a few days in South East Asia. The geography of India and South East Asia is now firmly etched in my consciousness. I am very grateful to the many people who helped me understand the rich, complex history of the region.

In India, Mridula (Mitty) Syed showed me boundless hospitality and was always ready to help solve any problem I encountered, large or small. At the University of Madras in Chennai, South India, where I was privileged to be writer-in-residence for three months, I am grateful to Eugenie Pinto, Dr C. T. Indra and Supala Pandiarajan for their assistance.

The historian and journalist Subbiah Muthiah kindly endured several interviews during which I besieged him with questions. His extensive writings on the history of Madras/Chennai were pivotal in helping me imaginatively visit India in 1910.

For their enthusiasm and friendship, and for offering me other windows into India, I'd like to thank Professor Pankaj Singh and Neelima Kanwar of the University of Himachal Pradesh, Meenakshi Francis, Anto Thomas, Anushka Ravishankar, Anita Roy, Maina Bhagat, Sonya Boylan, Anthony Ellis and Narender

Kumar. For assistance in accessing original court records I am grateful to Mr Jose John of King & Partridge, Advocates and Notaries in Chennai.

Also, many thanks to Janet de Neefe for introducing me to Indonesia and always being so welcoming.

The extract that Poesy recites to herself on page 94 is from Mary Coleridge's poem 'Unity'.

Thank you to Sarah Brenan, Rosalind Price, Kate Constable, Penni Russon, Kabita Dhara and Jocelyn Ainslie for their feedback on the incredibly convoluted drafts of the novel. And a million thanks to Ken Harper, who has shared the highs and lows of every stage of this book and is the travelling companion of my dreams.

Other Templar books you might enjoy...

VIII

by H. M. Castor

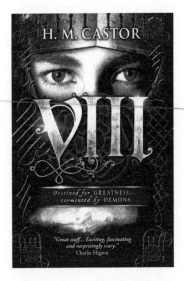

Destined for greatness...
tormented by demons

"Exciting, fascinating
and surprisingly scary."
Charlie Higson

VIII is the story of Hal: a young, handsome, gifted warrior, who
believes he has been chosen to lead his people. But he is plagued
by the ghosts of his family's violent past and, once he rises to
power, he turns to murder and rapacious cruelty. He is Henry VIII.

Hardback £10.99
ISBN 978-1-84877-499-5

A SMALL FREE KISS IN THE DARK

by Glenda Millard

"… a story of despair and hope, love and sorrow, courage and frailty. Millard… has created something exceptional."
Reading Time

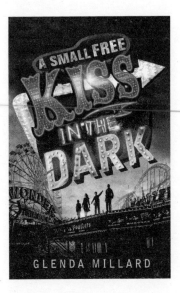

Skip is an outsider. Neglected by his parents and society, he's living on the streets. There he meets old homeless man Billy and, when war breaks out, they're joined by six-year-old Max and beautiful teenage dancer, Tia, with her tiny baby, Sixpence. As conflict rages around them they set up home in a deserted funfair. Scavenging for food, living on love and imagination – how long can Skip's fragile new family hold out?

Paperback £6.99
ISBN 978-1-84877-027-0

Wickedness

by Deborah White

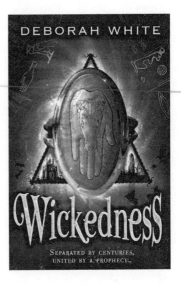

Separated by centuries, united by a prophecy...

"If you are looking for a historical thriller with strong characters, great plot and just a touch of terror then you need look no further."
Fantasy Book Review

Two flame-haired girls, both 14 years old and living in London, but four hundred years apart. A powerful and charismatic man. An Egyptian mummy and 20 spells written in hieroglyphics on parchment. An emerald casket, a gold ring and a rope-walker. All are united by blood and by a devastating prophecy.

Paperback £6.99
ISBN 978-1-84877-531-2